AUSTIN NOIR

EDITED BY HOPETON HAY, SCOTT MONTGOMERY, AND MOLLY ODINTZ

AKASHIC BOOKS

BROOKLYN, NEW YORK

Published by Akashic Books
©2023 Akashic Books
Copyright to the individual stories is retained by the authors.

Series concept by Tim McLoughlin and Johnny Temple
Map of Austin by Sohrab Habibion

Paperback ISBN: 978-1-63614-089-6
Hardcover ISBN: 978-1-63614-090-2
Library of Congress Control Number: 2022947063

All rights reserved
First printing

Akashic Books
Brooklyn, New York
Instagram, Twitter, Facebook: AkashicBooks
info@akashicbooks.com
www.akashicbooks.com

ALSO IN THE AKASHIC NOIR SERIES

TABLE OF CONTENTS

PART III: THIS LAND

INTRODUCTION
We Hear Dallas Is Nice

You've probably heard of Austin. You may have been here for South by Southwest. Your best friend may have recently relocated here from California. You might have thought about moving here yourself, then decided it wasn't worth it to live in Texas. You may have moved to Austin decades ago. You may even have been born and raised in Austin, and now you're on the outskirts of San Antonio or (god forbid) Waco because you can't afford to buy a house anywhere else. Or you may be living in a shiny new building downtown, watching the final stages of a sleepy town's transformation into modern metropolis. One thing you'll hear from almost any Austin resident: it was better when they got here.

Austin is so many different things to so many people. In the 1970s, '80s, and even into the early '90s, it was a beacon for many looking for the laid-back lifestyle and progressive attitudes that come with being home to a large research university and a thriving music scene. With its pro-environment leanings, big festivals, and intellectual fervor, Austin gained a reputation as a safe place to move from either coast while maintaining the same quality of life. And, most importantly, it was affordable.

It's the Live Music Capital of the World. It's a college town. It's weird. It's where college students, hippies, high-tech professionals, restaurant and service industry workers, and others can coalesce for a good time during music festivals like Austin City Limits.

And that's how some used to talk about Austin. It was a touchstone of sixties counterculture with a Texas twang that made it less pretentious. Everybody who was kicked out of their small town came here for harmony. Living was so cheap, you could support yourself by selling flowers on the street (like author Joe Lansdale did).

Then there was the music. Janice Joplin got her start at Kenneth Threadgill's converted gas station. Willie Nelson came to the Armadillo World Headquarters and brought the hippies and rednecks together. Clifford Antone created a blues club where young kids learned from the old masters, launching the Fabulous Thunderbirds and Stevie Ray Vaughan, and making 6th Street the spot. As Richard Linklater showed us in his 1990 film, Austin was a slacker's paradise.

More artists came in.

Then more people.

Then more money.

But there has always been another side of Austin in conflict with its liberal label. After the passage of the Voting Rights Act in 1965, cities across the nation began changing their electoral process, often going from at-large election of city council members to single-member districts in order to ensure fairer representation for minority communities. Indeed, at-large election of city council members was essentially put in place to water down the vote of minority communities. By the early 2010s, Austin was the largest city in the country without single-member districts. It was not until the municipal election of November 4, 2014, that the city residents could once again vote for city council in single-member districts.

Austin is not Silicon Valley, but it is a self-styled Silicon Hills that has seen its high tech–driven economic boom foster an explosive growth in the city's population, adding nearly 200,000 residents between 1990 and 2000, and another 300,000 between 2000 and 2020. And yet this has come at a cost. Housing prices have dramatically climbed and many predominantly Black and brown communities in East Austin have fallen victim to gentrification. The Black population in Austin in particular has declined as some residents have left the city for more affordable housing in the suburbs. Cities like Pflugerville and Manor, some fifteen to twenty miles from downtown Austin, have become destinations for many Black middle-class families.

The rising tide doesn't lift all ships, and those whose incomes haven't risen in turn have had to move farther and farther from the core of the city, losing access to such city amenities as public transit. And on the outskirts of downtown, there is a growing population of unhoused people. Austin is no longer a great place to live with little money. There's still always something fun going on, but even the nights out are growing too pricey for many people to afford.

As the city expands, construction never stops, struggling futilely to keep up with new demand. The running joke is that the city bird is the *crane*. Rents and property values keep climbing. We fear becoming Dallas.

The writers contributing to this collection represent a kaleidoscopic view of the city—not just in where they set the stories, but in their different social, economic, and cultural perspectives.

But to understand the stories, you first must understand the geography. East Austin, the setting to Gabino Iglesias's

"The Pink Monkey," is the historic heart of the Black and Latinx communities, now bulldozed and replaced by soulless condominiums. South Austin, which makes a disturbing appearance in Andrew Hilbert's "Bangface vs. Cleaning Solutions, LLC," is a locus of aging hippies and newly arrived tech gurus. Stratford Hills, perfectly captured in Alexandra Burt's "Sapphire Blue," is home to any number of, shall we say, Botox clinics and doggy-day-care spas. Miriam Kuznets's "Saving" takes place in Rollingwood, a wealthy area of South Austin where environmentalists and homeowners have forged an unholy alliance at the expense of urban density. The Great Hills area in Northwest Austin, the setting for Amanda Moore's story "Reflections," is an enclave of the upper middle class with its high-end hotels and restaurants. Jacob Grovey's "A Time and Place" is staged in an area of North Austin hovering between lower middle class and middle class, with apartment complexes, payday loan stores, and a housing development that seems a little out of place.

Downtown Austin, where Ace Atkins's "Stunts" and Lee Thomas's "Charles Bronson" take place, is the center of the music scene, now threatened by noise ordinances from luxury condos. It's also where all the government buildings are, but surprisingly, no one chose to fictionally kill off a politician for this anthology.

Then there are the smaller communities and neighborhoods that show up in these stories. Clarksville, near downtown Austin and the setting for Chaitali Sen's story "The Foundation," was established by freed slaves and is now inhabited by many law offices. West Campus, artfully explored in Amy Gentry's "Stitches," is the student neighborhood next to UT Austin, home to the city's many democratically owned and operated housing cooperatives, but sprouting new residential towers like mushrooms in a decades-long build-ing boom fueled by changing height restrictions. The Do-main, a mixed-use residential development and the setting for Richard Z. Santos's "Rush Hour," was constructed from scratch starting in the midaughts and is now a cross between a neighborhood and a giant outdoor mall, with more parking garage spaces than people. West Lake Hills, lovingly skew-ered in Jeff Abbott's "The Good Neighbor," is home to many of Austin's wealthier residents, while Scott Montgomery's "A Thousand Bats on an Austin Night" takes us to Lady Bird Lake, where we watch the bats fly off from under the South Congress Bridge.

Still thinking about moving to Austin? As the bumper stickers say, we hear Dallas is nice.

Hopeton Hay, Scott Montgomery, and Molly Odintz
Austin, Texas
February 2023

PART I

Money's tight, nothin' free
Won't somebody come and rescue me?
—Stevie Ray Vaughan

THE PINK MONKEY

BY Gabino Iglesias

East Side

The 2001 Ford Taurus idled in the far left corner of the parking lot in the back of the Pink Monkey. Every once in a while, one of the car's belts screeched like an angry banshee. Manuel was doing his best to ignore it, but with the windows open and his nerves on edge, it was hard. The sound was like a voice he couldn't understand yelling a warning he was forcing himself to ignore. Next to him, Carlos sat like a statue, his eyes glued to the back door of the place. He seemed calm, his breathing even. The only movements he'd made since they'd gotten there involved lowering the window and smoking. Manuel envied him. He knew some people were able to keep their cool under any circumstance. He wasn't one of them. Knowing they were about to commit a crime made him feel like a big python was curled around his lungs. The belt shrieked again.

"You could've put some WD-40 on that shit, you know."

Carlos peeled his eyes away from the strip club's back door, looked at Manuel, and smiled. It made Manuel think about the snakes in all his kid's books.

"Sorry the only car I could borrow on short notice isn't up to your standards, cabrón."

The joke stung. Manuel drove an olive-green Scion xB with no AC. The last four Austin summers had been brutal. After leaving a construction site, he couldn't even call home because his phone would overheat inside the car. He hoped this night would help him change that. He hoped this night would help him change a lot of things.

"How long do you think we'll have to wait?"

Carlos peered at him again. The hint of a smile was gone. His face had morphed into a battlefield where worry and impatience battled for control. It looked like both were winning.

"I don't fucking know, all right? We'll wait for as long as we have to."

Manuel felt the half dozen questions stuck in his throat wither and die. He swallowed their corpses and glanced around.

The parking lot wasn't full, but there were a decent number of cars for a Thursday night. Sasha Fire, a porn star who had quit the business and now toured as a dancer, was in town for the weekend. She was in there now, probably moving around effortlessly on heels so high she could stomp on a man's chest and puncture his heart.

Carlos exhaled loudly. The belt cried again. The sound reminded Manuel of the cats in the back alley of his childhood home back in Barrio Obrero. Sometimes a cat would curl up under his window to lick its wounds after a bad fight. Manuel was always sure the screams came from the evil spirit of a child that haunted the alley or from some angry demon that was going to break into his room and steal his soul. In the first place he rented after moving to Austin—a dilapidated bungalow near Speedway and 45th—he'd heard the same thing from time to time, and it still made his skin crawl.

As Manuel scanned the parking lot for the umpteenth time, his mind reeling and worry slowly eroding his resolve, two men pulled into a parking spot in an old LeBaron, exited the car, and stumbled to the front of the joint. They were both white and had the classic polo shirt and chinos that Carlos liked to call the "my daddy will sue you" outfit.

"They look like they've been partying for a while," said Carlos.

Of course they did. Manuel had nothing to say, so he pulled out his phone and looked at the screen: 12:59 a.m.

"This place shuts down in about an hour, right?"

"Yeah," said Carlos.

Silence settled between them again, an invisible presence that filled the car and amplified Manuel's nerves.

"You think—"

"Listen, man," interrupted Carlos, "my cousin said she likes to dip early, okay? She's probably also thinking about getting the fuck out while there's still security around, you know? These girls are always on the lookout for pervs. It's the only way they can survive. A guy might walk her out to her car. I don't know. If that happens, we'll follow her. If she comes out alone, we get the money and bounce. It's all good. You need to chill the fuck out."

Manuel checked out the trees surrounding the parking lot. It looked like all the other parts of Austin no one talks about. The Pink Monkey was on Reservoir Court, a place known for a nearby flea market and not much else. In fact, the flea market, a used car lot, and a place called Jesus Window Tint were the only businesses near the strip joint. They were all closed at that time, which was good. They could get the job done and get on 290 in no time. Manuel started to send out a prayer that Sasha would come out alone, but then thought maybe God wasn't exactly crazy about stealing.

The belt screeched again. This time, it was a fucking accusation: *You've accomplished nothing . . . and now look what you're about to do.*

Manuel knew this was a stupid, dangerous idea. Approaching a dancer with a gun in a parking lot was as dumb as it got. Following her to wherever she was staying was even worse. He'd known Carlos for a few years. They worked for the same construction company. But now Manuel felt like he didn't know him. He could tell there was something dark hiding behind Carlos's eyes, and he was afraid of what he might do if they had to follow Sasha Fire home.

"How's your kid?"

Carlos's question shattered the silence and pulled Manuel away from the toothy monster his apprehension was quickly turning into.

"He's good, man," said Manuel. "Hasn't had an asthma attack in a couple months. He started those allergy shots I told you about."

"The ones they pricked him a buncha times for?"

"Yeah, that was to identify what he's allergic to. You know, to figure out what was triggering all the attacks."

"Gotcha," said Carlos. "Them things are expensive, right? Pinches doctores . . ."

Manuel wanted to ask about Carlos's kids, but he knew asking was like slicing open a wound that never healed, so he just nodded.

Carlos was born to undocumented Mexican parents in Houston. He'd gotten lucky and married a white girl named Lisa right after high school because he got her pregnant. That got him papers and he landed a gig cleaning pools with a company that serviced hotels. Lisa had a girl and started working at a coffee place. They had a boy two years later. It was rough, but they got by. Lisa's parents were unemployed alcoholics living in a crumbling little house and refused to babysit, yet Lisa and Carlos made it work. Then Lisa and the kids were in a car accident. She was taking them to school when a drunk driver slammed into the driver's side at an intersection. The bastard was coming back from a long night of celebrating a new contract. He died in the crash. So did Lisa. That left Carlos with two kids, no partner, no help, no money, and no education. He'd heard of an opening in Austin that paid better and he applied. Being bilingual got him the gig and he moved down and became another lost soul in a city that seemed to attract them from all over the world.

Every day since his wife's death had been a fight for Carlos. His girl had pain in her legs from the crash and the boy had refused to talk for almost two years. Carlos couldn't afford what his kids needed—meds, doctors, therapy, toys, a better school—and that had slowly turned him into a lumbering shadow of a man who was perpetually searching for ways to make an extra dollar. He'd heard from a friend that Sasha Fire had pulled in thirteen thousand dollars in one night at a stage in Houston, but that she'd actually walked out with much more because she was selling blow, Oxies, and blowjobs on the side. According to Carlos's friend, who worked security at the strip club and got money from Sasha to look away, Sasha made anywhere between thirty thousand and fifty thousand dollars per night on a good night. Way Carlos figured, they could wait on her, pull a gun, and bring home some easy money. Manuel felt bad about stealing, but knowing the money came from preppy UT Austin students who were happy to overpay for snow made him feel better.

Manuel checked his phone again: 1:17 a.m. He looked at the building. On the roof, a giant neon pink monkey with a cartoonish smile moved its arms. The sign was horrendous, but it fit the place perfectly. Manuel was about to ask Carlos how much longer he thought they'd have to wait when Carlos spoke.

"What are you gonna do with the money, hermano?"

Manuel had thought about it night and day since he'd agreed to come along and split whatever they got. Anything would help, but a couple thousand bucks would make a big difference.

"Gonna pay some bills, man. You know how it is."

Carlos nodded. "Man, I remember how long money lasted when I had no kids. Nowadays holding on to a dollar is like kicking water uphill. Javier destroys shoes like they're made outta paper and Nina needs all these fucking things for school, not to mention clothes and the meds for her leg pain. I'm behind on my water, behind on my electricity, behind on my rent . . . I'm behind on life, you know?"

Manuel knew the feeling well. Back in Puerto Rico, his father used to say that people are divided into two groups, and that this has nothing to do with gender or the color of your skin: those born to win and those born to lose. He learned early on that the color of your skin played a role in which group you had more chances of falling into, but he also understood that poverty didn't give a shit about your skin color or your accent. In Austin, a place he'd moved to dreaming of a degree that would inevitably lead to upward social mobility, he'd been reduced to stealing toilet paper and food before he decided to quit going to school and get a job. Tracy, who he'd met at an anthropology class, kept going to school, but she cut her classes in half and got a job as a cashier at a dollar store on Burnet. After she found out she was pregnant, she gave up on her degree and put in more hours at the store. When she told her parents, devout Jamaican Catholics, they said she was dead to them, hung up, and never picked up the phone again. Thinking about his son's bright eyes and huge smile was the only thing keeping Manuel in this car. If all went well, he could buy his kid new clothes and toys and get Tracy something special. He could pay some bills, pay for the allergy shots, and get the student loan assholes off his back for a bit . . .

The back door opened and a large man in a suit that belonged to someone much smaller stepped out. He was talking on his phone. He pulled out a cigarette and lit up. A moment later, the door opened again and a short brown woman stepped out wearing jeans and a black T-shirt. She was carrying a large bag. Manuel sat up.

"Chill, pendejo," said Carlos. "Sasha Fire is a thick blonde with an ass like a truck. I googled her. I'll let you know when she comes out."

Manuel leaned back and watched as the woman walked to a car, opened the door, threw her bag in, climbed inside, and drove out. When she was gone, Carlos pointed at the man, who had stayed next to the door.

"That dude's packing. I hope he's the only one in there. I mean, it's a Thursday, right? Shitty joint like this probably only pays for one gorilla on weeknights, maybe two on Friday and Saturday. They probably get a bunch of students in here and not much else. You know, those too cool or too horny for 6th Street. Anyway, if he's the only one, he's definitely not walking every girl out because he has to make sure motherfuckers keep their hands to themselves during private dances. Probably was just about to step out for a smoke anyway. I mean, we haven't seen anyone else all night—"

The belt cried again.

What the fuck are you doing, Manuel? Go home to your kid.

"Did you check if there are any cameras here?" Manuel had been obsessing about this. People now had cameras everywhere.

"I checked. I was in here last Sunday too. Took a walk

around the place while pretending to smoke and talk on my phone just like Mr. Smallsuit over there. This place is shitty through and through. At least two of the dancers had C-section scars and one of them had dark scars under her boobs bigger than her implants. Oh, and the food is trash."

"You ate here?"

"Some of these places have decent food. The Yellow Rose sells a mean steak."

Manuel couldn't fathom cutting a steak with breasts swinging in his face, but he knew Carlos was a very different man.

Mr. Smallsuit was grinding out his cigarette under his shoe when the door opened again. He grabbed it and held it open. A short, thick blonde in black yoga pants and a white T-shirt with a smiley face on it stepped out. She was pulling a black box on wheels that was vomiting a chunk of pink feather boa into the warm night. Mr. Smallsuit said a few words to her. She smiled. The gorilla walked back into the Pink Monkey.

"That's her," said Carlos.

Manuel reached down and grabbed the gun from under his seat. It was a small revolver Carlos had gotten from someone at the site.

Carlos put the car in drive and pulled out of his spot slowly. When he stepped on the gas, the belt shrieked again.

Put the fucking gun down and go home, Manuel.

The damn belt sounded like his mother.

Carlos drove slowly. Sasha approached a red SUV and pressed a key fob. The car's lights blinked twice.

"I'm gonna pull up next to her," said Carlos, his voice a few octaves higher than before. "Just point the gun at her and grab that box she's pulling. Throw it in the back and then we're gone. We clear?"

Manuel nodded. He didn't want to do any of it. He had to do it.

Sasha was about to open the trunk when they pulled up next to her. Manuel jumped out, gun ready.

"Hey," he said. It was the only thing that came to mind.

Sasha Fire turned to look at him. The terror in her eyes was almost enough to make Manuel lower the gun. Almost.

"Get the fucking box, pendejo!"

Manuel took a step forward.

"Hey, what the fuck are you doing?"

Manuel turned. Two white guys were approaching. He needed to grab the box and bail. When he turned back to Sasha, she had a gun.

BANG!

Something punched Manuel in the stomach. The snake that had been curled around his lungs went up in flames and dropped down to his belly. He lifted his weapon, a question blossoming in the back of his throat.

BANG!

The second bullet caught him in the chest, right below his right nipple. Manuel took a step back and bumped against the car.

Carlos stepped on the gas. The belt screamed.

You fucked up, Manuel. You always fuck up! He rolled off the car and stumbled away. He made it two cars down and had to lean against the trunk of a small white sedan. His innards were on fire. His lungs refused to work properly. The world was beginning to spin around him. In his head, a thousand voices were yelling accusations. In the distance, the belt screeched again as Carlos sped onto 290.

Sasha screamed something. Before Manuel could do anything, he felt hands on his back. For a moment, he thought someone had already called an ambulance. He could explain things. They would take care of him. If he could get rid of the gun, he could claim he was holding his phone, wanting to take a picture with Sasha. This was all a misunderstanding . . .

"The gun, Joe, get the fucking gun!" said one of the men.

No. He had to throw it away before—

Someone yanked the gun away from him. Then he felt a fist explode against his left kidney and he dropped to the ground.

The two men started kicking him. Manuel wanted to curl up into a ball and protect himself, but his body was refusing to follow orders. He heard the word *wetback*. He wanted to tell them they were racist assholes . . . and that he was Puerto Rican, not Mexican, but the words wouldn't come out. A shoe connected with his temple and the world went black for a second. When his vision came back, the men were standing in front of him. So was Sasha. She still had her gun.

The men were on their phones. Manuel watched as Sasha moved back, turned, and opened the trunk of her SUV. She pushed the handle of the black box down, picked it up, and placed it in the trunk. One of the guys turned and told her to wait. Sasha ignored him and got in the car. The reverse lights came on. The two men moved. Sasha swung out of her spot and drove off.

Manuel had heard once that people aren't afraid of being alone in the dark; they're afraid of *not* being alone in the dark. Looking at the men in front of him, he understood that perfectly. He wanted to be alone. He wanted to get up and go home, to kiss his son and crawl into bed for a whole day. The pain in his gut told him none of that would happen. It was as if a thousand shards of glass were dancing in his torso, each pushing out a bit of blood onto the dirt he was sitting on.

Manuel looked up, praying for an angel, hoping for a paramedic. Instead, he saw the pink monkey's giant neon grin.

STUNTS

BY ACE ATKINS

Red River Street

Like the old song says, there's nothing like the life of a
Hollywood stuntman.

Saturday afternoon, three people were shot and another
killed outside a downtown Austin bar. According to police, the al-
tercation started inside the Royale Lounge, 701 Red River Street,
at what was supposed to be a fan-appreciation fundraiser for a
regular in the local movie scene, retired stuntman Jason Colson.

Colson, 71, is in stable condition at UT Health Austin. Police haven't identified the other two victims or the man who died
at the scene.

"I was in line for an autograph when we heard the gunshots
outside," said Scott Montgomery, 51, of Austin. "At first, everyone thought it was part of some kind of Old West show, like maybe
Mr. Colson was going to fall backward off the roof or something.
But when we walked outside to watch, the police rushed up and
pushed us back. That's when we heard someone was dead."

According to IMDB.com, Jason Colson worked from the
early seventies up through the early 2000s on films like Smokey
and the Bandit, Hooper, and the Cannonball Run films. He
was the go-to double and stuntman for the late Burt Reynolds.
In recent years, Colson had been a featured guest at several film
festivals and events for the Alamo Drafthouse.

"I don't know who would make trouble for Jason," said Lars
Nilsen, programmer for the Austin Film Society. "He's one of

the nicest guys in the business. Always willing to give his time and immense knowledge of the stunt scene in Southern California to fans. Anyone who has ever heard his story about jumping that cherry-red Trans Am over a ravine in Alabama for Hooper *knows that he was the real deal."*

A woman who answered the phone at Colson's home said she didn't want to comment on the shooting. Austin police say no charges have been filed in an active investigation. Any witnesses are asked to call the department at 512-472-TIPS.

"How do I look?" Jason Colson asked.

It was a little after ten Saturday morning and his daughter Caddy was in his apartment kitchen, sitting at his old wagon wheel table. She had a purse thrown over her shoulder and keys in her hand. Ready to roll even though the show didn't start till high noon.

"Would you be mad if I said the shirt was a bit much?" Caddy asked.

"This shirt?" Jason said. "Hell. Burt gave it to me himself. Had six of 'em made for *Smokey* deuce. Fans will get it. It's real silk and the red roses were embroidered by hand. Mexican woman over on Olvera Street made a dozen of 'em special for the crew."

"I'm sure the ladies loved it back during the bicentennial," Caddy said. "But how about that nice one Donnie and I gave you for Christmas? Maybe tone it down a little, Dad."

"That's not what folks want," Jason said. "They're not payin' twenty-five bucks a head to see an old man in a button-down collar and tie. This isn't some fancy church service."

"That's me, putting on pearls and lipstick before worship."

Caddy worked her tail off for some Christian nonprofit feeding homeless folks and immigrants in need. She had on an old threadbare Johnny Cash T-shirt, bell-bottoms, and hippie sandals.

She rolled her eyes as Jason walked over to the counter, where he reached for his wallet and then headed back to his bedroom. He stood in front of his floor-length mirror and checked out the spit-shined Luccheses, the tight black jeans, and black silk cowboy shirt. He ran a comb over his gray hair and gray mustache and decided his daughter was a fine woman and an amazing person but plain wrong on the shirt. 1976. Hell, everyone knew that *Smokey II* hit theaters in the summer of 1980.

"Ready, Daddy?" Caddy said, calling out from the kitchen.

"*I was born ready,*" Jason said in his best Roy Rogers.

Jason remembered the Red River District before the place had a name. He used to hang out at the One Knite Club back when it was filled with bikers, hippies, and old blues musicians. The bar had once turned away the boys from Pink Floyd because they couldn't name a Lightnin' Hopkins song. That wasn't long before they were shooting *Outlaw Blues* with Peter Fonda and Susan Saint James. He'd doubled Fonda in that picture, riding a police motorcycle along the concrete path of Waller Creek and up and down North Lamar and Lavaca. Fonda was playing a convict who'd had a hit song stolen from him by a sleazy country-and-western singer. Pretty damn good script written by his pal Bill Norton, who went on to write *Convoy*. Jason did stunts on both.

The shoot wasn't easy. Most days Fonda and a lot of the crew had showed up stoned out of their minds. Hard to believe he was gone. Burt too. Needham. His old pal Charlie Bail, who taught him just about everything he knew about gags. Almost everyone he knew from the old Hollywood days was either dead or tucked and fucked beyond recognition.

He missed old Hollywood so bad it hurt. But it was gone. He'd moved to Austin five years ago because he could make a buck or two as a consultant for young filmmakers. He worked on a vampire flick, some coming-of-age horseshit made with cell phones, and what was supposed to be a Western shot on a jerry-rigged set out in Bastrop. The script was so bad it made him physically ill to say the lines. (OLD MAN: *I'm getting too old for vengeance, son. Blood just begets more blood till there ain't no more.*)

Today was supposed to be a celebration. But now he wondered if it might be a crucifixion.

Damn if he wasn't still into Bobby Delgado for ten thousand big ones. At the moment, he only had four hundred bucks left to his name.

Bobby D won't show, right? Even Bobby D wouldn't want to piss on my parade.

The Jason Colson Celebration hadn't even started, the band hadn't played a lick, and already he had folks talking his ear off.

Some big fella in a black duster and black cowboy hat cornered him by the bar, asking him all sorts of questions about his trucker movies. When they'd shook hands, the duster parted like a curtain and he saw the fella was carrying a goddamn cannon under his right arm. Looked like a walnut-handle .44.

"Mr. Colson, I can't tell you how much your work means to me," the big man said. "I drove all the way over from Amarillo in my rig just to meet you. My daddy and me used to watch you on television when I was a kid. Is it true that *The Fall Guy* was really based on you?"

"Well," Jason said, "some folks have made that connection, although the courts saw it different. But like the bard said, partly truth and partly fiction. Just a walkin' contradiction."

"Who was that?"

"Fella I used to know back in the ole days," Jason said. He gave a quick wink and shook the man's hand again, trying to get back to the card table they'd set up by the bar.

"What's he like?"

"Who's that?"

"Burt."

"Third-finest man to walk this earth," Jason said. "After Jesus Christ and Elvis Presley."

"Did he do a lot of his own stunts?"

"When he could," Jason said. "When he was younger. But Burt had a bad back from football at Florida State and when he did his own stuff on *Gunsmoke*. We knew each other a long while. From *White Lightning* all the way to *Cop and a Half*. We shot that one in Tampa."

"He seemed like a regular guy."

"Yes sir."

"No airs about him."

"None at all."

"I knew it," the man said, hitching up his belt buckle. "They don't make 'em like that anymore."

"Broke that ole mold."

Caddy walked up on them, grabbing Jason's elbow, being a real pro at separating her dad from the crazy fans, and said it was time. Fans had started to line up outside and they'd soon be letting them in. Two-dollar beers and dollar tequila shots, as the event was sponsored by the Jose Cuervo distributor.

She ushered Jason over to the table where he eased into a hard chair, feeling that familiar lightning zap up his legs and into his lower back. Both knees. One shoulder too. Caddy had set out a bunch of Sharpies and Jason Colson swag: eight-by-ten action shots, T-shirts, ball caps, and belt buckles.

The band on stage started picking out the first chords of "East Bound and Down," Jason recalling how ole Jerry had come up with that one on the spot for Hal, saying if he didn't like it, give him a few hours and he'd write something else.

"Only one question," Caddy said, giving him the side eye. "What's all this bullshit about medical expenses?"

"You know," Jason said, "I've had a few over the years."

"Mm-hmm," Caddy said.

"I love you, baby," Jason said, "but can you please ease off on the sermon? Just for today?"

Red River.

Jason didn't know if it was his nerves acting up, but he couldn't stop thinking about that film he'd seen as a boy at the picture show in Tibbehah County, Mississippi. John Wayne bigger than shit in black-and-white with a six-shooter on his hip, leading that first cattle drive along the Chisholm Trail. Monty Cliff playing his adopted son willing to follow him into the depths of hell and madness until things went off the rails, the Duke killing off two of his cowboys for not keeping their word. Wayne and Clift damn well beat the hell out of each other until a good woman intervened and told them they really loved each other. *Loved each other?* If only it was all that simple.

Jason knew his own son thought about him the same way. Five years ago, Jason had decided to up and leave in the middle of the night in an old Firebird he'd gotten after *Hooper* wrapped. It had stayed in storage for thirty years until he had the time to take it apart and put it all back together after.

Ended up selling it for forty grand to a collector in Dallas. He never did get around to explaining to his son why he'd left again. Some things were just too rough and painful to discuss.

Jason knew that him shagging ass sure opened up some old wounds, scars made when he left his first wife back when the kids were little. But given the circumstances, he didn't have any other choice.

When Caddy and Quinn had been kids, there were epic trips out west. Visits to the movie sets. Disneyland, popcorn, and ice cream sundaes till they about burst. Caddy could always see the good. He sure wished his son one day might do the same.

Jason counted almost a hundred heads, hitting over 2K, as the rain pinged on the tin roof above the wide-open cinder block bar. They'd cheered for him as he made his way to the stage after a fine introduction by his buddy Lars, who ran the film fest. Lars was able to name a bunch of his films that most folks had forgotten, like *Billy Jack Goes to Washington* and *Moonrunners*.

Moonrunners hadn't paid well but was a hell of a fun shoot with Mitchum's son James and a real pistol of a gal named Chris Forbes. No woman, except maybe Lynda Carter, looked better in a pair of tight jeans.

"Never in a million years did I think falling off a damn horse or crashing a car would mean so much to folks," Jason said. "Those pictures we made were supposed to run for a few weeks at your neighborhood drive-in and maybe show up once or twice on late-night TV. But seeing so many young people here tonight shows me that we made something real and honest. And not to get up too high on my horse, but I think that's something lacking in pictures today with all that

CGI. I don't care how good the picture is, people can tell what's real and what's fake. And I promise you, everything that happened in those old movies happened in real life. I got a file cabinet of X-rays to prove it."

There was laughter and applause. Just as he was about to shake Lars's hand and return to the card table to sign some autographs, he saw Bobby Delgado walk into the bar. He had that short, mean fella, Angel Rojas, riding shotgun with him.

The men wore all black. They looked like maybe they should've worn hoods and maybe carried scythes too.

Delgado had on a black suit over a black shirt and bolo tie. He was thin and hard looking, with black eyes and slick black hair. Angel Rojas was shorter and squatter, walking low to the ground like a bulldog, with a pockmarked face and trimmed mustache.

When Jason locked eyes with Delgado, he was pretty sure he wasn't gonna be leaving the show with a dime.

So he stepped back up to the mic, cool and collected, and took in all the folks with their eyes on him. The beautiful women, so young they could be his granddaughters, and the aging hipster kids with their retro T-shirts and receding hairlines. He could smell the bar funk of weed and piss; there was a poster on the wall for a monthly burlesque show and another for some punk band playing later that night.

"When you get as old as me, you see things different," Jason said, offering a sad, introspective smile. "Y'all stop being fans and become family. I love you all."

People clapped, hooted, and hollered.

As he shook Lars's hand, Jason leaned in and asked, "Just where's the shitter in this place?"

The line wound its way past the bathrooms, the elevated

stage, and the extended bar with the longhorn skull above the bottles shining in bright neon. One fan brought Jason a plate of brisket and beans from Ruby's, another wanted him to sign an original half-sheet to *Moonrunners*, and then a middle-aged woman with frizzy hair and tattoos asked if he wouldn't mind signing one of her titties.

"Sure you don't want me to sign 'em both?" Jason asked. "Don't want the other to get jealous."

It wasn't the first time he'd been asked. Or told the same joke.

The woman leaned down and he signed her right cleavage with a Sharpie.

"Headed straight to the tattoo parlor to make it permanent," the woman said. "How about we do a shot later on?"

"I haven't had a drink in ten years," Jason said, "but I sure do appreciate it."

"My husband sure thought you hung the moon," she said. "He always said *White Line Fever* made him want to be a trucker. Hell, he'd be standing right here with me if he hadn't up and died."

"Sorry to hear that," Jason said.

He reached out and patted the back of her hand. She smiled at him while Jason glanced down the line to see Bobby Delgado and Angel Rojas getting closer. Bobby D never had been a guy to wait his turn, but he figured Bobby must've appreciated the drama of him and Rojas getting closer and closer, hoping that old Jason Colson would finally up and wet his pants.

Not a chance. That wasn't the Colson way.

"Happens," the woman said. "I told him to lay off the red meat."

Jason swallowed and looked back up at her. She pushed

her right titty back down into her tight tank top. "What can you do but keep on truckin'?"

"Yes ma'am," he said, "pedal to the metal."

"Darlin'," Jason said to Caddy.

His daughter looked over from where she was making change for a man buying two copies of Jason's autobiography, *From Tibbehah to Tinseltown.*

"You mind holding down the fort while I hit the head?"

"Can't you wait, Daddy? That line's stretching out the back door."

"Wish I could, but my prostate is now officially listed as an antique."

Jason stood up. Rojas turned to Bobby D and pointed right at him. Jason ducked his head and passed behind Caddy, smiling at all the people in line.

"If I don't come back," Jason said, leaning down and whispering in her ear, "I'll call you later. Don't worry. Don't worry about nothing, baby."

"Daddy?"

But Jason was already headed to the bathroom door.

The bathroom had a row of six urinals on the wall, two stalls, and no window or other way out.

Jason walked over to the lone sink and ran the faucet. He splashed some cool water in his face and looked into the rusted reflection. He could hold firm, maybe talk his way out of his arrangement with Bobby D. Or have Caddy pull the car around and drive like hell.

Bobby D didn't know about his new apartment. Didn't know a damn thing about his family. He'd get him back. It might take some time. But he needed to rest up and come up with a plan. He'd already sold his old truck, ran down his last few friends in California for some money, and even sold a silver belt buckle given to him by the late, great Chuck Roberson.

Jason was studying the paneled ceiling for an exit when the bathroom door opened and the big man he'd first met at the lounge walked in.

"Mr. Colson, there's two fellas here aim to do you some harm."

"No offense, son," Jason said, "but no shit."

"I think I can help you out."

"You got ten grand in your hip pocket?"

"No sir."

"How about you give me a boost then?" Jason said, pointing at the ceiling over the urinals. "I'm planning on finding an alternative exit."

The man nodded and then removed his duster and cowboy hat. He sized Jason up, then nodded. "Here, take 'em."

"Son."

"Come on. Those fellas want to rough you up good."

Jason started to unsnap the buttons on his black silk shirt with red roses. He took it off and handed it to the man.

"Always been my lucky shirt," Jason said.

"Looks identical to the one Burt had on in *Smokey II*."

Jason winked at him and slid into the duster and put the hat down on his head. It was a little snug but would work just fine.

"Tell my daughter she can find me saddled up to the Driskill Bar."

"You wrote in your autobiography that you quit drinking."

"I did?" Jason said, cracking open the bathroom door and

peering back into the Royale Lounge. "Maybe. But today sure seems like the day to start back up."

There wasn't much planning to it. Jason figured he'd walk past the country band and make his way outside into the rain before anyone noticed a thing. The Driskill wasn't too far away and he'd be high and dry within fifteen minutes, sipping on some Patrón. He felt terrible about leaving his own party early but figured folks would think he wasn't feeling well and had to rest a bit. After all, this was all about helping a man down with medical expenses.

Jason pulled the brim of the cowboy hat over his eyes just as the band started into "Slow Rollin' Low," the theme to *Moonrunners*, a film which later became a little something called *The Dukes of Hazzard* on CBS. He and Waylon had worked on both productions. He sure wished ole Waylon was still around so Jason could tell him about Bobby D and Angel Rojas on his ass. He could hear Waylon laughing about the current predicament. Maybe he'd even write a ballad about it. "The Last Days of Jason Colson."

He didn't get five feet from the men's room when Angel Rojas caught his eye and jabbed Bobby D hard in the ribs. But then Bobby D grabbed Rojas's arm and pointed to the man in the black silk shirt with roses on the shoulders. They turned in the opposite direction.

Jason passed the card table, Caddy not noticing as she was making excuses for him, offering half price on all official stunt gear. *Half damn price?*

He spotted two metal doors at the back of the bar. One had a padlock and a chain and the other looked like it might go into the adjoining bar. He didn't think twice, just pushed into it and found himself in complete and absolute darkness, tripping over something and landing hard onto a staircase. Feeling for the wall, Jason made his way up and then around the blackened staircase, spotting light up top at what looked like an exit. He could hear the wind and the rain now, the tin roof panels slapping up and down.

He tried the exit but it held tight. He leaned into the lock with his good shoulder but it wouldn't budge. Hearing voices and music below, Jason stepped back and kicked hard, the door slamming open. He walked out onto the roof, stepping lightly on the slick metal, looking down onto Red River and all the cars passing in the rain-slick street. The whole bar vibrated from the old Waylon tune playing below.

He saw where there was a small gap between the Royale Lounge and the bar next door, maybe five to six feet. He felt if he had a little wind at his back, he might just be able to make it across and slide down the other bar roof to the ground. It was tricky but he figured it was better than a shot in the back by Bobby D or Rojas.

Jason shimmied down to where the roof flattened out over a loading dock. He backed up, took a breath, and was about to make a run for it.

"Daddy," Caddy called out from below, "just what the hell are you doing? We don't have time for you to play around." Hands on her hips, she stared up from the alley separating the two bars. The rain coming down now, tapping hard at the cowboy hat and across his back.

Jason put a finger to his lips and shook his head. He gestured toward the end of the alley where he spotted Bobby D running like hell and yelling in Spanish. He had a gun in his hand. Caddy simply shook her head and walked away.

Bobby D immediately replaced her, peering up at Jason on the roof, and drew his gun. *Holy damn shit.*

More people followed. Jason could see the Royale Lounge emptying, people standing shoulder to shoulder on Red River and in the alley, pointing up to crazy Jason Colson on the tin roof. The crowd transfixed as they watched some man in a black suit, a villain straight out of central casting, aiming a big silver pistol up at Jason, yelling, "You have two choices, Jason Colson: easy or hard way down!"

The crowd started to laugh. Some clapped and whistled.

Jason raised his hands as if surrendering.

Bobby D wasn't smiling. He looked to where several folks had gathered around him. One was the big man from the bathroom wearing Jason's lucky shirt, the snap buttons about to explode from his chest. Jason could see he had his big gun stuck in the back of his blue jeans. The fella's hand reached back to grab that beautiful walnut handle.

"Oh shit," Jason said. "Oh shit."

The roof exit slammed open again and Angel Rojas came barreling out with a two-by-four in his hand. He was screaming something nasty and blasphemous when the first bullet ripped into his shoulder, and then another caught him in the throat. He fell backward onto the sloping tin roof and slid his way down fast into the alley and a pile of garbage cans.

Bobby D turned to Jason Colson's number one fan and raised his gun. The whole damn thing running slower than Peckinpah on Valium. Bobby D fired and caught the man in the arm and the big fella fired and caught Bobby D in the leg. The man fired again, the *BLAM* of the pistol sounding like thunder above, getting Bobby D in the chest, dropping him to his knees.

The crowd clapped.

Jason took off the cowboy hat and waved, while no one seemed to pay Angel Rojas or Bobby D a bit of attention. *Son of a damn bitch.* That big ole boy was bleeding right through his lucky shirt. This sure wasn't Jason's day.

That's when he felt the bullet slice through his shoulder and heard the crack. Two more shots and hot pain seared his right thigh. Goddamn Angel Rojas was on his feet in the dumpster, unloading his goddamn pistol. Jason didn't waste a second, taking a practiced fall onto his back as if the bullets had done their job.

Down below, Rojas's hammer finally fell on the sixth shot and he wavered on his feet until he tumbled back onto the black plastic bags.

Caddy was the first to reach Jason on the roof. She was twice as strong as she looked, reaching under his arms and dragging his ass off the rainy roof and into the stairwell, the landing now full of bright light. She held Jason's head in her lap and stroked his gray hair.

"What did you do this time?" She was crying hard. "God, your dumbass fans think it's just another show."

"But you know different," Jason said. Damn if he didn't feel like he was trying to stand up with bowling balls in his luggage. "You always knew."

"Will you ever stop?" Caddy asked. "When will you ever stop?"

Jason could hear the sirens and the drumming of the rain across the roof of the Royale Lounge. As he thought on what had just transpired, he wiped the wetness from his face and mustache. "I'm getting too old for vengeance," he said, eyes fluttering closed. "Blood just begets more blood till there ain't no more."

"I love you," Caddy said, "but damn if you haven't always been full of shit."

REFLECTIONS

BY AMANDA MOORE

Arboretum

I never liked mirrors. It didn't matter what I looked like. My reflection only provided a blunt and truthful reminder of my life's choices. Dark shadows under my eyes covered with brown MAC concealer. Thin lashes transformed with eye glue. By some miracle or mistake, my curly hair and dark natural waves allowed me to look the part. Thoughts about my appearance didn't consume me like a river. I didn't obsess over the stares from men in the courtroom or from the women at the restaurants. I dealt with the law partner with the wandering hands and lascivious smiles deftly, breaking his finger and his bank account before I left. No, the problem that haunted me daily was that when people saw me, they saw *her*. I had her face, but not her sneer. I had her mouth, but not her voice. I would like to have felt her love, but I only managed to secure her indifference. She channeled rage well, never allowing it to go beyond the surface where other people could detect it. It lived below her skin like an unused muscle, rippling like a wave, but never quite breaking through her flawless demeanor. Most would describe my mother as exquisite, lovely to a distracting degree. I viewed her like a carnivorous creature, attractive to the eye but fatal in its resolve.

I straightened the largest satin ruffle that lay next to my neck and removed my black tapered jacket from my suitcase.

I liked to dress moderately, classically, refined to a painful degree. From my many jaunts through the elite clothing shops on South Congress, I learned that as a woman of color, I received better service if I appeared as if I could own the establishment. I pulled my hair back from my face and brushed it gently. My hair was thick but pliable, easily pressed, twisted, or braided. When I wore it pressed like my European counterparts, I could assimilate effortlessly. No one would dare run their hands through my bone-straight hair praising its volume and vitality as they did with my natural hairstyle. In my formative years, it would cascade over my ears and onto my shoulders and move with the wind. Even now, I can still smell the chemical fragrance emitting from the white paste in the dark-blue plastic container from my quarterly appointments at the salon. The stylist, or the female magician of hair manipulation, would paint the smooth cream on the roots of my Z-pattern curls as if she were a hair contractor on a deadline.

Years later, I discovered why. Oh, the creamy substance felt cool to my scalp and pacified my nerves with visions of silky, socially acceptable hair—until the burn began. The sodium hydroxide seared my scalp like it was an enemy combatant. I held on as long as I could—the longer the burn, the straighter the hair. It was my mantra, my religion. I could be Black when I wore my pretty dresses to church, when I danced with my cousins in my living room, or even when I ate a Southern dinner for Thanksgiving. My hair, however, had to conform and not draw unnecessary cultural attention and disingenuous flattery.

My mother watched this ritual from her chair in the corner with her own hair wrapped in a thin plastic cap edged with hand-pulled cotton from Sally Beauty Supply so that her mane could absorb every drop of the deep conditioning serum. She saw my distress, noted my condition, then pointed to the parts that my tormentor overlooked. When I escaped central Texas, I embraced my curls and only reserved my flat iron for antiquated events. Today seemed fitting to sport the flattened hair she championed instead of the Senegalese twists that I preferred, undoubtedly a fitting end to the role I intended to portray. I reached into my velvet bag and donned the pearls that my father gave me. She would dislike the fact that I decided to wear them today—a day when others would judge *her* for once.

I stayed at the Renaissance Austin Hotel, near Arboretum Boulevard, vowing never to sleep in my old bed in my childhood home. My drive from Houston took the usual three hours, but it was worth it just to stay there. It had a certain lone grandiosity, sitting above the Texas Hill Country skyline like a modern-day castle. On my walks with my father through the Arboretum, I would often see it emerging from the trees like an ancient monolith surrounded by stores with designer labels and elite clientele. I have stayed in grander hotels than this one, but this place had a splendor to it that made me feel real, noble, and somewhat inspired. I treasured it because my father loved it first. I knew that I would spend the next few days here, though I never liked to unpack my things. It would feel too much like home, and I was only a visitor.

I picked up my legal notepad and placed it in my briefcase. I had stayed up all night reviewing the police report, but in the end it wouldn't matter. She would be arrested, and I would happily watch it happen. I placed my silk-lined Ralph Lauren winter coat over my left arm, allowing it to swing freely, and grabbed the hotel key. At best, her arrest and detention would not take long, and I would be back before lunch.

The hallway outside my room ran alongside an enormous foyer which allowed for a spectacular view of the restaurants and bars below. I watched for loners, easy marks who separated from the pack and who might need my services. The frazzled father who had to have that late-night drink at the hotel bar became an excellent candidate for solicitation. The frustrated fiancée whose fight with her man caused her to bury her sorrows in an early morning mimosa always brought spectacular daytime DWIs to my inbox. I had contacts who were ready to witness the tipsy person who deviated from the yellow line or turned left at a red light out of the parking lot. The police were on speed dial and so was I. The defendant always managed to call me first, usually after I ran into frantic family members in the sterile waiting areas or restrooms at the police station. They stayed in a perpetual state of desperation, searching for legal representation to save them from life's little uppercuts. It was not barratry if they approached me first. Fortunately, my hunting ground remained in larger cities, not this one. In Austin, the lawyers, judges, and police officers all knew each other. They would not think that my casual presence in a waiting room was coincidental, or that my strategically placed cards by the fish tank in a hospital waiting room were inconsequential. My mother would be so proud.

I walked into the open dining area, noticing the croissants and other lightly toasted delicacies drizzled with vanilla glaze at the breakfast bar. I could smell the sweet aroma of the pecan-roasted coffee beans drifting from another customer's cup, although by the look on his face, he wouldn't be able to keep it down.

"Anyone else joining you today?" The waitress reached for the empty glass in front of my place setting and began to fill it with water.

"No."

"We have a variety of choices on our menu—"

"I know. I'll have coffee, avocado toast, and fruit. No salsa, please."

"Yes ma'am."

I didn't know what it was about Austin restaurants that made everyone want to offer the ingredients for a breakfast taco on every menu. I enjoyed eggs, and I savored fresh salsa, but never at the same time and never for breakfast.

My phone chimed with an incoming message.

When will you arrive?

Soon.

That is not a time.

This morning.

That is not a time either. They will be here at 10 a.m. sharp. You need to arrive before then.

I will be there before they arrive.

That's not acceptable.

If you want me there, it will have to be.

I don't understand why you couldn't stay here. There is plenty of room.

You know why.

The coffee arrived. It was only eight thirty a.m., and the police detectives would probably arrive thirty minutes before the scheduled time. It would serve her right to have a few surprises to humble her, to make her feel less like she had control of the situation. Their scheduling a visit on a Friday morning, at a time that was convenient to her and only three weeks after the winter storm, stemmed from professional courtesy and a deference to her former position on the city council.

If hell and heaven could coexist in the same place, it did for one week during the Texas winter storm. I remember my mother calling me when the first snowflakes fell. She droned on for hours about the beauty of it as it blanketed the hillside. She sent pictures of her wood-burning fireplace with the snowfall in the window. She texted that she'd found heaven in the hill country and she didn't have to die to see it. I never replied. She sent pictures of the neighborhood children with their vacation skis and snow boots playing in the unpaved street. I deleted them. For three days, Texans believed that they could have the best of both worlds—a place where one could view all of the four seasons in a backyard. The weather started out magnificently, dropping eleven inches of snowy goodness across the state, mesmerizing Texans with its unnatural presence but welcomed beauty. We witnessed what we thought to be the upside of climate change, where we would not have to make snow angels in slush-covered grass. No, we had the weather that we only saw featured on the news, where we had little sympathy for people who complained of blizzards when we suffered from summer drought and heatstroke. Ironically, our comfort was short-lived.

I remember when the power grid failed. My neighbors and I did not have any means to warm our homes. Boiling water notices erupted across the news like confetti. While I sat in my well-stocked condominium trying to figure out how to boil water without power, I watched news reports of parents burning cribs and cardboard fruit crates for warmth. After a day, the water disappeared into frozen pipes and unpainted walls. Untouched snow that amassed on lawns found a secondary use in its melted state as liquid to flush toilets and cook food. My classmates who remained in Austin after graduation posted pictures of H-E-B, the local grocery store, overflowing with customers. The aisles swelled with customers and metal baskets to the point that store managers began to post laminated signs describing the limited supplies of toilet paper, beans, and milk. Customers stood in line like living statues, cold, desperate, and completely reliant upon the grocery food chain.

Heaven? No, Mother, that was hell.

I still called my clients, the ones who lived in jail, unable to secure bail money for their release. The brick walls kept the frostbite at bay, but the prisons were meat lockers and my clients were carcasses. Delayed court appearances due to county court shutdowns only exacerbated their misery, but I did my best with superior cell phone battery life and 5G cellular data services. Before the storm, an online law practice served me well. My files remained in a cloud, and I made legal appearances via Zoom. I set my own hours and fees, and kept minimal staff. I had two phones, and she called me on the one that I always answered.

She once bragged that the neighborhoods of 78759 never had as much violence as the other areas in Austin. Residents who lived near the Great Hills Country Club cared about the safety of their homes and neighbors. As a city council woman, she once proclaimed on the local news that the pathway to citywide safety resided in the relationships between those whose yards we shared. She declared that violence was a sickness that only kindness could eradicate, and our neighborhoods could return to the landscape of our childhoods. We only needed to believe in our capabilities and change our impoverished mindset. She ran her reelection campaign supporting neighborhood improvement and opposing citywide composting. She gained attention and the respect of some state representatives when she voted against allowing homeless people to camp out on public property.

She lost the election, but won a following. She discovered Twitter and Facebook and continued to post her views with pictures of what she believed to be the forsaken people of the Live Music Capital of the World.

No one deserves to be exposed to the natural elements, she tweeted. *It's not sanitary or safe.*

I found it interesting that she still tried to maintain that view even after her landscaper found a decaying body in her backyard.

I pulled out of the parking garage and headed toward the Capital of Texas Highway. I passed Eddie V's and the Z-Tejas Southwest Grill that had a breathtaking view of Northwest Austin and the Texas Hill Country foliage. I loved looking at the picturesque homes grasping the small mountainsides like a lover, their windows reflecting the skyline and the occasional Texas blue jay in flight.

My phone chimed.

Where are you?

Close.

I turned on Bluffstone Lane, a dead-end street lined with trees and office buildings. It was a straight climb up the hill, causing my luxury rental to automatically switch into another gear. Once at the top, I took another right onto Bluegrass Drive, the street that would lead me straight up to the Great Hills Country Club if I stayed on it long enough. It was a public street, but it was lined with trees as if it were a private drive. Many of the homeowners on this road sacrificed their backyards for hill country views and heavily wooded greenbelts, favoring titanic stilts and metal platforms over concrete foundations. The front yards were immaculate, the brown lifeless grass manicured and shaped to perfection. My mother lived at the far end of a cul-de-sac in a taupe-colored colonial-style one-story residence. She told my father that she did not want to live on the side of a road as if they could not afford the premium lots. If she could not have her ten acres of land outside of the city, she would have an entrance, even if the city maintained it. I pulled into the driveway noting that she had installed plants on either side of the garage. The small evergreens emerged like sentries, and I had the haphazard notion to drive into one of them. I glanced into the rearview mirror to smooth my hair and saw them turn into the cove. The unmarked police car drove slowly and cautiously until it stopped at the curb where my mother's lawn and the neighbor's shrubbery merged like long-lost friends. They waited.

I closed my car door and looked to the house as if unaware of their presence. I could feel their eyes on me as I approached. She opened the door before I walked up the stairs, acknowledging my presence but looking over my shoulder. Dressed in her light-pink cardigan and dark-blue Donna Morgan ensemble, she looked prepared for a battle she had no idea how to fight.

"I've been calling you," she said.

I walked through the door and rubbed my arms. She lit the fireplace, but turned off the heater. My childhood home was a museum with a plethora of substitutions and contradictions. She had portraits instead of my class pictures, vases instead of my trophies, and awards where my diplomas once belonged. The only exception sat on the mantel over the fireplace where she kept many of my childhood photos, though she remained visibly present in most of them.

"Why don't you ever pick up when I call?"

I glanced around the living room. She'd changed a few things, but I could still see the dark residue from the crime scene tape on the doorway leading to the back door. I walked up to it and gently placed my hand against the frame. I rubbed it until the plastic residue rolled against my fingertips.

"We need to talk about how I should handle this situation."

"It's too late for that," I said.

"You're the lawyer. Aren't you supposed to control the direction of this conversation? To make sure that it doesn't go somewhere that would cause more problems for me?"

I walked to the edge of the hallway that led to my bedroom. The little dove statue sat on top of the ceramic table outside the door. His little dove. That's what he would call me on the nights he came over. She claims that she and my father were too drunk to remember, partially stoned from the marijuana and the vodka-laced fruit punch that she kept in the refrigerator at the end of the day. I knew better. Douglas, my mother's former law school friend, always seemed to find time to drop by when my father was out of town. He had light-green eyes that would never stay on my face. He would talk to my feet, then slowly move his eyes upward until he reached the top of my head. He repeated this viewing every time he saw me. His constant presence made the inside of my skin itch. My mother welcomed him into the home, offering him baked goods or treats for his dog.

Doug would smile at her often, laughing at her idiosyncrasies and mimicking her somewhat girlish pouts. His casual glances in my direction grabbed at my skin, peeling back my childhood innocence like a rotting piece of fruit. One time after tennis practice, I remember walking to my mother's car in the parking lot at Anderson High School. I opened the back door to their laughter and watched Doug's hand as he slowly massaged her right shoulder. She grinned, her beautiful brown skin practically radiating from the front seat. He liked to comb his dark-brown hair backward and then push it forward like a 1950s movie star. He always wore suits, some with ties, some without. He worked as an attorney at the Capitol, but my mother used him as a consultant for some of her campaigns. I often wondered about their closeness, with the same resentment and distaste as I would for kissing cousins. He looked at her face as if she were a meal and her legs as if they were the appetizer.

"Where's Dad?" I asked one afternoon.

Doug's grin grew more subtle, but he still kept his hand on her shoulder.

"Your father is at work."

She started the car and pulled out of the parking lot. Her wedding ring shimmered in the sunlight, but I could not pay attention to it when her right hand was on Doug's thigh. Out in the open. Not even a hesitation anymore. Did she want my father to find out? My stomach turned.

"You did not greet Douglas when you opened that door and sat in my car. Do not forget your manners or upbringing. I didn't raise an ungrateful child, and I won't take any excuses about feminine cramps or muscle pains."

My face flamed. I turned my head to the window, but I could see Doug pull his lips into his mouth, suppressing his mirth at my expense. I could never win with her.

"Hello, Mr. Whitfield," I whispered.

"Hello, Sophia," he replied. He kept his eyes on my mom when he did it, his grin lifting the rest of his face. She smiled and winked at him as she turned onto Mesa Drive.

"You can start on chores when you get home."

"Yes ma'am."

Over a period of time, Doug continued to display an interest in my discomfort. "Accidental" entries into rooms that he knew I occupied. Showing up at my tennis practices without my mother. Buying me gifts that I did not ask for. Gift certificates to the Shops at Arbor Walk, the Container Store, or Nordstrom Rack appeared on my dresser like used lottery tickets. Mom said that he dropped these things off because he cared about me and that people often spoke of his unexpected generosity. I did not feel the same. Every object he touched projected some kind of smell, no doubt the stench of his questionable intentions.

One day I decided to tell my father about Doug while we walked along the pond behind the Arboretum. He had just ordered two new Jos. A. Bank suits and three new faucets from the Restoration Hardware store next door. We stopped at Amy's Ice Creams, took a guess at the movie trivia of the day, and carried our frozen treats through the hidden courtyard, past the cow statues and oak trees, and down the stairs to the pond. I carefully balanced my cup of Mexican vanilla ice cream mixed with strawberries and cinnamon in one hand and held his hand with the other. We emerged at the edge of the woods, watching the swans and ducks swim in different directions. We sat on a wooden table by the pond.

"I don't like Doug," I said.

He took a piece of his waffle cone and rolled it in between his fingers. He did not meet my eyes.

"And why is that?"

"He's weird, you know?"

He laughed. "Weird in what way?"

"Well, he's different from Mom's other friends. He hangs around the house and is always coming over for dinner. I can't stand his food."

"Well, sweetheart, he is our neighbor. He looks after the place when we have to go out of town. It's pretty convenient."

"Doesn't he have his own family?"

"Doug? I don't think so."

"I don't like him."

"What don't you like?"

I looked down at my spoon, moving it gently through the creamy mixture, scraping the sides of the orange and white container. I heard a shriek and watched a young mother chase a small child to the water's edge. The kid threw a rock at a turtle and the mother saved him from tumbling in headfirst as he laughed hysterically. She turned with him and paused for a moment when her eyes fell upon my dad. He had grown used to it over the years, but I hadn't. Lingering stares. Quiet smiles. I used to think that his light-hazel eyes drew their attention, but at some point I realized that his eyes coupled with that light-brown skin and curly dark-brown hair caused them to truly appreciate that male beauty could come in any shade, even the slightly darker ones. I had my mother's face, but my father gave me the complexion of my lighter-skinned ancestors.

"I don't know. I feel strange around him. It's hard to explain."

Dad wrapped the rest of his cone in a napkin and set it down beside him. He folded his hands and leaned forward on his knees. "Try to."

"She spends a lot of time with him."

"Yes, she does. They are good friends. Always have been."

"Yeah, well. He watches me, when she's around and when she's not. It's weird. Some of the seniors at school look at me the same way."

My dad's face changed. His brows furrowed and his countenance morphed from contemplation to consternation. "How do the boys look at you?"

"Like they want something."

"And what's that?"

I shrugged my shoulders.

He tugged at one of my curls. I looked up to catch his small smile. It didn't reach his eyes. "I'll take care of it."

"What do you mean?"

"Well, if he makes you uncomfortable, then we may need to revisit this friendship."

"But she'll be mad."

"She'll be okay. Once she understands, she will be fine."

We sat there for a little while longer. I confided in him about other things that were only real to my young teenage heart. Unmet expectations of a secretive smile from my current crush. A surreptitious hand brush by a sophomore in the crowded hallway. He gave me assurances and validation that I never received from her. To him, I did not appear as a stranger in my own skin, stumbling around puberty like an imbecile. He shared his own struggles as a young man, and even forayed into a short discussion about the circumstances of my birth.

"It was a miracle when we found out you were coming."

"A miracle? Me?"

He chuckled and stood up, bending down to collect our things and then searching for a trash bin.

"Yes, I didn't know if we would ever start a family. We had some false starts and bad endings at St. David's. One day your mother came home and told me that everything would be okay and that you would be here soon. Happiest damn day of my life."

We walked around the pond and up the long hill to the car. He saw me—the real me—and he loved me.

He died that night.

It was ruled an accident and no one even called Doug in for questioning. My dad always sampled things like sauces, soup, and pastries. He had mild reactions many times over the years. After an incident where his lips swelled when he sampled a new menu item at the Pappadeaux Seafood Kitchen off Highway 183, he removed his EpiPen from the car and always carried it in his back right pocket. He was always careful when we left the house, but never at home. Home was the safe zone, the one place where he didn't have to ask about the contents of a meal. When we returned from the pond that afternoon, he had disappeared into the back bedroom with my mother for several hours. I heard him raise his voice, though she remained quiet. When they finally emerged, she avoided my eyes, yet his watery gaze never left mine.

Where she walked by me, he stopped.

"Tonight's the last night. He is cooking dinner for us but won't be coming over here anymore after today."

She slammed a pan on the stove. I did not turn to watch her face—I knew what I would see.

"I'm sorry," I whispered.

He leaned away from me and placed both of his hands on my shoulders. "I'm not."

I should have known it then, but I do now. Dad's massive allergic reaction to Doug's casserole seemed like a joke at first, an implausible occurrence. It took three bites of the cheese-covered entrée before my father realized his breathing had changed and that his tongue had begun to swell. At first, I thought the spices caused it, or that our walk had triggered some kind of latent reaction to oak pollen. His throat-clearing attempts grew futile with every passing moment. When he realized he could not stop it from the inside, he reached into his back pocket. His eyes widened when he felt nothing but cloth—he never carried the pen on him in the house. His arm movements grew erratic and I watched in horror as he clawed at his throat, breaking his skin in the process. He tried to get to the bathroom, his lean athletic body stumbling in that direction, but he never made it. He fell, hit his head on the side of the knife drawer, and greeted death on his way down to the travertine floor.

She claimed that the EpiPen in the bathroom drawer had expired. Doug claimed ignorance and looked genuinely surprised to discover that my dad had a severe shellfish allergy. I believed him until I caught his smirk while the EMT tried to perform a tracheotomy on my father's lifeless body. I was fifteen.

I stood in my heels at the side of the kitchen island. She stood on the other side of the room.

"You don't have anything to say. Those people are sitting outside that door to talk about what they found back there and you are just staring into space."

"You can tell them whatever you want," I responded. "It won't make a difference. They will reach their own conclusions."

She moved toward me then, one hand wrapped around her own waist and one at her throat. Her face did not change though it looked like she was trying to express some kind of emotion. "You've changed."

I shrugged.

"Doug said this would happen, but I didn't believe him."

I stayed silent.

"They told me that it was a man's body back there, frozen beneath the ice. Can you believe that?"

Oh, I could imagine it. Hell, I dreamed of it. "Not my problem."

She dropped her hands. "You have always been difficult. If you're not going to help, why are you here?"

I nodded toward the door. "To watch."

"I am your mother. I deserve a little respect."

"You were never my mother. The only parent I ever knew is dead."

She flinched before she was able to control her reaction. The doorbell rang. I was surprised they had sat out there for so long. I stayed in the kitchen, looking at the front door over the island stove. She waited.

"Are you going to open the door?" she asked.

"No."

"Damn you." She turned and walked away, her footsteps echoing off the tile.

She opened the door to two police detectives. The man was dressed in a dark-brown suit with a light collared shirt beneath it. He did not wear a tie, but he wore a black leather belt. The woman was dressed similarly. She wore leather tennis shoes, and her hair was styled into a small chignon.

"Good afternoon."

"Hello, ma'am. Thank you for your time."

"Of course, please come in." She walked into the living room and gestured in my direction. "May I introduce my attorney? This is Sophia Cummings. She is one of the most distinguished and well-known criminal defense attorneys in the state. She is also my daughter."

The officers nodded toward me in the kitchen.

"It's nice to meet you ma'am. I am Detective Carl Jensen. This is my partner, Detective Laurel Thomas."

I nodded.

"My other attorney should be here soon, but I haven't been able to reach him. I left messages. His name is Douglas Whitfield."

The officers looked at each other.

"Can I get you something to drink?" she asked.

Detective Jensen spoke first: "Coffee if you have it, ma'am. If not, just water."

"Same here, thanks," said Detective Thomas.

She smiled at them before turning in my direction. She grazed my shoulder as she passed, causing me to change my position by the stove. I moved to the side and waited.

She spoke in a low tone: "Do you want something or are you going to just stand there?"

"I'll take some lemonade, thanks."

Her eyes flickered and her jaw tightened. "Fine, I'll take care of it. Just go in there and do something."

I sighed and moved out of the kitchen. I turned my pearls so that the clasp would fall to the back of my neck. I sat down on the brown leather couches and gestured to the detectives to do the same.

"How long have you two been at the Austin Police Department?"

"Nine years for me. Detective Thomas just joined us from the Houston Police Department."

"Oh yes, I'm familiar with that one. Did you enjoy your time there, Detective Thomas?"

"It was a challenge," she said. "I enjoy where I am now. How long have you been an attorney?"

"Long enough."

Both detectives watched as my mother walked in with her porcelain tray. She placed it on the square glass table and smiled in their direction. Steam rolled over their cups like a contained fog. The lemonade appeared cool and refreshing. She had placed a mint leaf in it, and from the light-brown shimmer, I knew that she had stirred honey in it as well. I reached for it and brought it to my lips, careful not to smudge my lipstick.

"Mrs. Cummings, we normally have these kinds of conversations at our office downtown."

"Yes, I know."

"We are here to talk about the body that your landscaper found in your backyard," Jensen began.

"Yes."

"Can you tell me why your landscaper discovered the body and you did not?"

"Certainly. I am one of the few residents on this street who tries to keep the edges of the woods in the backyard manicured. I was concerned about a young oak tree that we had planted back there at the end of last year. I called him to come check on it when he had the chance, especially after the freeze. He came over right after the streets were cleared. He told me that he saw a body and called the police. He didn't have his cell phone so he had walked up to use the line on my back porch. He tracked in a bit of dirt, but it was an emergency."

"Yes ma'am, that is correct."

"He said it didn't smell. I'm glad about that. I have a friend who says that the cold weather keeps that from happening as quickly."

"Yes ma'am, it does."

"Frankly, I don't think we pay the county medical examiner enough for what he has to review. Can you imagine having to process all of those homeless bodies?"

"You think the body belonged to a homeless person?"

"Yes, of course. I'm surprised they were in the area, but ever since they started talking about the camping ordinance being reinstated, people have been moving farther into the woods. It's sad really."

"The camping ordinance?" said Detective Thomas.

"Oh, pardon me. A couple of years ago, my colleagues on the city council decided to allow individuals to set up tents in public spaces across the city. Well, soon after that, little tent cities started popping up all over the metroplex. It became downright ridiculous. Every time I passed under the bridge to go to the Arboretum, I was terrified that I would hit someone walking across the road. I even saw a couch near a traffic light at Great Hills and Highway 183. I always spoke out against it. There is talk that the Austin folks are going to vote on it in the fall. Isn't it dangerous to live like that?"

"Yes, it is."

"That's what I said. Well, I heard that the police officers were going to start talking to these people and some folks were talking about finding new places to live. I assumed that the unfortunate individual could have been a homeless person trying to stay warm in the woods."

The detectives looked at each other. I looked at her.

"Well, do we know who it was? I haven't heard anything and I was wondering if you knew."

Detective Jensen shifted in his seat. "That's just it, ma'am. We have."

"I'm sorry?"

"We have identified the body, and it was not a homeless person."

"Then who was it? Do we have a name or some form of identification?"

Detective Jensen glanced at his partner, at me, and then

at her. I sipped the lemonade through the straw and waited. He placed his padfolio on the table and opened it. A familiar face smiled up at her. A low sound escaped from her throat.

"It was Douglas Whitfield."

I had never seen her face morph like that before. It looked as if she was experiencing five emotions at once and could not decide which one to feel first. Fear, disbelief, sadness, surprise, and rage all had a place at the table. I knew which one she would choose. It always remained while the others burned away.

"What in the hell do you mean, it was Doug?"

"We have identified the body on your property as a Mr. Douglas Whitfield."

"I heard you the first time . . . Excuse me." She stood then and crossed her arms over her torso. She walked to the fireplace and stood there facing it for a moment, her hand covering her mouth.

"Mrs. Cummings, I'm so sorry for—"

"Why wasn't I told this?"

"I'm sorry, ma'am?"

She turned around with her arms down to her side and her hands in fists. "Why didn't anyone tell me?"

"We are telling you now, ma'am."

"My God."

"We understand that you were close."

She looked at me for a moment and turned back to them. "We were. He was a good friend of our family. My . . . my only . . . I'm sorry."

Jensen stood, moved closer to her, and continued: "We were unable to determine the exact time of Mr. Whitfield's death because his body was encased beneath the snow and ice for up to four days."

"I can't believe this."

"Do you know anyone who may have anything against you? To do this on your property?"

Her eyes flickered at me again. They didn't notice. "No one."

"Mr. Whitfield did not have any children? Perhaps we could notify someone about—"

"Is that all, Detective?"

I finished my lemonade. The chilled glass started to make my fingers numb. I placed it down on the table with a loud clink. My mother looked at it and picked up a leather coaster in the center of the table, next to the fake fruit and pine cones. She lifted my glass and placed the coaster underneath it.

"A few more questions, ma'am. Can you tell me where you were the day before the storm?"

"Yes, I was at the club reviewing scholarship applications for my nonprofit association. I also had a long conversation with the events planner. We were planning a fundraising event there in the summer."

"You didn't see Mr. Whitfield before that time?"

"I did not."

"He didn't contact you or call you that day?"

"No, he didn't."

"What about you, Ms. Cummings? Did he call you?"

I sat up slightly. "No, he didn't. I barely knew him. He and I weren't very close. "

"You weren't?"

"No."

I felt her eyes on me then. I sat back slowly and crossed my legs. Jensen moved to sit down again and turned to my mother. "Ma'am, can you tell us more about how you knew each other? I understand you both attended the University of Texas School of Law."

She breathed out slowly. "Yes, of course. Would you like a refill on your coffee?"

"Uh, sure. Yes, please, thank you."

She removed the tray and took my drink with her. I waited, admiring my nails and cuticles. I saw the glass placed in front of me before I heard her voice.

"Well, where do I begin?"

Jensen leaned forward, completely entranced in the story that I'd heard a thousand times. She was the first in her family to go to law school. She met Doug and my father at the same time. They formed a study group that turned into a partnership for life. I sat farther back in my seat, surprisingly relaxed in the environment of a house I hated. I knew a different story.

After my dad died, Doug started showing up more than he used to, as if that were possible. My mom sent him to pick me up from practice on more than one occasion, and he would arrive earlier than the other parents to watch me play. My friends, who always asked for rides home with my mom, somehow found other ways to get home. I was often left alone with him in the car. Those were the longest trips of my life.

When I was seventeen, he brought over the same casserole that had killed my father two years earlier. He didn't say anything to me, but he winked at my mother as they put it in the oven to reheat. I never showed a reaction. Neither did he when I rammed the tree branch into his face, forcing the bones of his nose into his brain, three weeks ago. I thought about stabbing him with a kitchen knife, but I learned that natural weapons are much harder to trace.

He had greeted me earlier that day with a smile, standing

in my father's living room like he owned it. He said that he was proud of my accomplishments and that I had grown into a beautiful young lady. I nodded. His eyes, as usual, drifted from my face, but I was prepared this time. I shifted my hips to the side and peered at him as my roommate had taught me. He didn't seem to notice, but I did it anyway.

"Let's go for a walk," I said, "before it gets too cold."

I knew what the police would find. His eyes would have been wide open, fixed in the same expression like green marbles in his porcelain face. His nose would be unrecognizable, broken and misshapen, a lump of skin in the middle of his face. His fingers would have been broken. I heard them snap when he tried to block the blows to the back of his head. His arms would have been fixed at an odd angle as he died trying to keep the pieces of his raw face together. His mouth would have been wide open, his teeth broken from the multiple impacts to his mouth as he screamed.

"Sophia, do you have anything else to add?"

I blinked and looked at the officer. My eyes felt heavier. "No. I just find it amusing that my mother would recite her law school accolades during a time of sorrow."

"Ms. Cummings, your mother is not currently a suspect in this investigation, but we would prefer if she remained in the area in case we have any more questions."

"Of course. I don't believe she has plans to travel."

"Well, that is all we have. We thank you for your time."

Detective Jensen rose from his seat. His partner stood with him.

I felt a slight tingling in my feet. I wiggled my toes a bit, lifting my heels to alleviate the pressure and to create more circulation. A dull ache started to thrum in my forehead and behind my eyes. I reached for the lemonade and took another sip, drinking more of the melting ice than before. I looked at the officer. His jacket seemed bigger, and I could have sworn he shimmered a bit. My throat felt dry even after I finished my drink. I moved my hand across my face, trying to clear whatever was flying in front of it.

"It was nice to meet you both. My apologies, I don't feel quite myself at the moment."

"That's understandable, my dear," my mother said. Then: "Sophia has been under a lot of stress lately. She worries about me and the effect all of this might have on my health."

"We understand. We hope you feel better soon. We will let ourselves out."

"Thank you both."

I tilted my head back on the cushion to alleviate the pressure on my neck. The ceiling shifted a bit, moving left and then right. I could hear her, but for some reason I could not move my body. I heard the faucet turn on in the kitchen and glasses move against the sink, but nothing else to indicate that my mother was making any move in my direction to help me.

I turned my head to the left, my eyes roaming over the pictures on the mantelpiece. My father's photo was long gone, but there were plenty of her and me. My high school graduation, my third-grade piano recital—all memories of somewhat happier times. She had taken many pictures of Doug at one point. His image dominated the mantel even before my father died.

I cleared my throat, but the object I felt in it wouldn't move. I didn't remember ever seeing my baby pictures, but she had a small one on display today. She was dressed in a blue hospital gown, her face glowing but drawn as she lay horizontally next to a dark-blue curtain. The doctor's face hovered nearby. My father must have taken the picture because Doug stood there holding me, his light-green eyes wide and alert.

My breathing became more labored. I reached up to touch my throat, but my fingers didn't seem to work. I blinked and allowed my eyes to drift to the next frame. I looked eight or nine and Doug was holding me in his lap. Our faces were very close together and we were both smiling at whoever was holding the camera. I noticed for the first time in my life that his eyes and my eyes were the same shape. We held our mouths the same way and tilted our heads at the same angle. Our dimples were even in the same spot.

I blinked again, slowly this time, allowing my body to catch up with my mind. I made one last attempt to get up from my seat. I began to wheeze, but I needed to see. I needed to be sure. I forced myself up and grabbed the mantel, my eyes transfixed on Doug and a child who looked just like him.

"Impossible," I whispered.

I took in a shallow breath, praying that it would reach my lungs in time. My legs began to loosen, and one of my hands slipped off the mantel. I held on with the other and pulled myself up again, my face bent deeply into the picture frames. I caught my reflection in the edges of the photos— my face a portrait of pain, my eyes bloodshot and glazed. I could feel my insides shutting down, my body abandoning me when I needed it the most. I reached for the picture, but my grip slipped and I pushed it backward toward the brick wall. I searched for my reflection, but found her face instead, smiling at me from behind as I collapsed at her feet.

THE GOOD NEIGHBOR

BY JEFF ABBOTT

West Lake Hills

The funeral was lovely, everyone said so during the reception at Bill's house. Viv hovered, making sure there was enough food, making sure no one was cornering Peyton or Deirdre and exhausting them with sympathy. The crowd was a mix—Deirdre's friends from yoga, her and Viv's friends from the book club, Deirdre's friends from her old job where she'd met Bill. Twenty people left, and there should be enough food. This wasn't Viv's job to worry about, but it was what a good neighbor did in a time of difficulty and mourning.

Viv watched Peyton. The late Bill's son stood slightly away from everyone else, his anger and grief a fence around him that did not invite conversation. It was awkward. He could have given his father a kind sendoff, a respectful farewell. Instead, he had sat next to his stepmother Deirdre with clear distaste, scowling, refusing the offer of a tissue she made during the eulogy. Making a production of not looking at her.

It's okay, Viv told herself. He needs time. He's hurting.

As if Deirdre wasn't. Deirdre was only twenty-seven and Viv, like Bill, was thirty years older, but they were close. Viv had become a widow herself two years earlier and Deirdre was too young for this grief. Viv wanted to shield her, but . . . you couldn't. It was a fire you had to walk through.

The last guests finally left.

"Peyton, I'm leaving," Viv said. She had known him his entire life, watched him grow up from giggling toddler to football-playing teenager to a serious twenty-one-year-old man with one year left in college.

"Thanks, Viv," Peyton said. He gave her a hug, then turned and walked up the stairs without a word to Deirdre, who stood awkwardly next to Viv.

"Peyton," Viv said, and he stopped on the stairs without turning around.

"I know you feel alone. But you have me, and your friends, and your stepmother, and we all love you very much."

"But I don't have my dad." He turned and glanced at Deirdre. As if the heart attack was her fault.

"No, but you have the memory of him. And you have the knowledge of how he'd want you to act and behave."

"Sure. All right," he said, after several long seconds of hesitation. "Good night, Viv. Thanks for everything."

"Good night, Peyton," Deirdre said. He didn't look at her, he went up the stairs. Viv and Deirdre heard his bedroom door close.

Viv shrugged. "I'm sorry. You have enough to worry about. He'll . . . He'll come around. He's a good kid."

"He's an adult, not a kid, and he thinks I'm responsible," Deirdre said. "He blames me."

Heart attack, much younger wife, people always imagined the worst-case scenario, Viv thought. But Viv didn't want to say that. "You brought Bill happiness in his final years. Look, you and Peyton both loved his dad, you have that bond. You have that."

"He's never liked me and now he doesn't have to pretend with Bill gone."

"Do you want to come stay with me?"

"This is my home and I'm not leaving it. I can handle Peyton."

"It's his home too. But do you feel safe here?"

Deirdre let the shock play out on her face. "Of course I do. You're not suggesting Peyton could be violent?"

"No. No. But you call me if you need me." Viv kissed her cheek and headed out the door. She lived across the cul-de-sac. She glanced back at the Brant house as she walked toward her own. Deirdre and Peyton lived in a large house, five thousand square feet, on a circle with four other similarly huge houses. Viv's house was too much for her, being all alone now, but she was so fond of Peyton and Deirdre and her other neighbors that she didn't want to move.

Viv eased out of her funeral dress—same one she'd worn when she buried her husband—and crawled into the lonely bed. She missed her husband Clark, the pinewood scent of his soap, the easy predictability of his stacked books on the bedside table, the way he'd make little noises in his throat when watching his favorite sports and feeling dismay over his Astros or Texans losing.

She told herself it was ridiculous to have asked Deirdre to stay with her. That was her own loneliness talking, reaching out to Deirdre's sudden loneliness. Friends had asked Viv if she'd considered getting a job, or considered dating. Her dating, on a phone app? Lord no, she thought. Both prospects were too daunting for her. But if she needed a project, here was one: getting Deirdre and Peyton to get along better.

She could do some good.

She pulled her pillow close to her, and she closed her eyes, and sleep finally came.

Viv brought kolaches to Deirdre the next morning. Deirdre

said Peyton was still asleep and invited her in for coffee. A list of names and thank you notes were spread out on the table.

"Well, that's old school," Viv said, taking in the notes and the fountain pen Deirdre had been using. "I approve." This was the kind of reason why she adored Deirdre—she was thoughtful.

"My handwriting's not great but it seemed more personal than an email."

"How are you?" Viv asked.

Deirdre shrugged. "Numb feels like the new normal."

"How's he?"

Deirdre shrugged. "I haven't talked to him since you left last night."

Just then Peyton came down, hair tousled, in T-shirt and pajama pants, and stared at Deirdre and Viv and the stationery spread out on the table.

"Are those like actual thank you notes?" he asked.

"Yes."

"You could just send emails or texts."

"I know. This is just a nice way to say thanks. Your dad had so many friends. He was much loved."

"Yes. He was. Hey, Viv." Peyton poured himself coffee.

"Good morning, sweetheart. I brought kolaches."

Peyton snagged one, nodded his thanks, and went upstairs.

The doorbell rang. Another neighbor, Jenny, bringing over one of her famous cakes, just checking in on Deirdre. She was a good friend of Viv's and they exchanged a glance that said, *We're both worried about her being alone.*

But Deirdre seemed . . . okay, as if getting past the funeral was getting past the hardest part. Bill's heart attack five days ago had been sudden, the ambulance arriving in a rush and departing without sirens, Deirdre and Peyton left standing in their mutual yet separate grief and shock on the front yard.

Jenny was a talker, and almost always in a bright mood. She and Viv and Deirdre talked about the funeral, about what she was going to do with the house (Bill had left it to her, and left money to Peyton). Deirdre told them the house was the one Peyton had grown up in, she wasn't going to sell it while he was still in college, not when he wanted to come home to it. They fell silent as Peyton came down the stairs to the kitchen.

Jenny gave him a hug. He managed a slight smile.

"Do you want breakfast? I'll cook you breakfast," Jenny said. "Are you eating?"

"I already fed him," Viv said, with a slightly possessive tone.

"I'm fine, Jenny, thanks," Peyton said. "I can cook my own if I want it."

"Well," Jenny said. She was the mother of four boys, all had been Westlake High School football players, and she was used to cooking large meals. "Okay. You know it's okay to let us help you, Peyton."

He nodded but stayed silent.

"I have some news," Deirdre said suddenly, her voice sharp. As if forcing the words out. "I'm pregnant." She put her hand on her stomach.

"Oh!" Viv cried, clapping her hands together. Caught up in the joy of the moment. Then the cloud of Bill's passing eclipsed her smile. "Oh. Deirdre."

"It's a good thing. I'm happy." She hesitated for a second. "Bill knew."

"Oh, Deirdre," Viv said again. Jenny folded Deirdre into a hug.

"He hadn't told me," Peyton said in a flat voice.

"He wanted to figure out how to tell you," Deirdre said. "He was worried you would be upset."

The kitchen was silent. "No, I'm not upset," Peyton said. "I . . . I . . . excuse me." He turned and hurried up the stairs.

"It's a shock," Jenny said, patting Deirdre's shoulder. "He'll adjust."

"Just give him time. He'll be happy once it settles in," Viv added, but not with confidence.

"Why are you all so worried about his feelings?" Deirdre said with sudden heat. "I've lost my husband, I have a child on the way, and we're tiptoeing around Peyton's mood swings."

"Oh, honey," Jenny said, embracing Deirdre.

"I didn't cry at the funeral because I just feel numb. And Bill's left me behind, and my own stepson hates me or acts like he blames me . . . and I don't know what to do." Deirdre started to cry, and Viv joined in the group hug.

"Deirdre?" A voice behind them. Peyton.

The three women broke the embrace.

Peyton looked down at his feet. "Sorry. I shouldn't have acted that way. It was just a surprise. On top of Dad's passing."

"I know," she said, wiping tears from her cheeks. "Maybe I should have waited to say something. But I want this baby and I want you to know about it."

"I'm happy for you," Peyton said.

"Bill wanted you to be happy about it."

"His new family. Well, I'm grown up, I can't be upset about it."

"It'll be nice to have a little brother or sister," Viv said.

"I'll be more like an uncle than a sibling."

"Peyton," Viv said, "that's up to you. That's your choice.

You can be a wonderful big brother if you choose to be." Her need for this project swelled in her heart. More was at stake now! They had to get along, and she could help them.

Peyton didn't say anything.

"Think what your dad would want you to do," Jenny said.

"Well, he's dead now, so I can't make him happy or unhappy, can I?" Peyton said.

"Don't be that way," Viv said. She kept waiting for Peyton to give Deirdre a hug, but he stubbornly stayed rooted in place.

"This affects the will," Peyton said suddenly. "Doesn't it? The baby will get half of what was mine."

There was a shocked silence. "Maybe don't worry about that right now," Jenny said.

"Peyton has things he wants to do. Tour Europe. Start a food truck with a friend. Maybe go to film school. Just so many ambitions." Deirdre's voice was a knife's edge. "None of which Bill cared to fund, but now that's not a worry."

Viv glanced at her. Was Deirdre trying to pick a fight?

"I think I'll go back upstairs now," Peyton said. "Congrats on your insurance policy to get more of Dad's money."

"Peyton!" Viv said. "Apologize right now." She couldn't believe she'd said that, he wasn't her son, but he couldn't speak that way to Deirdre in front of her.

"Sorry," Peyton said, unconvincingly. He turned and went upstairs.

"What is wrong with him?" Deirdre said, shaken.

"It's a shock. And no, I'm not making excuses for him, Deirdre, it *is* a shock."

"It may not be the last one," Deirdre said. "I think I'd like to go lie down now."

* * *

Jenny lived on the next street down from the cul-de-sac and Viv walked home with her. They absolutely had to discuss the drama.

"He'll move out as soon as he has his money," Jenny said.

"He's stubborn and he thinks of that house as his," Viv said. "He might not."

"You don't think he'd . . . be violent, do you?"

"Jenny." Viv didn't want to admit she'd had the same thought.

"Did you see the hate in his eyes?"

Viv had, but didn't want to admit it, or bad-mouth a boy she had known since birth. "He's not been the same since his mother died." That was three years earlier, and Bill had married Deirdre a year later. They'd worked together at Bill's mortgage company, one of the largest in Austin. "Peyton was angry at Bill after his mom died. Now angry at Deirdre for Bill. He has a pattern."

"What should we do? Maybe Deirdre should move out."

"The house is hers."

"Then she should throw out Peyton."

"I think she wants peace between them. We could try and help with that," Viv said.

"It's kind of not our business," Jenny said.

"We'll do it for Bill. His memory."

"I'm not sure this can be fixed." Jenny shook her head.

"I'm going to try," Viv said.

Viv found Peyton where she thought he might be, walking the track at Westlake High School's stadium. He had played football and run track there. The high school was a focus of life in West Lake Hills, with multiple state football championships, a place of happy and proud memories for many.

Viv had thought it was ridiculous that the school district had spent so much for a football stadium, but at her first game, sitting in the comfortable seats and caught up in the suburb's pride in team, band, cheerleaders, drill team, and more, she had enjoyed herself. And she and her husband ended up buying season tickets. She still renewed every season, and often gave the tickets to friends. It was a little lonely to sit without her husband Clark, even in the middle of a crowd.

Peyton saw her and kept walking and she stood where she was until he reached her on the loop.

"Hey," she said.

"Hey."

"Can I walk with you?"

"Are you going to lecture me?"

"I'm trying to understand you." She started walking with him, not waiting for an invitation.

"I don't know what you mean."

"Your hostility to Deirdre."

He didn't answer.

"She's not exactly an evil stepmother."

"No," he said. "She's not. I guess."

"She made your dad happy after your mom passed."

He didn't look at her. "Sure. I guess."

"So what is it that you have against her?"

"Do I have to give you a list?"

"I think whatever this anger is, you need to move past it."

"Why do people talk like psychiatrists now? *Closure, move past it*—it's all meaningless." He took a deep breath. "I needed him after Mom died, and all he did was focus on his companies, his money, and then, when a pretty face comes around, *then* he decides to pay attention to other people. He ignored me after Mom died."

"He didn't know what to say, hon, you know what he was like. It was so sudden."

"Don't make an excuse for him, Viv."

She reached out and touched his arm. He flinched and she remembered that he didn't like to be touched. She withdrew her hand. "Sorry. Peyton, your dad was all you had left. But now you are going to have a sibling. And someone who I think if she can't be a mom to you, she can be a friend."

"Is this the part when the music swells in a heartfelt moment?"

"Please don't be that way," Viv said.

"She's just six years older than me, Viv. Six years. It's comical. I mean, it was. He was ridiculous with her."

"You act like you're the only person who's lost anyone. I know it was hard to lose your mom and now your dad. I'm trying to help you, Jenny is too, even Deirdre . . ."

He made a noise.

"Are you going to stay in that house, angry and defiant? Bill would want you to take care of her. Take care of that baby."

"They're not my responsibility. Dad's set them up for life. She won't have to worry."

"Are you mad you'll be getting half of what you expected?"

"I'll be fine."

"Don't resent that baby, Peyton."

"You really think the worst of me."

"And don't resent Deirdre. Are you going to stay in that house? A pregnant widow doesn't need your additional stress."

"She can throw me out if she wants, I guess."

"She won't do that. Unless you make her."

"I have my last year of college. Then I'll see where I live."

Viv stopped so he stopped. "Your dad loved you. He told me that. He told me he wished he had done better by you." Bill hadn't told her that, but who was to know? Words might help Peyton.

"Nothing was stopping him." Peyton started to jog.

She watched him head away from her, then went out the gate and back to her car.

Viv's husband Clark had passed three years earlier, six months after Peyton's mom had died. Clark died of cancer; Gina had been killed by a hit-and-run driver, on a long run back into West Lake Hills from the trails bordering downtown Austin along Lady Bird Lake. Just left for dead in the road; no one saw anything, no one was ever arrested. It broke Bill, it broke Peyton, and they'd wandered like ghosts in the house, haunting each other. Viv and Clark and Bill and Gina had always been close, couple best friends, with trips to Las Vegas and New Orleans and New York City. And Viv felt she and Clark were like an aunt and uncle to Peyton. He was two years younger than Viv and Clark's daughter, Miranda; the two kids had different interests and were always polite to each other but never close.

Miranda had moved to Boston, and got busy and occupied with her own life. Despite knowing Bill her entire life, and Viv pleading with her to come to his funeral, she had an important client presentation and said she couldn't reschedule. "I simply can't, Mom, I simply *can't*." The same excuse she gave when Viv asked her to visit. It was clear a retired Viv was expected to travel to Miranda, not the other way around. And while Viv wasn't on the cooler, hipper social media platforms, she knew how to search for her daughter there, and Miranda's postings showed she always had time for weekend trips to New York with her besties and jaunts to Martha's Vineyard with a new boyfriend. How hard, Viv wondered, was it to reschedule a stupid meeting for a man who was like family? She'd felt disappointment and anger with Miranda but pushed it down.

Viv hadn't really liked Bill remarrying a much younger woman—one just a few years older than her own daughter—but Deirdre was funny, smart, and charming, and Viv couldn't help but like her. It was almost like having a more considerate version of Miranda living across the circle and not across the country.

Now Viv stood alone in her empty house, watching the windows of the Brant house, wondering what was going on inside. If Peyton was still fuming, if Deirdre was figuring out her future. Or picking out colors and patterns for the nursery. Deirdre honestly should keep the house, she thought, just for the sake of the baby's schooling. People bought in Westlake even before their children were school age, for the schools, which were among the top-ranked in the state and the country. And houses here more than held their value; her home value had nearly tripled in twenty years, a side effect of the growth of Austin and the influx of corporate types and techies who put education as a priority. Sometimes it felt to her like West Lake Hills and Rollingwood existed just for the schools, the center of the modern suburban universe. Successful people trying to groom other successful people, to pass along the privilege and advantage that they'd had. Viv loved the Westlake area, but with her daughter gone she felt like an interloper. Friends had asked if she would sell—they knew a lovely family moving here from Seattle, or from the Bay Area, or from Chicago—but she had always said no, and smiled, and thought, *Where would I go that I like so well? Do*

I not belong in West Lake Hills if I no longer have a kid in the schools? Should I leave where I love? Should I make room for a young family to have the experience I've had here . . .

Then she heard the scream.

Clearly. A scream. From the Brant house. She hurried across the circle. She reached the door and knocked.

"Deirdre? Are you okay?" She leaned on the doorbell.

No answer. She hurried around to the back of the house. It offered several large windows; the curtains and drapes were all drawn, like the house had closed in on itself. She tried the door by the pool—it was unlocked.

"Deirdre? Peyton?"

Silence. Then: "Viv? I'm in here." From the master bedroom. Viv followed the sound of Deirdre's voice. She went into the bedroom—it was down a short hall, ending with a wedding portrait of Bill and Deirdre. Viv entered the bedroom; Deirdre was sitting on the edge of the bed. The windows were open, a breeze gusting in. The bed was unmade. The door to the adjoining bathroom was closed.

"I heard you scream," Viv said. "I mean—I thought it was you. Are you okay?"

Deirdre looked up at her. "Bill . . . Bill . . ."

"What about Bill?"

"I had a dream about him. A bad dream. I fell asleep. I'm . . . oh, my God, did you hear me scream?"

"Your window's open. I guess so. Where's Peyton?"

"You thought he was hurting me?" Deirdre said flatly. "No. He's not here."

"Deirdre. Do you feel safe here?"

"Yes. Of course."

"Okay, hon."

"How did you get in, Viv?"

"The pool door was unlocked."

"Oh. Okay. I should be careful about that."

"Do you want any tea?" Viv asked.

"No."

"Why would a dream about Bill make you scream? You had a nightmare about Bill?"

"Yes. A nightmare. But Viv, I'm all right now. You can go. Thanks for coming over."

"All right. Call if you need me."

Viv left, blinking hard, going out the way she came in, hearing Deirdre lock the door behind her.

She had seen it.

Seen it when she entered the bedroom. A T-shirt of Peyton's, lying next to the master bed, wadded up on the floor. And the imprint of a second body on the sheets. A man's body.

So what do you do? Viv thought. What's happening between them? They don't get along. But . . . maybe Deirdre had been asleep on that side of the bed. Maybe she dropped it while doing laundry.

Maybe it was none of Viv's business.

But Bill was dead, and two young people were living in that house. She shook her head. It couldn't be. But Peyton was nearly out of college, grown, and Deirdre was in her late twenties. Reverse it and no one would think much about a six-year difference with the man older. But they both loved Bill, she was sure of that, so maybe it was just two people reaching out to each other in their grief.

Or maybe they had reached out to each other before Bill was dead.

That thought struck her cold.

They killed him. They killed him to be together. The suspicion entered her mind, like a vandal intent on ruination. Why? Bill was rich, but could be distant and difficult, and Peyton was young and handsome . . . and would inherit.

Madness, she told herself. It can't be.

What should she do? Call the police . . . and tell them what? *Well, there was a T-shirt I think was Peyton's on the floor of her bedroom. No, I've never seen them kiss or be romantic or even be that polite to each other.* She had no proof. None. And Bill had died of natural causes, hadn't he? You couldn't fool a coroner. It had been clearly been a heart attack, but caused by what?

She went back to her window to look at the house across the circle. She felt like a nosy neighbor in a 1960s sitcom. Peyton was back, sitting out on the porch, drinking one of the hipster local ciders. Calm, unbothered. Even though half his fortune was going to his new sibling.

She had told Deirdre she'd bring them dinner tonight. Two nights ago, she had brought over a lasagna. She had a whole arsenal of casseroles for the days after a funeral. And she liked cooking for more than herself; it was like cooking for Miranda and Clark, when they were all together.

What are you going to do, she asked herself, play detective? Clark would say you're being silly and her daughter would say, *Oh Mother, you watch too many British crime shows.* It was a heart attack. Peyton was raw at being an orphan at twenty-one. Deirdre had just lost her husband and was expecting. Nothing was as it should be, and that's why they were acting strange.

She made the casserole—King Ranch chicken, she knew it was one of Peyton's favorites—and tried to stave off dark thoughts. She started to call Deirdre to see if it was okay to come over, and then she thought, no, don't give them any warning. Then told herself that was a terrible thing to think. This was Peyton and Deirdre, she was being ridiculous, wasn't she?

Her doorbell rang. Jenny, at the front door, with a cake. "I'm taking them"—she didn't need to say who—"dessert, you want to walk over with me?"

"Sure. Come in for a second."

Jenny followed her, with her cake, to the kitchen. "Your casserole smells wonderful."

"I want to ask you something." Viv was almost afraid to say the words.

"What?"

She didn't want to say it out loud. These were not words you could take back. She had to be careful, because Jenny would practically post any idle thought she had on Faceplace. "I'm just wondering how things are between Peyton and Deirdre. If you noticed anything."

"Oh, I think, in time, and when college starts it'll be better. The grief is so fresh. And I think Peyton will step up to help her with that baby. It's his own brother or sister." Jenny was an optimist.

Viv bit her lip. "I hope so. Did Bill say anything to you about how they got along?" Bill was close with Jenny's husband; they were fishing buddies.

"Well, Peyton wasn't happy at first about the relationship, I mean just given the age difference. You wouldn't think a boy would be sensitive about it, but I guess he was. Though he told Glenn they were really getting along a lot better. They went to a music festival at Zilker Park together a few months back. It wasn't Bill's thing, so he didn't go, but Deirdre tagged along with Peyton and all his college friends, and Bill said they had a good time."

"That's nice," Viv said. Maybe that's when it started, she thought. She hated the dark little coal of suspicion glowing in her heart. "Do you think it's okay that Peyton is staying there?"

"It's his house. Why wouldn't he?"

"Just . . ."

"I don't think Deirdre should be alone. I mean, she's going to have to be. I'd expected she'd sell the house, but with the baby coming, and the schools here . . ." The schools, always a central decision point. Always a reason to stay.

"I guess. I think she'll stay," Viv said, having no idea.

"You have to give Peyton a chance to not be hurting and hurtful," Jenny said. "Let's go take them their dinner."

They walked across the circle and rang the doorbell. Peyton answered. He was wearing a long-sleeved University of Texas shirt and jeans. "Hey. This is *so* appreciated."

"We can just drop these off . . ."

"No, y'all come in, if you want." He opened the door wider and so they did, moving to the kitchen. Deirdre sat at the table, a mug of mint tea in front of her. Before her were spread a bunch of photos of Bill and his first wife, Gina.

"Oh," Jenny said. "Sweet Gina. I miss her."

"Bill always said such wonderful things about her," Deirdre said. "Peyton and I had not really talked about her, but he was just sharing memories with me."

"Are y'all okay? I mean, I know you're not, but you know what I mean," Viv said.

"We're fine," Peyton answered. "Aren't we?" And the glance he gave her, that Jenny didn't see because she was slicing a bit of cake to go along with Deirdre's tea.

But Viv saw.

Heat in his eyes.

Secrets.

Deirdre didn't react. Like she didn't see it. She sipped her tea and then her gaze met Viv's.

"May I use your bathroom?" Viv asked, and Peyton said sure and Viv went down the hall, hearing Jenny's voice identifying the pictures of late, lamented Gina: "Oh, that was taken in Vegas after three mai tais, she wouldn't have wanted you to print that one."

Viv went past the guest bath and down to the master bedroom. The bed was made. Viv could still hear Jenny's voice, reminiscing about her lost friend. She stepped into the master bathroom. She saw two towels hanging. Touched them.

Both were still damp.

One woman in this bedroom, two damp towels. Was Peyton showering down here? Or maybe Deirdre had showered twice? Maybe?

If Peyton was showering down here, was he sleeping down here? It was a big house. No reason for him to shower here. No good reason.

She opened Bill's medicine cabinet—his side of the sink hadn't been cleared, still shaving cream, razor, deodorant. Or . . . these were Peyton's.

Pill bottles. Several of them. She scanned the prescriptions, memorizing the names. She could search online for them later.

She closed the cabinet, hurried back out into the hallway. She flushed the guest toilet, washed her hands, and returned to the kitchen.

Deirdre wasn't smiling, but Peyton was, laughing at some memory of his mother Jenny had shared.

"I wish I had known Gina," Deirdre said.

"You would have liked Mom," Peyton said.

* * *

"See?" Jenny chirped, as she and Viv walked back to Viv's house across the circle. "That was a bit of a thaw. They're making progress in becoming friends."

Friends, Viv thought. Friends.

On her laptop, Viv looked up Bill's medications. They were often prescribed after a mild heart attack. Had Bill had an attack before the one that killed him? He had not mentioned it to her. She had not heard anything from Deirdre, and surely Deirdre would have told her and Jenny and the neighbors.

Bill's mortgage company had a website. Under the *Leadership* tab, she found the names of the other execs that worked there and she wrote down their names. Then she went on a social media site she'd heard some of her friends who worked mention, like Faceplace but just about careers and such. LinedUp, it was called. She thought they might be here. She created an account (she didn't have a job, she had the life insurance and investments from Clark and family money, so on her new account she called herself a "consultant") and sent friend requests to the accounts of Bill's employees. In the connection request she mentioned she was Bill's friend (that sounded better than neighbor).

One person responded quickly, approving her for "connection," and she sent a follow-up note: *Thanks so much for helping me expand my professional network—we all miss Bill so terribly. The heart attack was such a shock. I thought he was in great health.*

And then the response: *Yes, terrible, but he'd had a mild heart attack before, here at the office. He just didn't like to talk about it. He asked us all not to mention it, but we worried about him. You know a certain kind of guy and his pride.*

He'd had a previous attack, was on medication . . . Could

either Peyton or Deirdre have withheld it from him? The police hadn't seemed the least bit suspicious. Maybe he skipped a dose.

The look, though, that Peyton gave Deirdre. Viv couldn't shake the look.

Viv said nothing more about her suspicions in the following days. The dinner delivery calendar kept going for two more weeks, and then Deirdre asked her to not continue it; she said she felt guilty with people bringing food. And she felt like cooking again; plus Peyton said he would cook sometimes as well.

"Food is love," Viv said to her. "You know we all love you." And it was true, and she didn't want to believe the worst of this young woman she'd grown to care for as a daughter and this young man she'd known since he was born. But. But.

Bringing the food had given her an excuse to go over and observe their behavior. With that gone, she had to think of an excuse. But what was she going to do? Snoop? That wasn't her. She was a nice person who gave people the benefit of the doubt.

Viv saw, from her front window (and how much time was she spending peering out at the Brant house?), Deirdre come out onto the porch and sit down in a wicker chair. She had a book with her. Viv could see it was the new Meg Gardiner novel their neighborhood book club was reading.

There, that was Viv's excuse.

She walked across the circle, and could see Deirdre's slight change of expression to suspicion, then broken by a smile.

"Am I interrupting your quiet time?" Viv asked.

"No, just was going to read a couple chapters."

"I just wanted to see how you are."

"I'm okay."

"How's life with Peyton?"

"Oh, he's all right."

"He didn't move back to campus with school starting?" Viv's stomach twisted slightly.

"No. He decided he would save money and stay here." Deirdre touched her stomach. "Since he's not inheriting quite as much as he thought he was."

"Is he okay with that?"

"Yes. I think he's decided he should help me, not hinder me. Or at least he's thinking about it."

"I'm so relieved. Y'all were rocky there for a while."

"You seem really interested in us, Viv," Deirdre said.

"I just want you both . . . to be okay." *To be innocent. That's what I want.*

"I don't feel okay," Deirdre said. "I mean, it's day-to-day how I feel. Hormonal and emotional rollercoaster."

"Do you miss Bill?"

Now Deirdre stared at her. "Are you serious? Of course."

"You said you had a bad dream about him."

"Bill could be a challenge some days."

Viv didn't know what to say to that. "It's just . . . you're an impressive young woman. You don't have to stay alone."

"I'm pregnant and newly widowed. I'm not up for dating." Now her voice was flat.

Was anything she was doing with Peyton . . . dating? She wouldn't call it that. Neither would the police. "I'm sorry, I didn't mean to suggest you were. I just—"

"You just what, Viv? I feel like you're dancing around a subject you don't want to bring up. My husband is dead, I'll be raising a child alone, and I don't feel up to indulging your odd little takes."

Viv felt like Deirdre had read her thoughts. "I'm sorry. I just . . . The dynamic between you and Peyton . . ." She couldn't finish the sentence.

"The dynamic," Deirdre said, and the words now sounded awful to Viv.

Silence fell, awkward and thorny, and then Deirdre said, "I was afraid of him."

"Peyton?" Viv said, almost hopeful.

"No. Bill."

"Why were you afraid of him?"

"He was very possessive of his first wife. I knew that from Peyton. From Jenny. He'd started acting that way toward me. Constantly suspicious. Like I'd done something wrong."

"He and Gina were very happy."

"Were they? Ask Peyton."

"You said Bill was happy about the pregnancy."

"No, I said he *knew*. You finished that sentence in your head. Y'all hear what you want to hear."

"Didn't he want to be a dad again?"

"He didn't want me burdened with a child. Not being there for him. You see, I was his retirement plan. Young wife, in love with him, I should be at his beck and call. A child distracting me would have upset all his plans."

"But it's his child. How could he feel that way?"

"Well, he did." Deirdre got up from the chair. "And so, if I had a baby, I made him unhappy, and if I didn't have this baby, I made myself unhappy. I think I'll go inside and lie down."

"Deirdre . . . I just want you to be happy."

And then Deirdre surprised her. She leaned over and

kissed Viv's cheek. "I know you do, Viv. I know. But maybe just let all this be." She went inside and closed the front door.

And Viv thought: *I have to know. I can't let this go. I have to know.*

Viv didn't much like herself as she eased into the Brant backyard, past midnight. The master bedroom of the house had a set of bay windows facing the pool. She worried about motion detectors or something else alerting them to her presence. But were they in the same bed? Were they? Had Peyton's antagonism been an act?

She knelt beneath the window. A dim light shone in the curtained window. Probably just Deirdre reading yet one more chapter in the book club novel; she was so diligent about finishing the books.

This was dumb. Embarrassing. If they caught her out here it would end the friendship, and rightly so.

The light went off.

Then quiet voices, Deirdre's, Peyton's. Talking softly. In the darkness of the bedroom.

Viv's heart froze.

And then silence, where she dared not move, and then the first soft moan.

Now you know. Are you happy? Viv covered her face in shame and slowly crept away from the window. And backed into one of the pool lounge chairs, which scraped and screeched against the concrete deck.

A light flashed on in the bedroom.

Viv bolted to the backyard gate, hurried through it. It felt like a thousand miles across the cul-de-sac, back to her house, realizing she'd left all the lights there on and anyone looking would see her rushing back home. She started to cry as she reached her front door, slipped inside, and locked it behind her.

They were together. The antagonism was an act. What had they done to Bill?

After several minutes, she peered back toward the house. The lights were all out. Maybe they thought it was a possum or a raccoon on the pool deck. Maybe they were back to their whispered sweet nothings in the darkness. Maybe they'd returned to their murderous conspiracy.

And what was she going to do?

Viv hardly slept. She lay in the bed, trying to imagine the police coming and escorting Peyton and Deirdre out in handcuffs. Would Deirdre have her baby in prison? They would take it away from her? Who would take it? Was it Peyton's or Bill's?

She got up, tried to distract herself by looking at cribs online, as if nothing was amiss and she was simply helping Deirdre prepare for the baby. She made coffee, afraid almost to turn on a light. In case they were watching her, across the circle.

But she didn't call the police. She had no evidence. Nothing to show or to prove.

She drank her pot of coffee. The sun rose. She couldn't settle her thoughts. She went back to the online crib store, trying not to think, trying to avoid calling the police.

Around eight the phone chimed. A text from Deirdre: *Hey, I made some coffee cake. Want some? Come over.*

So innocent sounding. But if she meant to hurt Viv, she wouldn't be texting her. That left an electronic trace, right? She stared at the message and wrote back: *Sure, be over in a few.*

* * *

The dark roast coffee smelled great, and the coffee cake looked wonderful. Studded with pecans, swirled with cinnamon. So homey.

And Peyton was standing there in the kitchen as Deirdre led her in, and he smiled and gestured toward a chair at the kitchen island. Viv sat.

"How are you this morning?" Deirdre asked, slicing some cake onto a plate with a lovely pattern, one Viv remembered Gina buying years ago.

"I'm fine, how are y'all?" Viv's voice sounded a little wispy, and she cleared her throat.

"We're good," Peyton said. "We did want to have a chat with you."

"What about?" Viv said, her stomach clenching.

"We heard someone in our backyard last night," Peyton said, "and then saw you walking toward your house, Viv, so maybe you saw whoever it was while you were out for your midnight stroll."

Viv stared at them. Peyton had moved toward Deirdre, in a protective way. *Our backyard.* "It was me," she said, the three hardest words she'd ever spoken.

"Viv, why?" Deirdre said.

"I . . . I don't think the two of you have a strained relationship. Maybe you did once. But not . . . not anymore. I think . . . you're together." She didn't know how else to say it.

They looked at each other, and then they looked at her, studies in innocence. "What are you saying, Viv?"

"Bill had heart medication. I know he'd had an attack earlier he kept quiet. I think he had another and maybe . . . maybe you caused the heart attack, somehow."

Ten silent seconds. Peyton took a big bite of his coffee cake; he let the accusation hang in the air. Viv trembled. The knife to cut the cake looked sharp. She should have told Jenny, come over with Jenny, but this was Peyton and Deirdre, they couldn't . . . hurt . . . her.

"I had to act to protect Deirdre," Peyton said. "I hope you can understand that."

"Protect her from what?"

Peyton took a deep breath. "From my dad. He killed my mother and he would have killed her."

Viv struggled to make her mouth work. "He didn't. He didn't."

"He killed my mom. He ran her down with a car that wasn't tied to him—I don't know where he got it, but somehow he did it. Because he thought she was having an affair with your late husband. Just because she helped y'all when Clark was sick and paid attention to him. That's how crazy he was." Peyton waited for Viv to speak, but shock had silenced her. "And if Deirdre left him, she might get half of what was his. He wouldn't risk that."

"The idea that your father killed your mother is insane. You're just saying this."

"For what reason would I lie?"

"So that I won't accuse you . . . so that I'll protect you. You want me to take your side, like Bill was the bad guy and whatever you've done is forgivable."

"You can accuse us." He shrugged. "But you have no proof. None."

"Is the baby . . . is it his? Or yours?"

"Wow, what a suspicious mind you have." Peyton cracked a smile, glanced at Deirdre. "Mine, I think. But it doesn't matter. I'm treating it like it's mine."

"Why would you . . . your father's wife . . ."

"I didn't like Deirdre at first, but I didn't want her to end up just like Mom."

"But the autopsy. The autopsy . . ."

"There wasn't one, but if there was it would show a heart attack."

"You caused it." Now she was sure.

"Yes, Viv, I waved my magic heart attack wand and killed my own dad. Do you hear yourself?"

"So how did he . . ."

"We told him that we knew. That he had killed Mom. And that the price of our silence was he was going to leave this house and leave us alone. It was too much for him—the guilt, the anger. But words don't leave a trace."

"Where's your proof he killed Gina?"

"We didn't have any, just like you don't have any against us. I had my suspicions. Always. But I guess Dad thought we did, because the heart attack came super fast. I'd say *that* was an admission of guilt."

Viv felt dizzy. Did *she* have a heart condition? She didn't know. She thought: I guess I'm about to find out. "Why are you telling me this?" She stood, her hands flat on the granite of the kitchen island.

"Because we didn't *know* he'd have a heart attack. It's not our fault." Deirdre sipped her tea.

That could be a lie. What if they'd hidden the medication? Well, Bill would have just gotten more. Maybe they were telling the truth. What would she do if this confession was all the truth?

"Viv, we called the ambulance as soon as he collapsed. It was just a really bad heart attack," Peyton said. "His guilty conscience, if you ask me."

"I'm sure you rushed to the phone if you thought he murdered your mom."

"I placed my call in a timely manner," Peyton said.

"Why act like you hate each other?" Viv asked. That was what had told her they were hiding something.

"Because we truly didn't get along at first. Then I realized he's what I liked in Bill but without all the darkness," Deirdre said. "And we don't want to be accused. Or even suspected."

"No innocent person does," Peyton said.

Neither does a guilty one, Viv thought.

"Do you think we want the baby's life to start that way, with us under suspicion of malice, when it was natural causes?" Deirdre said.

Viv, after a moment, shook her head.

"I mean, you could call the police. But Deirdre's staying here. She wants the child to grow up here, and why not, it's a great place. Great schools. Great opportunities. Every advantage. You could take all that away from her child with an accusation and no proof, I guess, or you can let that baby have a great start in life."

"I . . . I . . . So you cannot prove it? That your father killed your mother?"

"No. If I could, I would have gone to the police then and there." Peyton shrugged.

"I don't know what to believe," Viv said, almost crying.

"We live in a world where people believe what they want to believe is true," Deirdre said softly. "We see it every day."

"Are you in love?" Viv asked.

"We're kind of stuck together now," Deirdre responded, and for the first time since the funeral she smiled. "Yes, Viv, I love him."

Peyton made his gaze steady. "I love her. We'll raise this

child together, and probably that will explain us becoming closer in the eyes of the neighborhood. Don't you think everyone will talk if we marry someday? She wasn't my step-mother for so long. It'll be a little scandal, but just for a while, because people will also tell themselves they understand how we leaned on each other for the baby and how that turned to love. It's a happy ending, Viv. It's just a problem if it's too fast, or right away. People get used to all sorts of odd ideas with very little effort."

It was true, she thought. People would get used to them living together in this house, with the baby. And then they'd accept the reality they were currently hiding. Viv pushed away her coffee cake. "How do I know you won't hurt me? You won't shut me up?"

"Viv. We're not monsters. We're not killers," Peyton said. "We're who we've always been."

"You're alone now," Deirdre said. "Your daughter's an in-grate who never comes home. Your husband's gone. We could be your family, Viv. You wouldn't have to be alone."

Viv said nothing for a minute. She looked at them both. Deirdre took Peyton's hand. Then she leaned across the is-land and reached out her other hand toward Viv.

Viv stared at it for a moment. Stared at Deirdre. Then Peyton. He reached his hand out toward her as well.

Then Viv reached out and took both their hands. Squeezed. Closed her eyes for a moment, then opened them. Made her choice.

"I went and looked at cribs online, Deirdre. I found some really nice ones." Her voice was steady.

"Show them to me," Deirdre said. "Please."

A THOUSAND BATS ON AN AUSTIN NIGHT

BY SCOTT MONTGOMERY

Lady Bird Lake

J immy's knuckles glared white around the small outboard's steering as we approached the Congress Street Bridge hanging over Lady Bird Lake. "You're sure we need to be under it, Tin?"

I hoped to see their boat already at the location, but just saw spots of tourists leaning over the bridge. "That's what the man said."

Moonlight bounced off the water and the October breeze brought the smell of the trees and grass, mixing with the river water. Echoes of the Americana melodies from Warehouse District clubs from the north bank blended with the beats of the rockers and rollers on South Congress. If I was with my wife for a romantic evening, instead of Jimmy on assignment, the city would have reflected that perfect Austin night the Bastard Sons of Johnny Cash sang about.

"They should be here," Jimmy said.

"They're thieves." I surveyed the water for our party. "They avoid steady jobs. You can't expect punctuality."

I had accepted a touchier-than-usual job for Tin Man Investigations—theft exchange. A crew headed by someone who liked to go by the name of the Lynx hit Krietzer's Jewelers for $350,000 three weeks ago. The thief contacted their insurer, Pryor & Panowich, offering to sell the hot rocks back for $175,000, saving them from a larger payout.

I'd worked with P&P mainly on fraud, but had done one or two of these before, even one with agents of the Lynx. Still, I wavered on doing it. You could always count on someone on the other side holding a gun. That said, you don't have to chase insurance companies down for payment and they were regulars.

Plus, I had an ex-marine with me. Jimmy Metz married my friend Stephanie over a year ago after his final Iraq tour in '05. He contemplated going into security and worked under me to get his hours for a PI license. It allowed me to branch out into security for clubs and musicians I knew when Stephanie and I played in the Criminals, a band of some note in Austin's early Red River scene. At 5'6" with a physique described as a teddy bear at its most complimentary, I found it hard to sell myself on that side of the profession. Jimmy, however, resembled a fireplug and worked out and possessed a military background and a tough-guy accent from the streets of South Boston.

"Think the bats are gone?" he asked.

"They're out feeding now."

"All of them?"

"Some probably left the kids at home with a sitter."

Jimmy watched the skies. "The babies are called *pups*."

I glanced up as well, only seeing starlight. "Learn something new every day."

"You know when they come back?"

"I don't know, you're the one coming off like Animal Planet."

"I'm not crazy about them."

"I don't know anybody who loves them." My watch confirmed we were on time at eight. "Just the folks who watch them fly out. Leave it to the city to turn them into a tourist attraction."

Jimmy looked ahead. "I got a thing about them."

"What kind of thing?"

"A thing." Jimmy noticed his knuckles. "A phobia."

"You're afraid of bats?"

"All kinds of rodents, but those flying bastards are at the top of the list."

"You have problems with mice too?"

"I'm not fond of them."

"Who kills the mice and rats, you or Stephanie?"

"That issue hasn't come up in our marriage."

"It will." I smirked. "For the record, I do it."

"Then you get a smiley face sticker."

"I didn't mean to hit a nerve."

"Hey, I got my reasons."

"They have anything to do with a guy named Mickey?"

Jimmy snapped, "It has to do with the death of over a dozen of my men."

The words froze me on the bobbing boat.

Jimmy inhaled like he was about to take a deep dive, and then he did: "We were on patrol, searching for Sadam. We humped over this mountain they dropped us on the other side of to check a valley and some of the caves. My pack felt like a bitch."

He straightened up, wrestling the ghost pack. "This guy we called Windex spotted some insurgents. They were carrying a long box into this one cave below. Looked like one of the leaders. Might not be the ace, but we thought we could take a couple of the other assholes in the deck. We snuck down.

"Most of the squad was young and pumped up. Chuck

Norris had just visited the base and they were swapping jokes back and forth." Jimmy smiled a split-second. "*Chuck Norris drinks napalm to cure his heartburn. Chuck Norris once punched a man in the soul. Chuck Norris doesn't sleep, he waits.*"

"I always wondered where those came from."

Jimmy lost his smile. "This kid from Oklahoma, Bills, he takes point. Dumbass runs right into the cave. I told him to cover the perimeter until the rest of us got down there. I swear I did.

"Wasn't long before gunfire started popping and the kid was screaming. I grabbed our anti-tank man Anderson in case we had to carry him out. This guy was a monster.

"We press up against opposite sides of the cave. Was pitch black, except for some lights you could see way down where they were strung up on the ceiling. I called out to Bills. The kid screams back, saying he was torn up. When I asked him how many bad guys, he said he didn't know but he knew they were nearby.

"Anderson and I hit the ground and crawled toward him. I can still hear those fucking rats squeaking next to me. I got close enough to Bills to hear his heart beating. The rest of the idiots rushed in. It was exactly what they wanted.

"A burst came out of the darkness, then others lighting up the cave. I was able to spot one and get him. I crawled over to Bills. The unit was holding their own for a bunch of dumb fucks that walked into a trap. I got to Bills's hand. Then the fucking bats."

Jimmy froze with a dead-eye stare. "I guess the gunfire stirred them up. They swarmed out of the cave, flapping around us. My boys weren't used to them, especially in their fucking faces. Nobody was Chuck Norris.

"The Muhadi cut everyone down. I felt Bills's blood spray

on me. It attracted some of those fuckers. By the time I swatted them off, my guys were dead.

"Then I played dead. All day in bat shit covered by my men's bodies with rats crawling over me. Then the bats would fly down and pick off the insects the bodies attracted.

"I was able to kill a guard, sneak out, and make it to the extraction point. Nothing calms me more than the sound of chopper blades now."

I heard the purr of a speedboat motor from the other side of the bridge. A cigarette boat skimmed to a stop and turned sideways.

"I need you in the here and now, Jimmy."

Jimmy straightened up and saluted in a dramatic way that chipped at my confidence.

I looked over the slick watercraft. "Now I know why they insisted on us renting this bathtub."

Jimmy noticed too. "They can outrun us easy."

"The Lynx isn't dumb."

"Has a dumb name."

"For some reason thieves always have to use a cat name." I made out two figures in the cigarette boat. "I blame television."

Jimmy cut the motor and we drifted in. I caught my tough marine studying the underside of the bridge. His face turned to a kid's with a plate full of brussels sprouts placed before him. "God, I hate that smell."

The guano peppering the piers and underside of the bridge gave off a sour smell of old farts, but I found it less bad than handling one of my son's diapers. Jimmy bobbed his head like he was about to gag.

"Are you going to be okay?"

He exhaled and nodded.

"I need you to be okay."

Jimmy shoved his hand close to my face. "Just give me a fucking second."

I leaned back.

"Sorry." He put his hand down. "I'm good."

I noticed the figures were a male and a familiar female. "I'm guessing the woman is who I dealt with before when I did the switch for the ingots from Casey's."

Jimmy's eyes went from the bridge above to her. "So, this should be smooth?"

As long as something squeaky doesn't fly down from below.

The woman sported the same black ball cap and sunglasses, covered in the same khaki camo. Looked like she carried the same pistol as well. Approaching a mountain lion with her cubs would be safer.

We both briefly showed our hands to demonstrate we were not carrying. Jimmy had stuck a Beretta holstered in the back of his waistband, but it didn't seem dishonest since he wasn't planning on using it.

The cigarette boat driver carried as well. A large cowboy hat, Ray-Bans, and shit-eating grin covered his face. I found something familiar about him too.

He tipped his hat. "Always nice to meet someone with a big bag of money for us."

"I hate chipper crooks," I whispered to Jimmy, trying to place the man.

"He reminds me of a guy who always got someone else killed on patrol."

I picked up the two duffel bags full of cash.

"You can toss them to the lady there." The guy tried to put on a British accent, but his East Texas drawl turned it to a bad Australian one. I knew I'd seen him before. I worked at what handbill his face decorated.

"Either one of you the Lynx?"

The lady with the gun adjusted her stance and aim, making sure I was right in her sights. "Keep it anonymous and professional."

She glanced at Jimmy and picked up the case.

"I'll need to take a closer look." I shrugged. "Just being professional."

Cowboy Hat: "Money first, mate."

I realized I couldn't have recognized this guy from a handbill since half his face was covered. I remembered the hat. "I toss the first bag, you toss the case. If it's good, you get the other one. I have no reason to cross you two—P&P wants to play it safe."

Cowboy Hat chewed his bottom lip for a moment. "I don't know."

"I do." Danger Lady kept her fierce stare on me. "It's fair."

I tossed the first bag into their boat. She picked it up; I clocked her moves. "Feel free to count it."

Cowboy Hat relaxed with his gun. "You got an honest face."

Danger Lady went through the stacks, not every bill, but she flipped through them for a quick confirmation of no consecutive serial numbers, marks, or phony bills.

The squeal of a bat cut through the rippling water and flipping cash.

Jimmy's head shot up. He realized I'd noticed and dropped it back down.

"You're good." Danger Lady dropped the bag then tossed the case over.

I fumbled my catch and it clanged onto the floor of the boat.

Cowboy Hat laughed. "Good thing the boys at P&P aren't watching."

"We don't need your mouth," Jimmy said.

The cheeseball kept his grin. "Your mate can't take a joke?"

Another squeak got Jimmy's attention. "Just shut up."

Danger Lady yanked her gun out again.

"Deep breath, everyone." I showed my hands. "We're almost there."

She actually did take a breath. Then she put her gun on me.

I picked up the case and opened it. The jewels caught some of the moonlight, making a strong proclamation that they were worth more than five years of me working for insurance companies and pissed-off spouses. I shut the case, then clicked the lock down. At that moment I realized where I knew Cowboy Hat from.

The flapping of over a hundred wings interrupted my memory.

It wasn't birds.

Jimmy looked back.

A swarm of bats came in like a screeching fighter squadron.

Jimmy yanked out his artillery and fired at them.

Danger Lady moved her gun on him.

I decided to be crazier and leapt off our boat at her.

I hit the side of the cigarette boat and grabbed the railing. I splashed in the water, but jostled the boat, throwing off the thieves' aim.

Jimmy got himself together and put his gun on the man.

The bats flew into their nest under the bridge. Their off-harmony screeches shook up the night. Jimmy shut his eyes as they screeched over him. The thieves took aim.

I rocked the boat. The bitter water smacked my face.

Cowboy Hat fell on his ass, pistol popping off by accident. Danger Lady's attention went to finding her footing. Jimmy's eyes went back to her and so did his Beretta.

I spit out the water. A small wave slammed me up against the boat.

Cowboy Hat scrambled up, firing a wild shot for cover as he went for the wheel. The cigarette boat started up. It felt wise to let go of the railing.

I pushed myself off from their boat. It missed me by inches as Cowboy Hat swung it to the east, its motor spitting up a gallon of Lady Bird Lake into my mouth. It didn't taste good.

Jimmy kept his aim on Danger Lady. She did the same with him as they sped off with a jet trail of water that also slammed into my face.

I paddled toward our boat. Jimmy fished me out and got me over the side in two yanks. I coughed out rancid water. "We're never doing a meet here again."

Jimmy nailed me in the back and pushed the last of the water out. "You don't have to tell me I'm fired."

"It actually might work out." I coughed a couple more times, just air now. "If the gunshots didn't put APD on them, I recognized the driver: Benny Atkins, aka Hound Dog."

"You dealt with him in a previous case?"

"When Stephanie and I were in the Criminals. He was the bass player for a jazz-metal fusion band called Night Train. Not sure if he's moving up or down in the world."

Jimmy glanced up at the bats as they flapped into their nests. "Fuckers."

I looked up at the creatures too, picturing them hanging down from a dark cavern with several dead men on the floor. "Have you talked to anybody about the cave?"

"Some guys at the VA. It helped with the nightmares.

Outside of them, even Stephanie doesn't know." He put a hand on my shoulder. "I'd like to keep it that way."

I nodded. "I never thought about what you really went through over there."

"You're a civilian, you don't have to."

"All the reason I should."

Jimmy bumped his fist against my shoulder. I'd seen him do to some marine buddies.

I listened to the bats above me, their squeals as sharp as their teeth. "Let's get out of here—now."

PART II

NOTHING I CAN DO ABOUT IT NOW

And regret is just a memory written on my brow
And there's nothing I can do about it now.
—Willie Nelson

RUSH HOUR

BY RICHARD Z. SANTOS

The Domain

I should have let her jump.

Really, I mean it, she would have been fine. Okay, maybe not fine but she would have lived. We were no more than forty feet in the air and she was maybe pushing twenty years old. Oh, her legs would have gone to powder and there'd be a titanium hip or two in her future, but most of us would be so lucky to get a couple of those bad boys installed.

I wouldn't even have been on that level of the parking garage if this mall had enough handicap spots. I saw her out of the corner of my eye when I pulled in. Real quick, one of those images that, even though glimpsed for only half a second, stayed with me. I knew exactly what I had seen.

Still, I waited a beat before turning off the car. I get floaters and a weird zooming black spot sometimes, so maybe I didn't see a person dangling their legs over the wrong side of a ledge four stories up. I turned off the car, grabbed my cane, and started the humiliating process of heaving myself to my feet. I could have just kept walking to the elevator. Ten or fifteen steps and I'd have been fine.

But I looked over my shoulder. All I could see was her slouched back and the black hoodie that wouldn't fit a linebacker, much less her. Her boots thumped against the outside concrete and she wasn't looking down, but I knew *down* was on her mind.

"Oh, goddamnit," I said.

No one heard me because no one else was around. No nurturing maternal figure, no hunky security guard, no insightful asshole in a blazer. Just me and this tiny person about to ruin both of our days.

The smart move would have been to mind my own business. Getting dressed in the morning takes me about twenty minutes and my wife makes me shower with the bathroom door open. If I tried to keep a kitten from jumping off a couch, I'd somehow end up killing us both.

But look, I know my time is somewhat limited and I didn't want to spend what was left thinking about some jackass kid who offed herself. So I put my head down and tapped my way toward the figure in black. I moved slow enough that she must have heard me coming.

The posture and the ridiculous hoodie told me she was young, but when I got closer I saw how young. I'd taught eleventh-grade English for ten years before getting sick. I knew what teenagers looked like. And not movie teenagers with straight teeth and thousand-dollar haircuts. Real teenagers look awful. Even the ones with "good" skin are still spotty, their hair tends to be kinda greasy, and no one learns how to dress themselves until their midtwenties.

I positioned myself in her peripheral vision but didn't look at her. We were both staring at the condos across the street. It was a new building—everything around here was a new building—and I imagine the studio apartments in there went for more than my mortgage.

Maybe she enjoyed hanging out up here and staring into the open windows. I could see people sitting on their couches or making food; one apartment directly across from us was flooded with what looked like studio lights.

I got nervous after seeing her phone and earbuds. They weren't in her hand or in her ears. She'd set them next to her. The earbuds were on top of the phone, which sat in a comically oversized Hello Kitty case. On top of Kitty was a folded-up piece of paper. *Sorry Tyler* had been scrawled in capital letters.

I'd never taught a student who committed suicide. I'd taught those who threatened—everything from playful ideation in dark poetry to full-on "Mr. Alvarado, I'm going to do this tonight." Every year there were one or two in my classes who had just been released from various facilities or centers. The wounds on their arms were still fresh, and their social workers would drop by once a month to bring them a hamburger and "chat about how things are going." Most teachers hated having to deal with kids like that. Sometimes it's hardest to help those who need it the most. I never minded them, and they usually didn't mind me because I never treated them like Fabergé eggs.

"Hey," I said. "You go to LBJ?"

She didn't turn around but she rolled her eyes so hard I saw it in the back of her head.

"Where'd you go then? Or are you still in it?"

She rubbed the back of a hand against her chin. She wore a couple plain brass bands that had stained her first two fingers aquarium-green, but otherwise she looked healthy enough.

"I was homeschooled," she said.

"Ah, there's your problem then."

She shot me a look and was ready to tear me a new one before she caught herself. "Oh, you're funny, I guess."

"Yeah, that's me, I'm hilarious. Look, I don't know who you are and I'm not going to ask. But if you jump from there you'll regret it."

"If I jump I won't be able to regret anything."

"No, it doesn't work that way. That fall is only two or three seconds, but it'll last a lifetime. You'll claw for a ledge but you'll just rip your fingernails off. And you'll probably land in some bushes and end up paralyzed for the next seventy years. That'd suck."

She shook her head and didn't look at me. "I'm not falling for that reverse psychology or whatever clever thing you think you're doing."

"Ha, *look* at me, not much cleverness happening anymore. My name's Pedro, what's yours?"

"Sandra." She said it slow, like it hurt.

"They're still naming people Sandra?"

"At least two people did. Named me after an aunt I never met."

"That's nice."

"That's what everyone keeps telling me. Look, I'm probably not going to jump. I mean, I might, but if I do or don't it won't be because of you and whatever this is."

"I'm just here to buy my son a graduation present. But Sandra, I'd feel a lot better about spending too much money in this awful place if I didn't have to hear your body hit that ground."

She swung a leg over the edge and straddled the wall. This made my heart stop, but my reflexes are so shot I didn't move a muscle. She looked me up and down in that cool, easy way only teenagers can.

"Are you a teacher?" she asked.

I raised my eyebrows. "You *do* go to LBJ."

"No, you just seem like that kind of asshole. Clever and all."

"I *was* a teacher. Not anymore. Look, I can walk all day

once I get going, but standing here like this is hell on my balance."

Sandra peered over my shoulder into the parking garage. I wondered if she was looking for someone.

"Teachers are assholes," she said.

"Most don't start out that way."

"Then what happens to them?"

"Shitheads like you."

Sandra turned to hide her smile. "Did a shithead like me lead to that cane?"

"Cancer. Leukemia. I imagine stress doesn't help, but teenagers don't cause cancer as far as I know."

"Leukemia isn't one of those tumor cancers, right?"

"No, those are easy, just a few snips and you're cured. Leukemia is when your blood and bone marrow kind of . . . glitch."

"Glitch?"

"And then try to kill you."

She hopped down off the wall. Her dingy Vans, once white but now a sickly gray, barely made a noise on the concrete. "You're not a hero, you know. I wasn't going to—"

"Who's Tyler?"

She stuffed her phone, earbuds, and the note into the pocket of her hoodie. "Who?"

She walked forward and stopped right next to me. We were side by side, facing opposite directions, but she was close and it felt awkward. I gripped my cane. She gently swung her hip into mine. Not hard enough to knock me over. Just a tap. It was almost friendly.

"Don't talk to strangers," she said.

I watched her disappear into the parking garage. I glanced around for another witness to whatever just happened.

Someone to explain to me if I had actually done anything, but no one was there.

I spent an hour in a department store I couldn't afford picking out a pair of cuff links and a white dress shirt. Marco didn't have anything this fancy, and I didn't know where he would wear something like this, but it seemed like a real graduation gift.

I was halfway to the register before realizing I may have just picked out his outfit for my funeral. The white shirt went back on the rack and I bought a silky light-blue shirt instead. It didn't take cuff links and it kind of looked like something a Miami gangster would wear, but I couldn't only buy him cuff links.

When I got to the cash register, my card was declined. The salesclerk gave me one "Oh, that's weird, try it again," before turning serious and saying there wasn't anything he could do.

"This isn't right though," I said. "I know there's money in that account."

He tucked in his bottom lip like he felt so sorry for me it hurt. "Our system's been acting weird lately."

"I don't need that." I leaned my cane against the counter and pulled out my phone.

"I'm sorry?"

"I don't need *understanding*. There's an error with my bank account. I'm sick but I'm not broke."

"I see. Well, maybe if you have another card, or you can call someone for assistance?"

I had trouble logging into my bank's app because it was asking for a PIN, but evidently not my actual card PIN but some other PIN.

"Look, I'm just trying to buy a shirt, give me a second." I closed my eyes and tried to think of what I'd use as a second PIN. Who needs a *second* PIN?

"Sir?"

"Jesus Christ, will you give me a second?"

The clerk stepped back and that expression of pity turned into judgment. I knew what he was looking at. An old guy ready to snap into pieces. Another broke Mexican in a store that sold twenty-five-dollar socks. A sick man. Dying.

"What, you think you'll never get sick? You're maybe twenty-four and nothing will *ever* happen to you."

He turned around and picked up a phone. The punk was calling security but didn't mind turning his back on me. So I stepped forward, picked up my cane, and shoved him right between the shoulder blades.

The guy let out an "Ow" even though I barely touched him. He turned around and looked more shocked than mad.

"Hey," I said, "go fuck yourself."

My plan was to storm out of there, call my bank, fix whatever bullshit was happening, and then spend more money than I could afford just to rub it in their faces.

But I only made it about twenty feet before feeling dizzy. I gripped the handle of the cane and focused on breathing in and out through my nose like the physical therapist had recommended, but it was no use. There was a bench near the escalator and security was surrounding me before I could even plop my ass down.

When I got home, I didn't tell Julia because I knew she'd be worried at first and then later pissed at me for causing a scene. I got sick two years ago, and she started wanting to leave me six months later. I see it in how she shuts doors behind her and how the only emotion I get from her is concern. She'll help me put on my socks and she'll pick up my phone when it slips out of my hand, but I'll be damned if she'll kiss me on the forehead.

She's too Catholic to divorce an invalid. Her older sister took care of their parents until they died, and I know part of her thinks helping me up off the bathroom floor (something she's only had to do twice, by the way) is her lot in life. Us Mexican Catholics aren't living unless we're suffering, but if you complain about your suffering or try to end it, somehow that makes it not count.

I don't blame her for wanting to leave. The first few months after my diagnosis were, in some ways, the best part of our ten years together. We cried, we raged, we held each other like lovers in a tragedy.

But then I stopped reliving our best memories because it made me angry that those days were behind us. I stopped recording cheesy videos for Marco to see after I'm gone because they made me sad. I stopped joking about my bald head and my skinny arms because it depressed the shit out of me.

I stayed sick, and then the chemo made me sicker, and now I'm cured but broken and filled with bone marrow and blood that's out to get me. I want to be better. I don't like seeing Julia and Marco tense up when I enter the room. But I don't know how to care about living again.

Julia saw that I came back from the Domain without any gifts for Marco, but she didn't say anything and neither did I. Instead, I went into the bedroom and tried to figure out what happened to my money.

By the time I got someone at the bank to talk to me, my account had nearly been drained. Hundred-dollar charges had been hitting my account every five minutes like clockwork starting at eleven in the morning. The name of the merchant was *Kitty_Says_Hi*.

I remembered Sandra's stupid phone case. So massive and childish. And then I remembered her stuffing that phone into her hoodie and then bumping into my hip, against my pocket, where my wallet was.

I could almost laugh. Almost.

Growing up, Austin was cool because people around the country had heard of us but no one actually ever came here. Then computer guys and Californians showed up, and now my old neighborhood is nothing but condos and oat milk. We moved to north Austin back when it was the outskirts, but even this area is filling up with fancy cars and people who moved to a "weird" city but call the cops if someone's muffler is too loud.

I hated the Domain but now I was there two days in a row. Lucky me. This place is just a mall. Sure, it's a new mall because it's open-air and you can get a fifteen-dollar juice and a twenty-dollar cupcake, but it's still a mall where assholes walk around pretending like they have money and teenagers on skateboards pretend they enjoy riding skateboards.

I didn't really know what I was going to do when I saw Sandra again, but I'd find her somewhere. The Domain has about ten parking garages and I cruised up and down each of them, wondering if I'd catch her fishing for another sucker like me. But I had to stop after a while because going around and around started to make me nauseous.

Like I said, this place is a new, fancy mall, which is another way of saying they piled condos and hotels on top of stores and also snaked a bunch of two-lane roads between everything. There's a constant war between drivers and pedestrians. The walkers make you wait at your stop sign for ten minutes while they trudge through the intersection, and then they make it back to their cars and get stuck at the same intersection. The angry guy who yells at a car for coming too close to his kids is the same one peeling out at a stop sign a few minutes later.

Honestly, the place reminds me of the hospital. Hospitals and giant malls aren't like anywhere else in the world, yet they operate under the same twisted logic. They pull you into their vast systems and you can try to fight the schedules and the patterns, but you'll lose so it's easier to let yourself get washed away. We enter as humans, then we turn into another product to be scanned and processed.

Also, at both places it's very easy to be surrounded by people and remain completely invisible. I was stuck at a stop sign and watched the river of pedestrians. Young couples drinking expensive coffee, high schoolers feeling oh so grown up, families either starting their day bright and cheery or ending it red-faced and sore.

There was a kid waiting on the corner, maybe seventeen years old, wearing a black T-shirt and a green hat. He was letting knots of pedestrians pass him. Every few seconds he'd put his phone into his pocket, and then he'd bring it back out and raise it to his face. It's the most common gesture in the world, but each time he'd do it, he'd let his hand rest a little too close to a woman's purse or he'd just graze the back of a man's pants, so light that no one felt it, and besides, he was just another kid lost on his phone.

I don't know how it works though I'd heard about devices or apps that let you skim the numbers off certain kinds of credit cards. They spoof a merchant and try to run a transaction without tripping any fraud alerts. It probably only works once out of every ten tries, but that's enough if you're patient.

I rolled down my window to yell at the kid in the green hat, but then the guy behind me started honking. The kid looked up and saw me staring at him. He spun around, nice and smooth, and went up the sidewalk. I tried to follow but lost him when he ducked into Banana Republic.

I'd need to do this on foot. Somehow.

I found a spot on the street and made it to a bench near an Astroturf-covered playscape. This was a good vantage point. I could see a few different strips of stores and I wasn't even the frailest person sitting here watching the world go by.

Now I knew what I was looking for. Young people lingering by themselves and messing with their phones. God, imagine if I tried to explain this to a cop?

What are you doing here, sir?

Oh, just watching teenagers play with their phones because I think they're part of some underground circle of high-tech thieves.

Julia would take me to get a CT scan if I said a word of this.

It was Friday, midday, but still the waves of people were relentless. Where were these people supposed to be? Should I have spent my life dragging Julia and Marco to places like this in the middle of the day?

About twenty minutes later, the kid in the green hat came walking down the sidewalk. He held his phone in front of him and then kept looking around, like he was lost. A few times he lifted his phone as if taking a selfie; a woman walking behind him had to stop quickly to keep from running into him. When he apologized, he brought his phone down and held it next to her purse. She smiled and kept moving without looking back.

The kid walked over to another teenager, a girl in a yellow sundress, who was sitting on a concrete ledge near a food truck. They huddled for a second and then the kid in the green hat walked away. I watched the girl for a few minutes. She was totally absorbed in her phone, but every few minutes some guy would approach her and lean close. She would smile and gesture like she was waiting for someone. Each guy would creep a little closer and then, *swipe*, she'd hold her phone against his pant pocket for just a second. Then she'd ignore him and he'd wander away, only to be replaced ten minutes later by another loser trying to pick up a teenager. These kids were good.

Then the girl in the sundress stood up and started walking in the direction the kid in the green hat had gone. After a few steps, she turned over her shoulder and looked right at me. I tried to tell myself it was random, just a quick glance behind her, but I met her eyes and I swear I saw a quick grin.

I should have just gone home, of course. The bank was reimbursing me and it's not like these kids were shoving guns into people's ribs. But honestly, I thought they were pretty clever, and I was curious.

The girl in the sundress rounded a corner ahead of me and I tried to keep up. My muscles are tight and my bones hurt all the time, yet I can walk long distances once I get moving. Quick turns are tough and standing in one place is hard, but if I keep my feet moving, I'm good.

She'd turned off the main strip of stores and was standing in front of a movie theater. The kid in the green hat was across the street at a restaurant's side door. Both looked like any other teenager—only half interested in the tangible world.

I started to form a plan. Yeah, I knew it was a little late to come up with a plan, but it wasn't like I did this regularly. Figured I'd keep it simple. I'd ask if Sandra was okay and then, well, I guess I'd just see what happened after that.

I was about twenty feet from the girl when I felt the lightest touch against my left side. I almost lost my balance, and when I righted myself I couldn't see anyone. Or, rather, there were people everywhere and I didn't know who had touched me. Then I felt another person brush my right side; maybe I saw a kid in a baggy white T-shirt. And then some-one else was right behind me but all I saw was a red polo before they blended in with the crowd.

I glanced up and the girl in the sundress had crossed the street. She was standing next to the kid with the green hat. They were staring at me like I was a butterfly pinned to a board. These little vampires were trying to drain me, and they knew I couldn't do anything about it.

I put my hand in my pocket and held onto my wallet, as if that could stop RFID waves or whatever they were using. But that just told them where my cards were, and then the guy in the red polo was back and he was touching me and asking if I needed help. I shook him off and then a kid in a white T-shirt took his place and offered me water and a chair.

A passing mom gave them a warm look, like they were just the sweetest fucking do-gooders she'd ever seen. I put my head down and kept walking toward the sundress, though I had to wait at an intersection while teenagers kept step-ping in front of me or swinging their bags against my hip. I couldn't tell how many of them were swarming me. Could have been two or three circling, or a dozen, or maybe they were just idiot kids not paying attention.

The cars weren't letting any pedestrians cross. Those two could vanish any second, so I just yelled, "Who's Tyler? Where's Sandra?"

The kid in the green hat whispered something to the

girl in the sundress and then ran off. The girl walked into the intersection and cars slammed on their brakes, but she kept advancing at me. She looked like she'd walk right over me, crunching my kneecaps into the concrete if she needed to. Someone was tapping a bag against my leg over and over again. I could feel my phone buzzing, alerting me to a withdrawal and a withdrawal and a withdrawal.

The girl in the sundress was just a few feet away. She raised her finger, pointed it at me, and opened her mouth just when Sandra stepped in front of her. Sandra grabbed the girl's wrist and brought it down to her side. She whispered, and the girl in the sundress looked ready to floor Sandra, but then she disappeared into the stream of people.

Sandra put her hands on her hips and looked at me the way I used to look at kids caught skipping class.

"Clever," she said.

She walked over to some concrete chairs that were low to the ground and shaped like somewhat ergonomic teardrops.

"If I get down onto that thing, I won't be able to get back up."

She laid back on the swooping chair and the way her feet were elevated made me think of a hospital bed. "I'll help you up, just sit down before you don't have a choice about it."

"Fine, but I'm going to make some really obnoxious groans while I position myself."

"Okay, Grandpa."

It took longer than I'd like to admit, but once I got settled the chair was pretty damn comfortable. I felt my feet pulse as the blood that had pooled in my ankles started to flow again.

Sandra looked concerned, which is totally different than looking like she pitied me or was worried I'd croak on her. "So you still have leukemia or what?"

"No, I'm cured."

"Yeah, sure, you look it."

I laid my cane next to me on the chair and folded my hands over my stomach. I closed my eyes for a second and let the cool concrete relax me.

"It's called chronic graft-versus-host disease. They cured my leukemia with a bone marrow transplant, but GVHD pops up pretty often. My blood, my *new* blood, thinks my body is a foreign object, so it attacks my muscles and bones."

"Your blood is attacking you?"

"It's not my blood, or it wasn't before my bone marrow was replaced. Magic of science, right?"

"Does it kill you?"

"If it gets to my heart or brain. Or kidneys or liver. Or lungs. But for now, it's content chewing on my muscles." I held up my arm.

Sandra reached over and squeezed my forearm. Graft-versus-host turns the soft muscles rigid as it breaks down the tissue. She seemed curious and a little disgusted. I could feel her hand on my skin, but when she squeezed my arm it felt like I was wearing a parka.

"Feels like rigor mortis," she said. "Some kind of shuffling dead over here."

"Thanks."

She smiled and we relaxed for a second. I scanned the crowd, nervous I was about to be swarmed again.

"You nearly drained my account yesterday. That's what you do, right?"

"That was a glitch."

"A glitch?"

"Yeah, we just do one-time skims, fifty or a hundred bucks, but the program freaked out on you. People around here don't even notice. Even if they looked at their statements later, and who does that, they probably couldn't remember each store and each brunch. We don't even need to change out the merchant accounts all that often because complaints are so rare. Would you have noticed just one charge?"

"I'm here because of a glitch?"

"I don't know why you're here. Your bank will make you whole. Maybe you pissed off a clerk and lost a couple hours, but that's it."

"A couple hours mean more to me than they used to," I said. "And the clerk wasn't pissed until I hit him with my cane."

She closed her eyes and laughed silently. "You hit someone?"

I shook my head. "Well, pushed him."

Sandra started to say something, but then she looked around and clammed up. She was scanning the faces around us, searching for someone.

"We're stealing from people, okay, but we're not . . . bad. You're not a cop but you are a threat. Cane and graft-versus-host and all. What are you even doing?"

I closed my eyes again. "I don't know what I'm doing. I avoid everything like this."

"You avoid gangs of criminals?"

"Y'all are just kids. You're making some money, but you're just kids. No, I mean I avoid all of this. I don't sit in the sun because my skin is so thin and dry it burns like kindling. I don't lounge in ridiculous chairs because they don't seem worth the effort. And my immune system is shot so crowds scare the hell out of me."

"Do you want to do a round?" Sandra pulled her Hello Kitty phone out of her hoodie pocket.

I looked at her and then shook my head.

"Oh, but you'd be good at it. You could bump into people and *they* would feel bad. It's hard if you can't tell where their cards are, we have to guess a lot of the time, but if you asked someone to help you into a chair you could scan purses, pockets, backpacks—anything."

I laughed when I pictured myself taking down tourists and tech guys a hundred bucks at a time. She was right, it would work.

"I get sick of people trying to help me," I said.

"Me too. But you also *need* help."

I looked Sandra in the eye and raised an eyebrow.

She shook her head. "Don't give me that teacher look. You think *I* need help, but I wasn't going to jump. I wasn't. Though I do enjoy thinking about it."

"But why? That's why I'm here. I just want to know why."

"Maybe I'm just a moody teenager."

"Who's Tyler?"

Sandra rolled her eyes. "Obviously he's the one who got us these phones and taught us how to use them, he's—" Her mouth closed with an audible click. She was checking out something behind me and for a second she looked scared, then she gave me a sad smile and I realized she wasn't scared for herself. She was scared for me.

I turned my head and all I saw was a rush of red, and then the world spun off its axis and I wondered how my cheek could hit the ground since the ground was so far away, and then I don't remember anything at all.

Until waking up in the hospital.

Every morning, just before being fully awake, I wonder if I'm still in the hospital. Four rounds of intensive in-patient chemo, weeks of recovery time, and then being admitted every time I fall, get a cold, or something else fritzes out inside has conditioned me. Before opening my eyes, I take inventory. If the blanket's soft, I'm at home. If I have a strip of plastic around my wrist, I'm in the hospital. If my back is sore and my ass is asleep, I'm in the hospital. If I'm swimming in a milk of pain and pain killers so deep that I can barely see straight, much less think clearly, I'm in the hospital.

I was in the hospital.

Julia and Marco were in the room. Julia leaned forward and looked worried, but even though she was only a few inches away, she kept her hands locked together on her knees.

"Pedro? Pedro, are you with us?"

I squinted at her. "Yeah, just a headache."

"They did an MRI because they thought you might have fractured a vertebra in your neck, but the results came back—"

"It's just a headache. I'm fine. But what happened?"

"No clue. You were at the Domain and someone called 911 when they saw you on the sidewalk. The doctor's going to want to hear what you remember. You hit your head, but did anything else happen?"

"Why the hell was I at the Domain?" I looked at Marco. "I already got your gift."

He nodded and then looked at the floor.

"I must have been . . . shopping, I guess, right? Or returning something." I tried to push myself up on my elbows, though Julia rushed to lie me back down. "Hang on," I said. "Just let me sit up a bit, will you?"

She sat back down and tried not to appear frustrated and, God bless her, she mostly succeeded. She let me fish for the bed remote for a minute before handing it to me. Sitting upright helped clear my head but it also allowed each bruise to scream at me.

I peeked under my gown. My chest was covered in a plum-colored bruise that stretched from under my neck down toward my stomach. My skin had cracked in a few places, and I knew this pain would really start humming as the bruise turned dark green, then yellow. It'd take months for the bruise to fade away, if it ever did.

"You weren't robbed," Julia said. "We have your wallet."

"A red polo. Yeah, the kid in the red polo. But of course I have my wallet, they're too clever to actually take anyone's wallet."

Julia's eyes slid to Marco for a second, as if trying to push him out of the room with a look. "Who . . . who do you mean?"

"These fucking kids, they're like little hacker genius orphan thieves, and I tried, I *tried* to help that one girl with the . . . the hoodie and Hello Kitty, she didn't jump but later she said, I think she said, she wasn't ever going to jump. So did I help her?"

"Marco, honey, can you go tell the nurse your father's awake?"

Marco crossed his arms and nodded but it took him a long time to stop staring at us. The poor kid was scared, and I must have sounded like a lunatic. Or, no, not a lunatic, like a dying man. Finally, he left but didn't shut the door behind him. I wondered what it would take to push him out of the house and into the arms of Sandra or Tyler or the girl in the sundress.

"Pedro, why don't you drink some water."

"Sandra."

Julia sat back in her chair.

"That was the kid's name. In the garage. I think she actually might need some help. Something spooked her. That's what I saw. The last thing before the kid rushed me. Sandra was scared."

"Honey, you're scaring *me*."

"No, I mean it, I—" I went into a coughing fit that brought Julia to my side.

She helped me sit up more, and brought a cup of ice water to my mouth. Hospital water. I was in the hospital again. I let Julia hold me for ten minutes, until the nurse came in, while I cried and cried.

Took me two days to get out of the hospital, even though I was fine. I mean, I'm never totally fine. The graft-versus-host is always chewing on me and the doctors are having a harder time acting optimistic each time I get admitted. But I was walking and nothing inside me was bleeding, which was good enough.

After I was discharged, Julia took more time off work, which meant I couldn't leave the house. Finally, nearly a week after that kid slammed me to the ground, Julia went to the grocery store and I was able to head back to the Domain.

I had started out worried about some strange kid, then I was curious about their operation, and now I was pissed.

I wanted to get to the Domain early so I could park on a street along the sidewalks. I took my iPad and figured out how to prop it on the dashboard so I could record what they were doing. Just to be safe, I left my wallet at home.

I sat in my car for almost two hours, right in the middle of their prime hunting hours, but I didn't see anything. No solo teenagers idling at intersections, no bumps and apologies, nothing. Maybe they'd moved on, or maybe they'd spotted me. I began to wonder if Sandra and her friends were messing with me. Maybe they had been livestreaming all this to their

Snapchat or whatever and I was just a clown for high schoolers to laugh at.

Julia had been calling and texting. I had put her off with
some vague assurances that I was getting some air, but Marco
would be home from school in an hour and I didn't want him
to worry.

This whole thing was a bad idea anyway. I shook my head
and knew I deserved whatever Julia was thinking about me
right then. On the way out of the Domain I passed the garage
where I had seen Sandra.

On a whim, I turned around, pulled into the garage, and
headed up to the empty fourth level. She was in the same
spot, of course, staring out at the building across the street.
I pulled up directly behind her. I was so close, she'd have to
step on the hood to get off the ledge.

I took my time getting out of my car, although it's not
like I had a choice about that. Standing hurt a lot more than
usual, and every time I took a breath I could feel the bruise
across my chest ripple.

I stood in the same spot I had the week before, just in her
peripheral vision, staring at the apartments across the street.

She glanced at me once, just a quick swivel of her head.
"I thought you might have died."

"Sorry to disappoint you."

"Quit that. I didn't say I wanted you to die. But you went
flying off that chair." She looked down at the ground. "Made
a hell of a noise when you landed."

"Your friend in red sent me to the hospital. Doctor said if
I had hit my head any harder I'd have bleeding in the brain.
No one knows how I didn't crack half my ribs." I put my hand
to my side. "Although I definitely cracked a few."

"Hey, I'm sorry that happened. For real, that wasn't the

plan, he got nervous, freaked out. That guy doesn't always . . . think through his actions."

Even if I'm only in the hospital for a couple days, my muscles go weak. It's almost as if my body starts to shut down the second they admit me. Some kind of self-destructive muscle memory. I leaned my back against my car with a groan.

"Every time I go into the hospital, I think it'll be the last time," I said. "It'll be something simple. When I go for good. They'll tell me I need to stay for a night or two just as a precaution, but then my body will just say, *No, no thank you.* And that'll be that."

Sandra turned halfway toward me and brought her left leg up on the ledge. "Sounds like a really stressful way to live."

"I think we're both leading stressful lives. You know, I came here today to record y'all, maybe turn you in. But I really didn't think you'd be back up here. Are you trying to leave Tyler and all this?"

Sandra tucked her hands into her hoodie. An image popped into my head, Marco as a toddler, wrapping blankets around himself and rolling on the floor of his room, giggling as he bumped into his furniture but unable to feel a thing.

"We're branching out. Trying new things." She pointed to the apartment across the way that was flooded with studio lights. "Some 'influencers' have joined us and they're making a ton of money talking about makeup and video games. It's clever. And it's not technically stealing."

"How many of y'all live there?"

"But Tyler had a new idea for me. Bought me a little dress like the one Kaitlyn wears. You saw her the other day. Wanted me to flirt with guys, older guys." She turned to me. "Not as old as you. String them along, giggle, bring them into a dressing room, and then threaten to scream if they don't give me their wallets."

I leaned my cane against my car and brought both hands to my eyes. "That's so dangerous."

"And mean. And antiwoman. And it's a *good* idea. But, I mean, if I *want* to bang a dad in Banana Republic, I'll do it. If I *want* to skim his wife's cards on the way out, I'll do it. I don't need Tyler giving me a quota and then taking 30 percent."

"Are you thinking about killing yourself?"

"I came up here because I wanted to see the horizon. Something new. But—" She gestured toward the apartment.

I sat up straight and pointed to the other wall of the garage. "Over there you can see the highway."

"I fucking hate traffic—why would I come up here to contemplate rush hour?"

"Those people are going places. All at once. And yeah, they're slowing each other down, but they'll get there."

Sandra raised her eyebrows. "That was actually clever."

"Yeah, it just kind of came out." I picked up my cane and stared down at the ground. "Hey, look, I don't have much but I can help you get away or back to wherever you're from?"

Sandra was silent. When I glanced up, she was looking so sad, and I knew someone was behind me.

"You can *what?*"

I turned around. The kid in the red polo was just a few feet away. I looked at him and then back to Sandra. "That's Tyler?"

He was older than Sandra but just by a few years. Maybe twenty-two, but with his ruddy cheeks and slight build he could probably slide down to seventeen if he needed to. He was skinny yet coiled, and the look in his eyes told me he was ready to slam me into the ground again.

"What are you doing?" he asked me. "You can barely move, I flattened your ass the other day, and honestly, I think you might die before I even finish this sentence, but you're trying to take Raven away from me."

"Raven?" I looked at Sandra but she was stone-faced. She had slid forward on the ledge and her feet were resting on the hood of my car. "Hey, look, Tyler—"

"Do not say my name, old man."

I held up my palms. "I'm not here to disrupt what you have going on. I met . . . her and thought she needed some help. That's it."

Tyler didn't take his eyes off me when he stabbed a finger at Sandra. "Do you need help?"

"No," she said.

Tyler moved forward and I shuffled backward until I could feel the ledge behind me.

"Well," he said, "I guess you're free to go, sir."

I was scared. I was so scared that I could hardly breathe. Tyler wasn't a big guy, and a few years and a hundred pounds ago I could have stared him down and left him shaking. But I had dropped my cane somewhere along the way and he could topple me over this wall without straining a muscle.

"You're free to go." Somehow Tyler was now even closer to me. His face was just inches from mine, and I could smell his breath of sickly energy drinks and junk food. "But she's coming back with me and we'll talk about you for a good long while. Are you okay with that, sir?"

Then Tyler was coming right at me, though his eyes were surprised and I realized he wasn't moving toward me, he was falling on me. I slumped to my side, landing on the hood of my car. The pain in my chest shot through my body and the world went white with pain, yet I could still see my cane in

Sandra's hands and Tyler flailing toward the ledge. I kicked out my leg and caught him in his hip, which spun him around and allowed him to see Sandra jab him, hard, in the chest one more time before he went over the side.

By my count, it took about six years for his body to hit the sidewalk. A week ago, I told myself Sandra would have lived if she'd jumped.

I guess I was wrong.

"He was a kid," I said. "He was just a kid."

Sandra helped me off the hood and handed me my cane. "Tyler was young. But he wasn't a kid." She peered over the ledge and grimaced. "Now he's not much of anything. You all right?"

I shook my head.

"Yeah," Sandra said, "neither am I, but look, I've got to go. I can't be here when the cops come, though you need to stay because there are cameras on the entrances. This is fine. He tried to mug you, you whacked him, and he fell. Look pitiful, tell them he was on drugs, and they'll give you a medal or something. But I've got to go."

She turned to leave.

It took me a second to catch my breath and even then my voice was barely a whisper: "Wait."

Sandra stopped and looked back at me.

"What happened here? Where will you go?"

"You helped me. You did, you really did. But," she pointed her palms toward the sky, "I don't have to go anywhere now. Call your wife and kid, then tell the cops you defended yourself. You'll be home before rush hour is over."

Then she was gone.

SAPPHIRE BLUE

BY ALEXANDRA BURT

Stratford Hills

The tires of the Subaru sail across the gray asphalt. Redbud Trail crosses the Colorado River and Nina's in meditative bliss. Her eyelids are heavy. She should be in bed right about now but Hank, her boss, called her just as she got out of the shower.

"I wouldn't ask you if it wasn't urgent," he said. "Help me out here, I'll pay you double."

Nina finished a move-out cleaning downtown earlier and she's drained and there's the lingering hangover from the cheap red from the Valero the night prior. And there's Belle, she's only seven, and Nina can't leave her home alone. Money's tight and so she calls Belle's father, who, true to form, doesn't bother answering the phone. He's either at his shift at Brown Distributing Company or on top of some woman. He barely shows for scheduled visits and she doesn't bother leaving a message. If bringing Belle to work is going to cause problems with Hank, so be it. It's not like there's any other option.

A car with blinding lights passes and a howling horn knocks Nina from her stupor. She checks the rearview mirror. On the backseat, Belle stares out into the night. She is a quiet, sullen child. She's skinny but healthy, with freckles on the bridge of her nose and untidy black curls.

Nina turns onto Stratford Hills Lane. She slows to a

crawl and beholds the clean, tree-lined streets. Various structures are perched on steep roads within lush rolling hills. Stratford Hills looks unfamiliar but construction has been booming around Austin since, well, forever. She hasn't been in the area for quite a while, doesn't recall any of the Bel Air–meets–Park Avenue vibe. Look at those hills, she thinks. And the trees. So many oak trees. Boxwoods everywhere, neatly trimmed. Some shaped into globes, some half-erect, others weeping. Her bedroom window at the Spanish Palms looks onto the dumpsters and if she leaves her window open and the wind blows just right, she can smell the stench drifting by. The clutch slips and a grinding sound escapes from the bowels of the ancient Subaru. The car has been giving her trouble but tonight's job will more than cover a mechanic to take a look and fix it up.

Nina passes an L-shaped ultramodern structure, spreading like a concrete snake along a sandstone embarkment. She glances at her phone and pulls into the adjacent driveway. A gaudy French country facade stares at her and oversized stairs lead to grand iron entry doors. She spots Hank's van immediately. *CSI*, the vinyl decal reads. *Clean Scene Incorporated*. It's funny and stupid all at the same time. Nina pulls up next to the open doors of the van and rolls down her window. Hank turns and does a double take on Belle in the backseat. His eyes narrow.

"You're kidding me, right?" he says.

"Couldn't be helped," Nina replies.

Hank's a short, stocky guy. If one were to compare him to an animal, he'd be a walrus. Round face, rosacea cheeks, mustache untrimmed, small, round glasses. "Well," he says, and strokes his facial hair downward, "it's blood and guts, so you'll have to think of something."

Blood and guts mean death scene. Even if he had let her know over the phone, she couldn't have made arrangements, but she's not telling Hank that. Instead, she cocks her head and says, "And when did you plan on telling me?"

"It's common sense, Kowalczyk. Don't bring your kid to this kind of work." Hank pronounces her name *Cow-wall-sick*. It's *Ko-val-chick*, but she's given up on correcting him.

"The kid can hold a mop," Nina says with a smirk.

"What the fuck's wrong with you?"

"Just chill, okay. Joke's on you, her dad's coming to get her," Nina lies, and steps out of the car. "He's on his way."

"Look," Hank says, "I don't know what to tell you, but this isn't a place for a kid."

"Like I don't know that." Nina grabs a hazmat suit and a mask from the back of the van.

Not a place for a kid.

Her grandmother cleaned houses; her mother cleaned houses. Nina cleans houses. She used to accompany her mother on jobs and there were years of her life when she thought the entire world was divvied up into those who clean and those who don't. Death pays, she found out. Hank's been giving her jobs here and there, it's his side hustle, that's what he calls it. It's a hustle because he's not certified, but she's seen her fair share of hoarding, squalor, and trashed properties. There've been a few homicides, suicides, all kinds of death scenes, really. Once she did a methamphetamine lab cleanup. When she tells people about the meth labs, they gasp, never see it coming. She's only been working those jobs for a few months but she got a lifetime of death and stench and squalor during her first week. She hasn't set foot in a death scene without a mask since.

Behind them a high, groaning sound, like a rusty gate

swinging shut. They turn and watch Belle use the weight of her bony body to push the Subaru door shut. The girl stares at them, her eyes blinking rapidly. Nina sighs.

"Stay in the car, your dad's on his way," Nina says, and watches Belle as her eyes widen and she cocks her head to the side. You can't fool that little girl, she ain't with the bullshit. "Get back in the car and wait, you hear?" Then Nina turns to Hank. "Let's do that walk-through."

"So here's the deal," Hank says. "Something came up and I have to drive to Waco to get my son. He, well, let's not get into details but I need to bail him out. So you're on your own. Nothing you haven't done before. Just be finished by morning."

Nina zips up the hazmat suit and pulls the hood tight. Once a house infested with fleas did a number on her. She slips on a mask and in the reflection of the van door a long-horn beetle stares back at her.

"All the equipment you need is in the house. Just to be clear, I don't know anything about your kid being here. Never saw her, she never saw me. But she can't be inside. Okay?"

Hank opens the front door and Nina steps into a foyer and from the foyer into a kitchen. Through the mask she hears herself breathe in a soothing in-pause-out-pause rhythm. A HEPA air scrubber sits on the tiled foyer floor next to chemical-spill boots, fifty-five-gallon biohazard waste containers, and a large plastic bin. Stacked in the corner are mops and buckets. Arranged like a terra-cotta army, an array of spray bottles and cans, flanked by sponges, brushes, and putty knives, crowd the kitchen counter. There's a bunch of rags and more gloves and more suits. Sometimes the suits rip. Nina doesn't have the proper training—but it's all common sense, Hank said.

Nina observes a giant potted fern in front of a window nearby, its palm-like fronds long but listless. Above it, flies are buzzing sluggishly up and down the window pane. Once she notices the flies, she's tuned into movement and she spots hundreds of gnats circling a fruit bowl like an ever-changing slow-motion murmuration of birds moving in unison through the sky, performing a highly synchronized ballet. The oranges are globes of white, green, and bluish spores.

"You scrape that off, it's pure penicillin." Hank's voice is muffled through the mask. He stoops down to inspect the oranges.

"Put one in your pocket then," Nina says jokingly. "I hear it works for gonorrhea." She takes a step toward the counter and spots coagulated liquid on the kitchen floor. "What's the story?"

"Probably a murder-suicide. Isn't it always the same: the woman pisses the man off and there's a gun and that's that?"

Nina can easily imagine countless other scenarios but doesn't say anything.

"All kidding aside, it's nothing juicy or scandalous. Just an old lady," Hank says. "Welcome to the death scene of Barbara Martin. Sixty-one. They caught hell recovering her body. She weighed somewhere around six hundred pounds. Needed special equipment and the fire department to get her out. Died all alone in the house. A cleaning service comes once a month and found her. Here's the kicker, though: there's problems with the electricity. Something about faulty wiring. When you run equipment, it might cut off. The lights flicker. Either way, never lasts long." Hank flips a nearby switch several times. "Couldn't tell you if it's on or off." His phone rings and he runs his hand along his thigh and curses, unable to retrieve the phone underneath his hazmat suit. "Damnit. I can only be in one place at a time."

Nina snaps on her gloves and explores the kitchen. Boxes stacked six feet high obstruct the view to the dining area. Stamped on the sides are the words *McKesson Underpads*. The kitchen opens up to a large family room which in turn opens to a vast stone terrace. The living room is the size of Nina's apartment. She follows steps down to a subterranean room which is filled with wine racks all the way to the ceiling. The room next to the wine room is an eight-seat home theater leading into a game room with a pool table and its own bar. Everything is clean but looks abandoned at the same time.

She makes her way up the stairs. The bedroom right off the top landing has a fireplace and an adjacent sitting room which opens directly onto an upstairs terrace. A photograph sits on the bedside table. A woman with permed hair and chunky oversized glasses. A cheesy eighties-style portrait taken at a mall, a sideways shot hovering on a black background and a different portrait image floating above the main one. The woman's neck is a triple layer of flesh. There's a visible hump on her upper back between the shoulder blades. Barbara Martin. Nina can somehow hear the woman's voice as if she's introducing herself. Breathy and croaky at the same time. *Bah-bra.* Nina can hear her low and rough voice bounce off the venetian plaster walls. *Bah-bra. Bah-bra.* The California king has one of those adjustable bases with a dingy mattress. Two oversized walk-in closets flank the bath, and very few clothes leave the space vast and empty. The only shoes Nina can make out have stretched at the seams as if they're about to disintegrate. She makes her way down the hall and opens a small metal door—an elevator.

Back downstairs Nina calls out to Hank, "I can't find any

type of death scene anywhere. "Is there a room I missed? A basement maybe?"

The overhead fixture comes on, bathing the kitchen in a harsh light.

"Just in time," Hank says. "Cleanup's behind those boxes in the kitchen. The woman was bedridden. Fire department told me her housekeeper fell ill and died and no one bothered to check up on Barbara. I have no idea how she ended up down here."

"There's an elevator," Nina says, and points in the general direction of the metal door.

"I guess that's what happened. Well, you have everything you need, I'm gonna leave you to it then . . ." His voice trails off and the front door slams shut behind him.

The house is silent until Nina hears a sound. It's not the gurgling waterfalls off the lower terrace, it's musical, like a melody. Not one you hear on the radio but an intermittent whir followed by loud beeps accumulating in a chime.

A door slams and Nina jerks around. Belle stands in the middle of the foyer.

"The man left," the girl says.

"Jesus, what the hell!"

With one hand, Belle presses a wad of papers against her body, with the other she clutches her prized possession, a purple velvety bag with gold embroidery. One day she'll realize the bag is a Crown Royal sack.

Nina guides the girl toward the long kitchen table. "I guess it's just you and me. How about you sit over here and I'll see what needs to be done, okay?"

"Where are the dead people?" Belle's voice is small and timid but demanding at the same time.

"No dead people. Just what's left of them." Nina swallows

hard. She feels uncomfortable in her skin, which is clammy underneath the layers of clothes and the hazmat suit. "Go sit, and don't move."

Belle's eyes blink rapidly and she slides between a chair and a table so large it can easily seat twenty people. She looks even smaller than she really is.

There's the sound again. It's so . . . celebratory. Nina slips off her mask and pulls the hood down the back of her head. She takes in a deep breath and faintly detects the layers of death: feces, mothballs, rotten eggs, a foul garlic-like odor. The stench isn't too bad—the body has long been removed and there's no carpet or curtains where the odor could linger.

"Do you hear that melody?" Nina asks. She feels disoriented. It's not the smell, it's more a *I don't have a good feeling about this place, not a good feeling at all.*

Belle just blinks. "It stinks in here."

"I know," Nina says.

"I want a mask."

"They don't make those for children," Nina says, and places a finger to her lips. She tilts her head. "Listen! It sounds like, like . . ." She can't find the words but the melody originates from near the boxes. She steps behind the cardboard box wall.

A slot machine sits in the corner with a metal swivel barstool in front of it. Nina takes in the space and knows immediately what's happened. The bedridden woman took the elevator downstairs and sat in that padded swivel barstool and died playing slots. She doubled over but the slot machine must have kept her upright. Six hundred pounds don't just tip over. She was an unmoving blob but then toppled with only one way to go. The stool must have given way and sent her onto the floor where she hit her head and her wispy thinning hair became a crater of crimson. There's a dark patch on the tile, a pool of blood that has curdled and caked and turned the color of copper. Then her body bloated and decayed and *Bah-bra* poured her life out on the travertine tile as enzymes began eating her cells from the inside out.

"What happened?" Belle appears next to Nina, unaware that she's standing in pinkish sludge. Her glitter high-tops with the unicorns are ruined.

"I told you not to move. Go sit down."

"But it's boring."

Nina wants to say, *I told you not to move, I told you to stay put, but you don't listen.* But what's that good for? It's as if the girl can't remember what she was told mere moments ago.

"I used to go with my mom when I was your age. With grandma. I was always a good girl."

"When I grow up, I want to be just like you and Grandma," Belle says.

Nina hears a buzzing in her ears, doesn't know if it's the flies or not, but regardless, it's making her stomach heave.

Nina used to accompany her mother cleaning houses, watched her scoot around on her knees, stand on top of footstools while her very own tiny hands held her mother's ankles, observed her kneel in tubs and listened to her barking and hoarse cough from oven fumes. Her mother cleaned every inch, every tile, every counter, every baseboard, nook, and cranny in those houses. She must have scrubbed and wiped and scoured away layers of floors and walls and tiles and windows.

She watches her daughter as she situates herself on her knees, scooting forward and reaching across the table for crayons. "*Bah-bra* was a big woman," Nina says to Belle. It isn't lost on her that she uses this imaginary voice she's convinced the dead woman sounded like in life. "Wherever she is, probably in a drawer at the morgue, she's left the cleaning to others."

Belle doesn't look up from the picture she's drawing. She seems frozen in place until there's a faint movement, a ripple in her demeanor. She raises the crayon. "Did she know she was going to die?"

"No one knows when they're going to die," Nina says.

Nina plugs in the ozone machine, sprays enzyme solvent, and starts up the wet vacuum. She begins with the boxes of underpads. The bottom ones are soaked with body fluids and it takes her about an hour to tear them apart and stuff them into red *BASURA INFECCIOSA* bags. Once the area is cleared, she inspects the perimeter of the fluid leakage.

As she begins the cleanup, she goes on autopilot and lets her mind wander. She thinks of one thing and one thing alone: sprinklers. No longer recalling how it began or when or for what reason, she's found solace in a memory she can't assign a year or place, but it's nevertheless comforting. A sound of old-fashioned rotating sprinklers with no moving parts to wear out; a pleasant hissing of water escaping from a hose; water droplets spewing upward and whizzing round in ever-decreasing circles. She adds an image of a young girl running through the sprinklers, a memory so beautiful, so innocent, so comforting to imagine not knowing of any evil in the world, to just feel the sun on your skin and the water cool you down. To be protected from the world. The world and all its stench.

On the edge of her perception, as she intermittently drags bags outside so Hank can pick them up in the morning, Nina thinks of Belle's words: *When I grow up, I want to be just like you and Grandma.* What kind of a mother is she, really? To allow Belle to be here with the fluids and the air, so hazardous, but what is she supposed to do? Who is she kidding anyway? The double pay for this job will cover the rent and the mechanic for the car, but that's the end of that. She'd have to do three jobs like this a week, and she'd have to put most of the money away. But school's out and day care is expensive and Baby Daddy is a loser who says he's not responsible for a grown-ass woman. She can twist and turn it any way she likes—she'll never get ahead. Whatever plans she's made in the past have been foiled, and why would the future be any different? There's always something—the car breaks down or the landlord drops by unannounced, never fixes the water tank or a dripping faucet or the fence leaning toward the ground but asks for late fees, and before she knows it she owes double rent. If she could count on jobs like this one, she'd be all right. But all things being equal, everything would have to go perfect from here on out and she knows it won't. And Belle wanting to be just like her.

Nina gets so hot she thinks she's burning up, so she rips the mask off her head and unzips the hazmat suit from around her neck. The lights flicker but then it's dark and she can't continue to work, and Belle sits in darkness but the crayons still scrape across the paper and Nina says, "Let's go outside until the lights come back on, let's look at the stars."

The sliding doors leading onto the back terrace purr gently along the grooves and then come to rest. The terrace stretches the length of the house and the waterfalls splash into the lagoon-like oversized basin. There's a pool to the right but Nina can't make out the perimeter with the moon above barely three-quarters full. The electricity cuts on and the terrace is lit by hundreds of lights and the pool shines so blue as if mirroring a summer day's perfect sky. Nina has never seen anything as blue as this, sharp like crystals and shiny and sparkly, and for a second she imagines penetrating the surface with her eyes closed and her arms outstretched, her heart skipping a beat as she dives into the cold and crystal-clear water.

"I want to go home." Belle's voice is so small and resigned.

"Lights are back on and I have to finish up so we can go home. If you're tired, I'll find you a couch or something?"

Belle nods and Nina leads her into the sitting room. The girl climbs on the couch and lies on her side hugging her upper body.

"It won't be long."

"It's too quiet."

"I'll turn on the radio."

In the kitchen, Nina fumbles with the radio sitting on the kitchen counter but there's only static and all she can make out is a crackling and rasping, and she hits the top of the mahogany device with the palm of her hand but it just continues to click and pop and maybe it's some sort of electrical interference, and when she glances around the corner, Belle's eyes are closed and her mouth gapes open, so she abandons the radio.

The baseboards around the kitchen island don't react to the spray solution and she's glad she doesn't have to dig into the wood and pull the island apart. The spill boots jab into the backs of her knees. She's spent and it's three o'clock in the morning, and her thoughts begin to ramble. The lights have been on for the better part of two hours, and if luck will have her, if she powers through, they can hit an IHOP on the way home, and if she doesn't have any coffee, she'll be fine and she can get some rest and Belle can watch TV. She hasn't formed an idea in her mind of when rest will come, with her next job at noon, but it's a comforting thought.

Nina covers the slot machines in hospital-grade disinfectants and then in industrial-strength deodorizers, and there's not a bubble to be seen, and as she wipes the glass, her eyes stare at the reels of numbers and cherries and crowns, but her mind is in those sprinklers again. There are flashes of spray and the sun blinds her (a rainbow, she throws in a rainbow for good measure!), and before she knows it, everything is clean and sparkles and it's done and she's looking forward to the IHOP bustle, the smell of coffee, and the tender sweetness of syrup, and the salty crunch of bacon, but just as she rests her shoulder from the circular scrubbing motion, the lights flicker again. Her eyes are so tired. Maybe she imagined it? The sky will brighten soon and maybe they can stand on the terrace and wait for the upper arc of the sun to appear on the horizon. The view of the canyon will be breathtaking.

In the sitting room Nina finds the couch empty and the blanket bunched up on the floor. She pulls her mask off and listens intently. She calls out her daughter's name but the only answer is the silence of the house and the stench of the chemicals.

Nina becomes aware that there's a gap between the sliding glass doors and the flies and gnats have long escaped, but now there are moths and crane flies bumping against the doors and the walls and the ceiling. Nina is dead tired yet immediately arrives at a state of a painful alertness and shouts, "Belle! Belle! Belle!" but there's no answer, and when she steps out onto the terrace the lights cut off again. Behind her, the celebratory jingles croak and the melody dies a sudden death and all is dark.

Nina rips off the mask. She can't see a thing. A thought enters her mind, one she shies away from naming, but it's of no use, her brain feeds on it, it can't be placated.

I don't have a good feeling, she thinks. Not a good feeling at all.

She makes out the breaker box on the wall and unlatches it, wants to swipe the circuit breakers back and forth, though there are no breakers, it's just the sprinkler box. She must talk to Belle, tell her how important it is for her to understand that she shouldn't be just another problem for Nina to deal with. She is a child, yes, but it's just that Nina is terrified of the world on her daughter's behalf.

The lights kick in and bathe the terrace in a glorious shimmer. There's something in the water. A lump disturbing the beauty of the deep and pure rectangle. The pool glows from within, a saturated sapphire blue with a diamond shimmer atop the surface. Belle's body is floating on the water, her hair fanned around her like a halo, her glitter high-tops bobbing.

Nina runs as quickly as the rubber boots allow, and even before she arrives at the lip of the pool, she dives forward and cuts through the water's surface. The boots fill with water and the suit's legs puff up and she swims as hard as she can but she just can't get to Belle, it's like moving in slow motion in a dream, she just doesn't have any control. Regardless of how fast she paddles her arms, the distance between her and Belle doesn't diminish. She reaches for the lip of the pool, pulls herself up, places one knee on the ground, and falls on her back and pulls off her boots and tugs on the suit, but that zipper, that temperamental zipper, won't budge, and she prays, *Please please please.* She wants to scream but she hears a voice inside her head, or maybe it's her mother's: *Save it, no one can hear you.*

She puts her hands on her neck as if to choke herself, then rips off the suit and her wet jeans and her soaked shirt. She stands there in her dingy bra and underwear and out of the corner of her eyes, smooth and quietly, sprinkler heads emerge from the ground and the water makes lacy wings as clear as glass all over the lawn.

How calm she is. How gathered. Just then the sun breaks through at the horizon and the day lights up in all its beauty and the canyon is on fire and the city lies below her, and then she races into the sprinklers and chases the droplets, she's circling and circling, but never reaching them. She runs and runs and she can't stop.

CHARLES BRONSON

BY LEE THOMAS

Hotel Van Zandt

Parnell Durst entered the hotel lobby and experienced a moment of claustrophobia, as if he'd just stepped into a holding cell. His chest grew tight, and ripples of tension ran down his neck. It took him a second to realize that the constricting atmosphere had nothing to do with the space itself. Blue brick arches ran twenty feet into the air, and the area beyond was spacious, enormous even. It was the opulence of the place that clamped tight against him, told him he didn't belong. This oppressive ambiance had started in the lungs of rich pricks who wouldn't give him a second glance and was exhaled like smoke to envelop and smother the less fortunate, the unworthy, the Parnells of the world.

A man with cash named Shepard waited for him in the hotel's lounge, and Parnell was already twenty minutes late, so he forced himself forward. He veered left beneath a chandelier made of brass tubes, like a loose knot of trumpet parts. The click of his cowboy boots echoed in the high-ceilinged hall, and the noise drew his attention downward. The pointed toes were scuffed, he noted, and then reminded himself the boots were the swankiest part of his attire, the rest of which consisted of a pair of blue jeans, one size too small in the waist, an untucked button-down, and a brown sport coat that no longer fastened over his gut.

The tight atmosphere constricted further, and his pace

slowed. Ahead, finely dressed assholes filled the lounge, holding martini glasses and cell phones, faces aglow with news and humor and digital intimacies. A cool jazz number droned in the dim light. Each step was another crank of the vise. As he entered the room, a few faces turned toward him and then turned away. Expensive perfumes and colognes blended into a thick, sweet ooze that slithered into his nose and took hold like a flowery parasite. He rubbed at his nostrils with the back of his hand and noticed an arm rising slowly on his left. Parnell stopped until the guy attached to it nodded at him.

"Mr. Durst," Shepard said, "have a seat."

"Yeah, thanks."

Though his host had not stood to greet him, Parnell pegged him as being on the short side. Wiry. A black sweater set off the white, salting his stubble and pale skin. He looked too soft to be involved in anything significantly shady.

"You're late," Shepard noted.

"Traffic's a bitch tonight," said Parnell, leaving out that his son's home health care worker had dragged her ass getting to the apartment, and Parnell had needed to feed his kid saltines while a can of chili heated on the stove.

"Every night, from what I've heard. This town needs half the cars and twice the lanes. It's changed a lot since I left."

"Right," Parnell said. Something in the guy's voice nettled him—again he thought of softness.

"Let's get you a drink."

"Jack and Coke."

After the drink was ordered, Parnell wriggled against the low back of the leather chair. "Why am I here?" he asked, unable to find comfort on the stylish misery.

Shepard reached beneath the table and produced an envelope, which he set on the table. He inched it forward with his index finger. Parnell checked over his shoulders for indications that others in the room might be curious about the transaction. They were not.

"I appreciate you coming out," Shepard said. "That should be sufficient compensation for your trouble."

Parnell took the envelope and slid it into his pocket. "What can I do for you?"

Shepard smiled and gave a measured nod. "I need something of an assistant here in Austin. I own a few properties and businesses, and I'm interested in several more. I have competitors and partners. Money moves from point A to point B, and I keep certain payments off the record. I can do some of that with crypto, but you'd be surprised how many of my colleagues here still deal in cash."

"Really?" *What the fuck is crypto?*

"Plus, there are other duties that need tending to, and I can't be here to manage all of them. I need boots on the ground. I'll set you up in an office with a title and some boring day-to-day in case anyone asks. Your background in warehouse logistics will prove useful."

Parnell pulled his lower lip between his teeth and drew a loud breath. "Somebody send you my résumé?"

"Mr. Durst, you don't think I'm going to enter into an agreement with a cypher, do you? You've been more than thoroughly vetted. Do you honestly think I'd lay any of that out to someone if I didn't have a steel-trap grasp on the guy with whom I'm speaking?"

"So what do you know?"

The waitress bent between them to place Parnell's drink on the table and then hurried away. He lifted the glass and pulled in a sip. Out of habit, he crunched on the ice cube that had slipped between his lips and pain exploded across his jaw.

"Problem with the drink?" Shepard asked.

"Bad tooth," Parnell replied. "This job got dental?"

Shepard smiled and shook his head.

"I still wanna know what you found out about me."

"Do the details matter? Should I list your arrests, your convictions, your tenure with the Dollar Store or Home Depot or the furniture warehouse in Round Rock? Should we delve into one of your three marriages or your son Lucas? What matters here is you haven't shown up on a police report in more than a decade, and your current career path makes you a reasonable candidate for the public-facing side of my interests here."

Parnell bristled. His throat closed tight hearing his son's name pop from between the too-white teeth. The guy's voice irritated him, but to hear it enunciate Lucas's name brought a harder emotion.

"Look," Shepard continued, "I'm going to head out. I'm interested in a property down the street and I want to check out the neighborhood."

The abruptness startled Parnell. He'd come all the way into town for a three-minute chat? "That's it?"

"You were running late. I have a schedule."

"You haven't told me anything."

"You know enough for now. Give what I said some thought. Look, I wasn't expecting to be in town this week at all. It just worked out that way, and I've got a lot on my schedule. I appreciate you taking the time to talk with me last minute."

"The trip wasn't planned?"

"Not exactly. I was hoping to have a couple more months to get the operation together, but things happen."

"What happened?"

"A funeral." Shepard stood and retrieved his cell phone from the tabletop.

"Sorry," Parnell offered, noting the man was even shorter than he'd thought.

"No need. The guy was a piece of shit, but his sister did me a favor, and she asked me to come down."

"Must have been some favor."

Shepard's eyebrows arched, and he gave a shrug. "We can talk about it tomorrow."

"Sure."

"Order yourself another drink or two. It's on me. Have a good night, Mr. Durst."

Parnell stared into his glass as the man walked away. Part of him felt like he'd assed up an important job; another part felt like he'd just gotten dumped by some bitch he didn't even like, but whose desertion still chewed his ego. Shepard was never going to call him, he knew that much. The only wages he'd ever collect from the man occupied the envelope in his pocket. So it was back to the warehouse, back to ten-hour days, back to painting his molar with benzocaine just to get through a meal, back to scraping together the cash for Lucas's home health care.

Sorry, kid. We've got a lot of canned chili in our future.

When the waitress returned, Parnell ordered another drink and then instantly canceled it. He stood and hurried from the lounge, clicking his way down the tiled hallway, headed for the exit. Shepard had said he was checking out the neighborhood. Maybe he was going on foot. Parnell had probably fucked up the whole thing—nothing new in that—but he needed to show Shepard he was a serious candidate, show the man he had tenacity.

He exited the fancy reek of the hotel, sloughed off the

disapproving air, and immediately saw the man. Shepard stood across the intersection looking through a chain-link fence at a paved lot. A cloud of smoke rose around his head, and Parnell found himself unsettled by the sight until he realized the guy was having a smoke or pulling on a vape rig. Even with the realization the scene disturbed him.

The fog wove into the chain link; it framed Shepard's shoulders and head.

A car sped down Red River Street, momentarily obscuring Parnell's view. When it passed, Shepard faced him. He couldn't read the expression on the man's face from such a distance, but he lifted an arm for the second time that evening, beckoning Parnell.

"I should have thought to ask you along," Shepard said, drawing on his vape rig. "I'm just walking a few blocks. We can discuss business. It'll save you a trip into town tomorrow."

"Thanks. Yeah. It's hard to find a sitter."

"A sitter? I thought your son was grown."

"Twenty-three. He's different."

"That must be difficult."

"He's a good kid," Parnell said, picturing his son's exuberant grin. All Lucas ever wanted was a hug and some watercolors to splash across swatches of butcher paper torn from the roll Parnell kept in the pantry.

"I'm sure he is," Shepard said. "As for the business, I'm going to be replicating the model I'm using in Denver. Granted, I'm about ten years late for the property revolution in Austin, but there are still significant opportunities."

As they walked, Parnell checked the street, looked behind his prospective employer, and along the sidewalk. It was his habit to stay aware.

Strange how busted up it all looked. The glittery asshole

palace stood only about twenty yards away, but this block was a wreck. A latex glove hung from the chain link, slapping quietly as they passed. Random cans and junk lined the ground below, as if to show elegance couldn't gain hold on this side of the street.

"So, like what are you talking about? Houses? Apartment towers? Shopping malls?"

"Yes," Shepard said, and then chuckled. "Long ago, I used to think about some of the great buildings in this town, the ones with real history, and I wanted to come in and save those. Renovate and restore them. Most of those are gone now, and it was all just nostalgic masturbation anyway. Austin, the Austin I knew, is lost. It became this cool, battered antique that some morons decided to refinish. Once the nicks and gouges were filled, and a few coats of paint were splashed on, the value tanked. I don't mean the financial value, of course."

"No, I get ya. The city used to have some cool. Now, it's just popular."

"Exactly."

At the corner of Willow Street, Shepard paused. He lifted his vape rig and inhaled deeply.

"So, what kind of work would I be doing?"

"Let's go down this way," Shepard said, setting off on Willow.

"The property's down there?"

"Not the one I'm thinking of. I just want to see how the place has changed."

"Well, this block is a shithole. You could get your throat slit out here."

"I assume you have a gun," Shepard said, eyeing him through a dense cloud of vapor. "I'm sure you can keep the *iffy* sorts away."

It was true Parnell owned a gun, but he'd left it at home. He hadn't thought it necessary to discuss a job opportunity in a hotel lounge. Add in the fact that the weapon wasn't registered, and he carried no permit—as a convicted felon he'd felt better off without the thing. This block changed his mind about that. The ground had been razed, and the lots were framed in chain link. Litter was scattered everywhere. The area looked like an apocalypse had just rolled through.

Besides, he knew this block. So much had changed he hadn't even thought about it driving in, but on foot his mental compass had clicked to north, and he knew where he was. The dismal buildings were gone. The greenery had been cleared, though he conjured the neighborhood's ghosts, one of which proved particularly unsettling.

A queer bar had been hidden at the end of this street, on a low pocket of land, cloistered by trees. Is that what pulled Shepard down the road?

"Yeah, but why come down here?" he asked.

"I told you, I want to get a feel for the neighborhood as it is now—see how the place has changed. I used to come down here a lot."

"Here?" Parnell said. A tickle of uncertainty danced along his neck. He didn't put much belief in coincidences, but he also didn't believe Shepard was psychic, and no amount of vetting was going to reveal the incident that connected Parnell to this area. If the police hadn't done it after twenty-five years, no one else was going to.

Fences ran on either side of the road, rising from the cracked sidewalks. Signs threatened trespassers with prosecution and alerted drivers that only those with permits would be allowed to park. At the end of the block, a wall of trees rose. A black SUV sat like a tumor amid the dark and sickly landscape.

"Used to go to a bar just down there."

So, he'd been right about that.

Parnell kept his eye on the SUV. "Doesn't look like your sort of neighborhood."

"Nothing says we end up where we started. I've done pretty well in Denver."

"Yeah, but real estate takes money."

"True, but I didn't start out with any. I got up to Colorado. Made friends. Got them to invest in a couple properties when I didn't have a dime. The properties turned a good profit. Then I did my own investing."

"Good deal," Parnell replied, catching movement in the front seat of the vehicle ahead.

Halfway along the block, Shepard crossed the street, and Parnell followed. At the fence, Shepard moved faster toward the trees to get a better view of the last lot. "Damn," he said, "would you look at that? I wonder who bought the place."

Parnell gave the SUV another glance and then turned to the empty lot. He couldn't remember how the bar that had once occupied the space had looked. He thought it had been a low building, run-down even then, but he couldn't be certain.

"All I see is nothing," Parnell said.

"For now," Shepard said, visibly disappointed. "Won't last. They're probably just waiting for permits to come through. Such a shame. Spent a lot of time here when I was sewing my oats. This place has history."

Parnell again turned to the SUV and the shadows within. "I think we interrupted something," he said.

"I can only imagine. I used to buy weed off a guy that parked along this strip. I'd toke up, go in for a couple of drinks, cruise around. They had this courtyard in back. Huge area. Tall fences. A lot of shadows. Shit got crazy. I couldn't tell you how many men I—"

"Look. I don't want to shit on your trip down memory lane, but you said you might have a job for me."

Shepard's mouth drew down in an exaggerated frown. "I'm making you uncomfortable."

"Whatever you do on your own is your business, but I don't need to hear about it, not even if it leads to a paycheck."

"Not a liberal thinker?" Shepard said, and now the asshole was just playing with him. "You hate thinking about what went on there. Kinda makes you sick, right? Angry even?"

"Something like that."

"So, you know what used to be here? You knew the bar?"

"Knew of it."

"Fair enough. Let's change the conversation. I told you I was here for a funeral. I mentioned a woman who did me a favor. Apparently, her brother's brain was rotting, leaving him to babble confessions to every little thing he'd ever done in his youth: he stole a car from his uncle; he abused his girlfriend; he hurt people. In fact, he confessed to a murder at one point. Now, his sister knew about his minor infractions, and some of the major ones. When the ramblings about murder came up, she had no reason to doubt him."

What the hell was this? Parnell checked the SUV again. Still movement there but indistinct. How many people were in that thing? "Well, you said he was a piece of shit."

"Yes, I did. There's really no other way to describe a man like him." Shepard paused. Eyed Parnell intently. "The boy he confessed to killing is of interest to me. So are the men who helped him with that murder."

"Right." The tone of the evening had shifted dramatically, and Parnell didn't like the direction it was taking. "How did you get my name?"

"Friends," Shepard said.

"How would your friends know me?"

"My friends wouldn't. But *your* friends can be exceptionally chatty."

The pieces fell together, perhaps slower than they should have, and Parnell stepped forward, taking handfuls of Shepard's sweater in his fists before pulling the diminutive man forward. "We're done with this shit."

Shepard's eyes twinkled. He wasn't smiling, but it appeared to Parnell that he really wanted to. "You can back off now," he said.

"I don't think so."

The road lit up. Parnell whipped his head around to see the headlights of the SUV blazing. He struggled against a current of panic welling in his gut.

"Mr. Durst, you don't want those men to leave that vehicle, so get your fucking hands off of me and step back."

Parnell did as he was told. "What the hell is this?"

"You know what this is. Actually, you figured it out faster than I had expected."

"Yeah, but you left me at the bar. You didn't know I'd come after you."

"Of course I did. Steel-trap grasp of the man I'm speaking with, Mr. Durst. Remember? I appeared to be of no physical threat to you. You needed the job I was offering you. Needed it quite badly. Why wouldn't you try to lock that down? Even if you hadn't behaved predictably, we'd be right where we are tomorrow night or the next night. I'm in no hurry. I've waited more than twenty years."

Shepard drew on his vape pen. The headlights went dark, the street returned to gloom.

"So, you came down for Gully's funeral? And what? His sister sent you after me? Don't suppose it occurred to you that she was lying? She's hated me since we were kids."

"Mavis Gulliver didn't mention you at all. She did mention a man named Hawkes and said there was another man involved. I chatted with Hawkes, and your name came up. You and Hawkes and Gulliver made quite a sport of bashing queers back in the day—just grab them off the street and beat the shit out of them. You'd all have a good laugh. You believed you were allowed to do it because they weren't like you, because you saw them as *lesser*."

"I'm getting out of here," Parnell said.

"No, you're not. Not yet."

"My son—"

"Can wait. How long he waits is wholly up to you." Shepard gazed toward the SUV, and then returned to lock his eyes on Parnell's. "One of your victims probably wasn't what you expected. He probably fought back or at least called you what you were to your faces. You didn't like that. You expected begging and crying, and he wouldn't give those to you. So, you dragged him into the trees. Hawkes told me you were the one with the screwdriver."

"No, fuck this," Parnell said. "I can snap your neck, and you'll be cold on the ground before your buddies get out of the truck. I'm going home. I'm not playing any more games just because we got a little rough with some faggot twenty-five years ago."

"His name was Joseph Allen."

"I. Don't. Care." Parnell's system was burning, a blaze that seared his mind and roiled his belly. He was trapped, and that knowledge fed the fire. For all he knew, the guys in the SUV were no more threatening than their boss. Probably just a couple more fairies whose only threat came from Parnell's imagination.

He stepped toward Shepard and the lights of the SUV returned to bathe the street. He froze.

"I worked late that night," Shepard said. "Joey liked pancakes, so we were going to meet at the IHOP down the street. When he didn't show up, I walked down to the bar, but couldn't find him there either. Hawkes told me you grabbed him back there." Shepard pointed to the intersection where he'd paused on their way down this street. "The next day, they found his body. That was the only thing that ever appeared in the paper. He was forgotten very quickly by most of the world."

"What did you do to Hawkes?"

"Well, Mr. Hawkes has seen better days. He was only willing to cooperate so much. I suppose I could have turned him in, but let's face it, your friend Gully wouldn't be considered a star witness, even if he'd lived. His sister's account would be nothing more than hearsay. Plus, I doubt they gathered much in the way of physical evidence back then. It's not like a lot of resources got expended in investigating the murders of guys like me."

"You think I'm going to confess?"

"That is one option."

"You're fucking looped. You don't have anything on me."

"Hawkes used those exact words." Shepard lifted a finger, indicating to Parnell he wasn't done speaking yet. After he drew from his vape rig, he exhaled a cloud and lowered his hand. "Let me try to recall the coroner's report. Multiple contusions. Five blunt-force blows to the head, likely with a rock, and . . . thirteen puncture wounds. Some were shallow, showing a cross pattern, consistent with those a Phillips-head screwdriver might cause. The others were more severe. Deeper. They ruptured his kidneys."

"You talking about the kid or Hawkes?"

"Yes." The twinkle in Shepard's eyes was gone, leaving a callous stare. "Now, make a call to the police and we're done here."

"I'm not going to ruin my life for something I did twenty-five years ago, when I was a goddamn kid."

"Joey was a kid too. He didn't get those twenty-five years, and I am certain he would have made a lot more of them than any of you fuckheads. There are only two choices here. Hawkes took one. He is no longer able to express his dissatisfaction with that choice."

"No way you killed him."

"Why, exactly?"

"You just . . . You wouldn't."

"Because I don't look the type? That's a terribly fragile logic, Mr. Durst, and you are staking everything on it. I'd think you should look deeper. If only for Lucas's sake."

"Are you threatening my son?"

"No. I am explaining that the decision you make here, now, will be the difference between leaving him for a while and leaving him fatherless. Though I hate to admit it, if you turn yourself in, you aren't likely to see much time in prison. With a good lawyer, you might spend less than a year away. It's fucked, but at least it's a semblance of justice, and I will consider the case closed. If you don't confess. If you recant that confession. If you send anyone after me to investigate your buddy Hawkes, then you'll meet those gentlemen across the street."

This was bullshit. If he'd offed Hawkes the way he

claimed, Shepard wouldn't be offering anything as weak as a short stretch to Parnell. That was too far for the pendulum to swing. Revenge didn't operate on a fucking dimmer switch. But even as he created suppositions about a man he didn't know, other thoughts wrapped and weaved through them. For a man Parnell's age, even a short stretch would be disastrous. With nothing but a piddling forgery charge on his sheet, he'd fought to get hired into the stockroom of a crappy retail chain. Later he'd all but begged a buddy from high school to get him on at the Home Depot. He hadn't even been able to get shared custody of his boy until his income had doubled when he'd been hired to manage shipping and receiving at the furniture store in Round Rock. He'd been thirty years old when he'd gone away for the bad checks. He'd never recover from another conviction, particularly if the charge rolled in as murder.

How would he take care of Lucas? He'd never see custody again.

"I'm on a schedule," Shepard said. "Any thoughts, Mr. Durst?"

"I need to see my son. You have to let me say goodbye."

"As a point of fact, I do *not*. I would, however, allow you to text Lucas's mother and let her know she needs to pick him up."

"She lives in Dallas. It'd take hours. I can be home in twenty minutes."

Shepard's brow knit. He looked at the ground and shook his head.

"I have to see him," Parnell said. "He won't understand."

"*I. Don't. Care*," Shepard snapped. "I've been as generous as I intend to be."

Parnell whipped his head toward the SUV, then spun

for the intersection. He heard Shepard's voice, but the rapid pulse in his ears drowned out the man's words.

Then he was running. Headlights covered him like mist. The SUV roared at his back, and Parnell shot a glance over his shoulder in time to see the vehicle speed around him, cutting him off. The brake lights flashed, and the tires squealed. He veered to the left as the doors flew open on either side of the vehicle. His heart throbbed loudly in his ears. A weight hit him in the back, and he dropped facedown on the street. Pebbles and pavement ground into his cheek and jaw. Agony screamed from his bad tooth. Breath drifted over his ear and neck.

"He said you'd do that," a thick voice rumbled.

Shepard's goons had Parnell on his feet seconds later. They jostled him and turned him toward the van. Shepard stood at the back of the vehicle. He exhaled a cloud and seemed to vanish. Dazed, Parnell thought the man had disappeared into the fog, but he'd simply stepped to the back of the SUV.

Parnell was dragged forward; thick biceps supported his weight under his armpits. Shepard stood, holding the back hatch of the SUV open.

The men lugged Parnell around Shepard. He blinked several times to clear his vision. When he was able to understand the bundle he saw there, he squeezed his eyes tightly closed.

"If our roles were reversed," Shepard said, "if I had murdered someone you loved and you were near the killing blow, many would applaud you for bringing justice to a homicidal outsider. There are a hundred movies with that exact plot, and the crowd always cheers the hero. No one boos Charles Bronson."

As Shepard spoke, Parnell allowed his eyes to open.

Wrapped in plastic with only his face exposed, Hawkes had, as Shepard noted, seen better days. His lips had been split in several places. Dried blood drew lines like drool from the edges of his mouth. Where his left eye should have been was a dark, scabbed pit. A shallow dent marred his forehead. The skin there, all the exposed skin, was pale and appeared gray in the dim light. Blood had gathered inside the plastic tarp, creating a dark pool in which Hawkes bathed.

"I'm not interested in cheers. I loved him. You murdered him."

Parnell's arms were yanked behind his back, and a zip tie was quickly applied to secure his wrists. A moment later, he was thrown into the back of the vehicle. The corpse of Hawkes softened his landing. Cold fluid began to seep through his jeans from where he'd torn the plastic wrapping the body. Shepard stood several feet away, exhaling a cloud of vapor that trailed from his lips, seemingly without end.

"I'll confess," Parnell cried, looking at the man in the cloud. He tried to scramble forward and slipped, falling back on the plastic and the body beneath. "I'll say whatever you want."

Shepard slammed the hatch.

SAVING

BY Miriam Kuznets

Rollingwood

Spring 1987

"I'm fixing to ask you questions," Detective Lee Ferguson said. When his secretary scheduled this meeting, I'd envisioned Ferguson as a potbellied man. Instead, I found him to be a substantial *her* with close-cropped smoky-gray hair, navy pleated trousers, and oxblood lace-ups.

"Questions? Shoot." I was wearing my uniform of black tee, Levi's, and black flip-flops, a Yankee in the Southwest.

Aside from askew diplomas and brass plaques, Ferguson's office felt homey, decorated with a terra-cotta vase sprouting dried baby's breath, a menagerie of windup toys, and an ironic poster depicting Day of the Dead masks. She asked whether Olga had a motive to commit suicide or if anyone might have wanted her dead.

"What? Car crash. But you already know that." I grabbed a windup pig and spun it on her desk.

"If she killed herself, what would her motivation be? Illness? A soured relationship? Erratic moods?"

"She ate and drank life. Lapped it up." Ferguson's questions were gouging the flimsy scabs lacing over my grief. "Are you reading from a textbook? That's like saying that if I killed you, what would my motivation be? I haven't murdered you, and I have no intention of doing so." Not yet, thought I, the pacifist. "I knew her for decades." I'd even defended Olga when she'd lured away my college boyfriend two decades back.

The whir of the windup pig was trickling away, and I rewound it. A hint of Crest toothpaste wafted through the claustrophobic office. I used Colgate.

"I understand your shock and anger," Ferguson drawled, hauling out the five-stages-of-grief nonsense. Psych 101 had taught me that the grief stages were developed to describe what someone with a terminal illness might experience, and only later were the stages sloppily applied to someone mourning. Anyway, grief couldn't be fewer than ten thousand stages.

Ferguson was waving an expensive-looking pen back and forth, a sketchy hypnotic pendulum. Nonetheless, I was a dupe. I began to succumb to the intrusive images that jangled like those in all those noir films I'd first studied at NYU. Ferguson's pen back and forth.

For the past two decades, Olga had been living testimony that I existed as a seventeen-year-old. She'd sparked the rooms that I'd slouched through way back when. We'd both known the stairs with the shaky bannister leading to her posh apartment with its fireplace and the wood floors painted four coats of impractical glossy snow-white. Olga and I had frequented the warm bakery near the college, the bakery that had since morphed into a generic Radio Shack. An hour before closing, she and I would arrive at Piece of Cake and though Olga had wads of cash stuffed into the pocket of her cigarette pants, we'd split a small coffee. The bakery manager, who of course had a crush on Olga, would sidle up to our table, offering free food. While we plucked the fresh blueberries off the top of the tarts, while we devoured slivers of cream-cheesy frosting from the carrot cake, we'd listen to the manager prattle on about Bob Dylan.

Concentrate, Beth, I thought. Just focus on the fact that you're being questioned, and this should be scary.

"Are you okay, Ms. Jacobs?" Ferguson said, clearing her throat, grating.

Trailing off again, I thought of asking why she wore a crisp-collared shirt instead of a guayabera to fit the Tex-Mex tone of her office. Or maybe she could do the tie-and-vest Annie Hall thing. Or a muumuu. Oh, right—she was on the job.

Being the sole historian of all those hours with Olga was like dining by myself in a bistro where the waiter said with disapproval, *Only one?* and herded me to a cramped table in the corner beside the kitchen door. The food might be as advertised, but with Olga I could have relaxed at a roomy table near the window, a lure for customers, everyone beaming at the two of us, or at her.

"From folks I've spoken to already, I gather that Ms. Johnson seemed an admirable woman."

What did she mean by *seemed*?

One year earlier

Though I applied lipstick at home, my reflection showed a garish smear in the Four Seasons lobby mirror, so I rubbed my lips with the back of my hand.

I rushed toward Olga as she descended in the glass elevator. After a bear hug, we locked eyes, hers a green amber. Her standout feature was her hair—long, voluminous, blond ringlets springing, grown wilder than ever, in contrast to the smoothness of her white silk sweater and ivory linen pants.

"My best Beth." No matter what the subject, she spoke with the oddly compelling tone of a newscaster.

"Been so long." I squeezed her tight again.

Till recently, our contact had consisted of a flurry of calls and a dribble of postcards. After I moved to Austin for my then-husband's job, she globetrotted. Every May, a package arrived for my now-sixteen-year-old Ray—a leather jacket, a lava lamp, and other goodies that earned Olga the reputation of fairy godmother.

When the estrangement in my marriage reached critical mass, and I was too ashamed to agonize about it with my local best friend or my marriage-at-any-cost mother, I called Olga, who was then living in Los Angeles. For months now, she had been phoning me long distance, dismissing my protests that the calls should be on my dime. She built me back up and, at my request, distracted me with tales of her cooler life, complete with a celebrity or two.

We arrived at her room and Olga ordered three desserts for us and a bottle of real champagne. We swigged the booze as we lounged on her balcony overlooking Town Lake and the magenta-streaked sky.

She said, "One thing happening for me is how sick I am of LA—it's getting claustrophobic. Superficial. I need something different."

"Come to Austin," I said. "I know it's a little town, but—"

"It might be just right," she said.

Her trademark lime-scented perfume weaved into the fabric of my shirt when she pulled me close for another hug.

That weekend, she procured a well-coiffed realtor to drive us in his Mercedes around Rollingwood, expensive for Austin, inexpensive by LA standards. The labyrinthine, lush area reminded me of the Hollywood Hills where, on my one getaway from parenting and marriage, I last saw Olga.

Back then, she lived with a wealthy Swedish guy, whom she called an "entrepreneur." He was out of town, but I had studied the Instamatic pictures strewn across their marble coffee table. In one photo taken from above by a mysterious third party, the Swede, muscular with large hands, wore a tiny swimsuit. In a scarlet bikini the size of fig leaves, Olga lay on a plush towel, and the Swede covered her belly button with his fingers. I envied Olga's seemingly carefree life—few domestic obligations, a sporty car that she raced around the hairpin turns of the hills. "Where's the fire?" I would ask. "I want to live!" She would slow, then speed up again.

The coiffed realtor turned toward the next house, which was obscured by live oak trees. A wrought-iron gate encircled the property, and the house had a tailored, less-is-more style. Through the sunny rooms with high ceilings, we swept. The curtainless windows, the realtor explained, were the kind from which you looked out, but no one could see in.

I couldn't resist comparing the house to mine, an old bungalow with paint that flaked like dandruff, scant natural light, and dingy bathroom grout. My well-worn house allowed us, and our guests, to relax, I told myself. Still, I'd chuck that for the brilliant finish of this house, a blank canvas in which to start over.

From a slim purse, Olga pulled bank statements, which the realtor perused and said, "You'll be fine." Out of the corner of my eye, I saw that she wrote a whopping check for the whole year's rent. No references or deposit required.

On her new back deck, Olga donned designer sunglasses; we reclined on canvas lawn chairs that must have cost more than all my living room furniture combined. So much for not comparing.

She brought out a pitcher of iced tea, with lime slices on a cobalt-blue plate. "Nobody can see me from here. Good sunbathing." Olga's skin glowed porcelain, as if even the sun couldn't burn her.

Her lawn ended in a steep cliff, with the only visible neighbor being the gorgeous chaos of nature, swathes of trees and scrub. Austin's landscape still entranced me: the oak's enormous gnarled branches, the magnolia's white flowers, the mimosa's bursts of fuzzy pink. The star of the show was the spring crop of bluebonnets, of devil's paintbrushes, of red and yellow flowers called Indian blankets. Austin was like Massachusetts and Southern California and Arizona, like hope and melancholy, all tossed into one.

The temperature was plummeting, and I unclasped my cold glass. I rubbed my hands together to warm them and tucked my flip-flopped feet under my bottom.

"I'm not only doing what you think I'm doing—the art dealing. I've branched out," she said sotto voce.

"What do you mean?" The sun made me squint, and she became a golden blur.

"Experimental medicines can help people with AIDS," she explained. "You know, while the FDA bides its time, people just die. Remember Frank and George from New York?" Both friends of Andy Warhol, and of Olga.

"You told me they were gone. It's so scary."

Leaning closer, she said, "I've joined a movement that gives people like them more choices."

The word *movement*, though it implied healthy change, made me picture Jim Jones and his Kool-Aid-drinking cult collapsed grotesquely in the grass.

"Responsible doctors and pharmacists are involved. We give our clients experimental meds or meds already being tried out in other countries."

"I wish you had been around for my friend James." The

hub of the work group that visited the Vietnamese restaurant every Wednesday, James had also raised his own vegetables, distributing bright cucumbers and tomatoes to the rest of us in our dim office with the blinking fluorescents. In the last months of his life, he had been the twenty-nine-year-old in diapers, disappearing in a prison of pain among the seniors in the nursing home. My other coworkers and I filled in for the family that abandoned him, then found the one place in town that accepted his body for cremation. My stomach twisted now as I pictured him.

Olga wrapped her warm fingers around my chilly wrist. "You told me about him. With this meds movement, we give people the chance to live. It's called a *buyers' club*." She leaned back and positioned her sunglasses on top of her halo of hair. "So," she said, a lawyer resting her case. In college, she'd aced her LSATs, though she'd ended up in the art world instead of law school. "Come work with me. You told me you want more meaningful work. This is it."

My job at a computer call center felt trivial and underpaid, but it was stable.

"You could be my tech person, my assistant, and I'm sure I could beat your current salary."

Part of why I'd dreaded divorce was the financial insecurity.

"Besides, you're trustworthy, so smart and sweet." She skimmed her hand up and down my forearm.

During the time Olga had known me, I'd descended from summa cum laude cinema studies egghead to phone drone with a failed marriage. Being near her revived me.

"Nothing bad has happened with the movement. Only good."

"Sounds like an excellent cause, but I couldn't just leave my job." Or could I? "Is this a charity? Is it legal?"

"We take expenses and salaries. These are like clinical trials, just bypassing the bureaucracy. And as we grow, we'll be able to serve lower-income folks."

I gazed at the lawn ahead of us, neat, dependent on a laborer's care. Past the abrupt drop at the end of the lawn, in the distance, stood hills, full of thirsty plants, animals gentle and harsh, all growing, then decomposing.

My manager opened my manila personnel folder. "You took thirteen sick days last year. You spend too much time on non-work phone calls, and your lunch hour is always more than an hour." He stood too close. "I've been watching you."

It was true. The other day, I tripped over a wire to my terminal, loosening a plug from the wall outlet, losing a day's notes because I'd neglected to do the required "save" move every fifteen minutes. I failed to do it at all. The manager forgot to add to my offenses the time off I took to accompany my sixteen-year-old son's new wave trio to performances in other cities.

"You know my numbers are top." Even when my co-worker James was dying, even as my marriage disintegrated. "I get the best customer reviews."

"I don't like your smug attitude." My manager now avoided my eye. "You know Texas is an at-will work state." He meant that legally an employer could fire a worker with-out cause. "Do you really care?"

"Not enough." I slammed his door on my way out.

After a dozen years at the job, I took from my desk only a paper bag with a box of tampons, an old class picture of Ray, and petrified sticks of Juicy Fruit. My arms trembled as I hugged a few coworkers goodbye for now.

I jammed my Ramones tape into the car's player and

shouted along to the music. When a driver at a stop light waved at me, I didn't know if it was a friendly greeting, but I gave him a genuine smile. Then we were off.

I felt giddy about working for Olga, about giving choices to suffering people. Each morning, I woke without the alarm clock, and instead of my son grabbing toaster waffles for breakfast, we feasted on poached eggs and homemade sourdough. True, he scarfed down his food in three minutes before he dashed for school. Since he was growing up and spent Thursdays and every other weekend with his father, I was missing him.

My new office, in a room next to Olga's living room, overlooked her backyard. Hanging on the wall opposite the picture window was a painting I admired by Olga's sudden new boyfriend, Martin. The painting depicted three wispy figures in a forest of tree trunks, pretty and creepy.

"Now that you're here," Olga said, "I can take more business trips, and you can hold down the fort."

"Where do you go?"

"It's best if you stay on the periphery, Beth. Probably overkill, but . . ."

I felt uneasy about the murkiness of the movement, and to friends and family I described my job as assisting Olga with her art dealership. I reassured myself that other worthy missions started this way.

She asked me to become the point person for a few customers who came by the house for their meds. Before a fellow named Alex arrived, Olga mentioned that he'd contracted HIV from his wife, who got it from a tainted blood transfusion and who'd died a couple of years before. Having a terminal disease seemed sad enough without the vast stigma attached to it.

In preparation for Alex's appointment, I unlocked the safe in which amber bottles of pills lined shelves; only numbers served as descriptors on the bottles' labels. As instructed, I transferred seven greenish capsules of *22B* to a small amber vial.

After he arrived, Alex accepted my offer of a glass of tea and took a polite sip. He was slim but not gaunt, his eyes and skin somewhat sallow, though the same might be said of mine. For a few minutes he was standoffish, but as he grew more comfortable, his shy smile drew me in.

I gestured toward the kitchen table, where we each took a seat.

"Is it hard to be dealing with all these . . . all us sick people?" he asked.

"I don't know most of the customers very well. I mostly just do administrative work, helping with the computer and such."

"I hope I'm not keeping you from something."

"No. Am I keeping *you* from something?" I topped off our drinks.

"I have a lot of free time now."

"What do you do with it?"

Alex had old-soul eyes. "When I worked at 3M, I used to fantasize about what I could do if I had all the time in the world. But those fantasies included my wife. We wanted to travel."

"Olga told me what happened. I'm so sorry."

"Thank you, Beth." His eyes moved to the window. "Those last few weeks of hers, I fantasized about sleep. I didn't tell her I was positive too."

"What a burden."

"Now I'm on 'sabbatical.' My body's okay, relatively

speaking." With mock seriousness, he held out an arm and flexed his bicep.

"Impressive." I allowed my impulse to put my index finger on his sleeve, feeling the solid muscle underneath. "You look in good shape."

"Thanks. I guess looks are deceiving."

After Alex left, I tossed our disposable cups and washed my hands thoroughly, following the safety protocol that I'd read about in the newspaper.

On subsequent visits, Alex described his recent activities, as if my interest egged him on. He described a day at the Fort Worth museums and a dusk watching the sunset from the top of Austin's Mount Bonnell.

I asked him if he had symptoms, and he told me that sometimes at night he struggled to sleep, his teeth chattering, the sheets soaked with perspiration, and he couldn't imagine warmth until some thermostat inside of him went to the other extreme and he burned. Quenching his thirst after the sweats was painful if he had sores in his mouth, as he often did now; they stung when touched even by purified water. Despite his digestion troubles and sore mouth, he said he liked anything with sugar and butter.

Baking was one of the few activities my son agreed to do with me, but I also had Alex in mind when Ray and I started making snickerdoodles and Toll House cookies on a weekly basis.

When I told Olga that Alex had invited me to go for a walk one lunchtime, she said, "He seems healthy, yes? Meds must be helping. He's handsome too. Be safe."

"Oh, please. I have enough troubles." Of course, her thoughts mirrored mine.

* * *

The day after Olga rented a car and left for a business trip, I received a call in the middle of the night from her boyfriend Martin. In my dream, I'd been trying to puzzle out the nature of a "bilious campometer."

Martin's loud exhale surprised me. "Listen. I got a call from a sheriff's department. Olga was in an accident." His ragged breathing sounded like weeping, and my tears formed in anticipation of Olga in a coma or a limb lost—or that she'd killed someone with her breakneck driving.

"Is she okay?"

Martin sounded underwater. "She was trapped in her car. Burned."

"The car burned? Olga burned?" I wound the phone cord tightly around my wrist.

"The car went through the rail."

"Is she alive?"

"No, she's not. Oh god." He gulped for air.

After we hung up, I hid in my bedroom closet, my arms shielding my head, as if I could escape my vision: an avalanche of ashes smothering Olga and James and Alex and his wife. And me.

Forcing myself into a scalding shower, I tried to share a thousandth of the heat Olga had felt, though her brain must have had mercy and shut off as the fire swallowed her.

In my backyard, I tossed the ball to the dog, and listened to the Cougher, who seemed to be outside all the time hacking away. I'd never seen her because her six-foot solid wood fence was dividing us.

With the dog's chin cradled in my palm, I whispered to him, "Don't you dare leave me." His expressive eyes soothed me for the briefest moment.

* * *

The movement medicine club coordinator from Houston phoned Olga's house, where Martin now lived and where I showed up for a week, in limbo, trying to get in touch with clients to share the news both about Olga's death and the abrupt end of the medicine supply.

Though I'd never met this club coordinator, we'd spoken on the phone about supplies. "What'll happen to Olga's clients?"

"Don't worry." She assured me someone would be contacting the clients as soon as possible.

"I *am* worried. Do you have the client list?" I paced in a tight circle like the miserable polar bear I once saw at a broiling-hot zoo.

"Of course."

"Is there anything I can do? I keep up with the latest HIV news, and I'm an ace at research. These clients are so vulnerable."

"We'll take care of it. I'm sure you have your hands full. Too bad about Olga."

All she could muster was *too bad*?

The adoptive mother of a girl who'd contracted HIV from her birth mother called Olga's work line. I'd seen the gray-skinned girl in her tiny pink cowboy boots on her visits to Olga's house. "She's not doing too well," the mother said.

"I'm sorry I can't help you more. A movement coordinator should be calling you." I'd been trained to placate at my old call center job, but now the stakes were so much higher. I referred her to the scanty local resources.

"Thanks for nothing." She slammed down the receiver.

That day the little girl's face kept appearing before my mind's eye unbidden: the rash on her cheek, the distended stomach and emaciated legs, not unlike those of my coworker James before he died.

I didn't have the combination of the safe where Olga locked the medicine, though I tried again and again. Searching the computer for any shred of information, I failed to find it. The precautions Olga had taken left me with no trail to follow.

Alex had no word from the movement, but he decided against pursuing it or another buyers' club. "Honestly, it didn't seem to be helping," he said, when we met for breakfast tacos one Saturday.

"That sucks."

"There's a legit specialist in town now, and a place called AIDS Services just opened."

"Great news." Then I deflated. "But I can't believe Olga's gone."

"Horrible year, in so many ways." He sipped his sweet tea. "Still, I'm glad we met."

I laid my hand on top of his, felt the veins in his coursing with life, then withdrew my hand to fuss with my napkin.

"How are you paying the bills?" he asked.

"I lined up some temp work." As an underemployment capital, Austin has various nicknames, including the Velvet Rut.

"You seem to really care about the cause."

"I do." I told him about James, and he told me more about his wife.

"I could see you working for a place likes AIDS Services. You're a comforting person. I might even volunteer there myself."

"Do you have any of Olga's pills left?" I ate pico de gallo straight up, enjoying the tingle in my mouth.

"I'll look."

When the check arrived at our table, Alex said, "My treat, please."

My ex-husband and our son Ray drove Olga's boyfriend Martin and me to the airport. We were headed to the memorial Olga's parents had arranged for her in DC, where she grew up.

Ray even initiated a hug goodbye with me, and I watched his back as he walked away, down the scarlet-carpeted corridor, photos of bluebonnets and longhorns nailed to the terminal walls. For a moment, I wished my ex and I were still married; he knew Olga when Ray was little. Back in New York, Olga took breaks from her whirlwind to read *Bread and Jam for Frances* to Ray dozens of times on the stained carpet in the minuscule apartment where my triad lived.

Up in the air, Martin asked, "What did you do when you were little, to make the time go faster on trips?"

"We sang."

He fiddled with the latch on his tray table. His thick brows and long eyelashes, his nose with what my mother would call "character," made it simple to project my dormant romantic wishes on him.

The plane took off, and Austin's university tower, the one from which a sniper once shot a dozen people, disappeared. Before, I never feared flying, but now my sweat glued my shirt to my back.

"All together now," Martin sang softly, *"Row, row, row your boat, gently down the stream. Merrily, merrily, merrily, merrily . . ."*

"Life is but a dream," I whispered. Both of us closed our eyes. While I pretended to sleep, he may have too.

* * *

That night, lying in bed in my solitary hotel room, I told myself, "Stay still."

An institutional print of a white boat on a glazed turquoise ocean shone in the otherwise dim room. Olga disparaged art made to match decor, but the painting charmed me.

Martin's room, just a few feet away, shared a wall with mine. On the bureau sat a tray with a leatherette ice bucket and plastic-sealed glasses, so I unwrapped a glass and stuck it to the mutual wall but heard nothing except doors in the hallway whooshing open and closed.

I pictured leaping from my bed to knock on Martin's door, asking him to hold me. Ridiculous. In my imagination, handsome Martin transformed into sweet Alex. How could I stay safe?

The next morning, in our rented car, we drove to St. Alban's Church. When Martin made a sharp turn, I clutched the door handle and squeezed my eyes shut, but still the bloodred sun penetrated my eyelids.

On the tour of DC on which Olga once led me, she explained that the facade of St. Alban's, a work in progress for over a hundred years, was crafted by a gifted group of stone carvers who used their own faces as models for the gargoyles. When the stone carvers died, their sons took over the carving, then the sons' sons, and now a daughter or two. Still, the project stood unfinished. I studied those faces, hoping one of them might bear a resemblance to Olga.

Before I entered the church, I pinched my finger to hold back tears.

People crowded the pews, whispering among themselves, and I longed to tell Olga she'd received a fine turnout.

Dark wood and shadows. Olga called all religions bullshit, and I had debated her on that.

Olga's parents sat in a front pew. Her mother's chin hugged her chest, obscuring her face, and her father froze, unmoving as a patrician portrait. I feared that when I gave my condolences to Olga's parents, I'd make it about me. Behind my breasts lay a burning, aching blister, while a gawky minister with thick glasses read aloud from the Bible.

When the door of the church opened midservice to admit a late arrival, I craned my neck to look. I half hoped, half expected that the witty guy Olga had stolen from me would have seen the *Washington Post* obituary, but the latecomer was another unfamiliar face, a slender woman with short red hair and clever glasses.

Her brother intoned, "All my friends were in love with her! Olga." For the umpteenth time, I heard "Olga" as "Oh god."

The memorial speeches dwelled on her "beauty," with an occasional strained stab at humor, mostly anecdotes about when Olga was a girl. I wondered if her looks and money ever became a burden, if she feared no one would love her without those lures. Would I have loved her as much? The tributes failed to capture her dimensions—her ease, her need for little sleep, her passion for novelty. I should have gone to the front and spoken, but words failed me. She would have given me an eloquent homage, even off the cuff.

Mourners' perfume and aftershave nauseated me. As soon as possible, I found the ladies' room and sat on a closed toilet seat till other people clamored to pee.

For the rest of the day, I managed to act calm, but after too many glasses of bloodred wine, when I tried to fall asleep, a whiff of Olga's burnt hair seemed to fill my nose, Goldilocks no more.

We, of that time, are no longer the same. That line from my favorite Neruda poem kept echoing in my head. I didn't even know what poetry Olga loved, and maybe I'd failed her by not knowing her well enough. If Martin ever invited me to Olga's former house, I could peruse her books.

That night, I woke at two. The starchy top sheet smothered me as I tried to drift off again. Nearby, a woman laughed on TV, or was it a dream? The laugh reminded me of Olga.

I ran my hands over my arms, then covered my bare breasts with my fingers, hoping to lose myself in a fantasy. No such luck.

One afternoon, I took Fiestaware cups and saucers that had been a wedding present to the backyard. With the accompaniment of the Cougher, I smashed them into shards with a hammer.

In my bedroom, I began to glue the Fiesta pieces to the top of my bureau. A mosaic emerged—chartreuse eyes, gray lips, rose-colored skin, and forest-green hair. The face, quite loosely, became my friend James. The cat rumbled on the unmade bed. Art from fragments soothed me, and I slept through the night for the first time in months.

Alex invited me over for brunch. I considered him a genuine friend now, but his suffering and my growing feelings for him scared the hell out of me. I pictured his salt-and-pepper hair, his brown velvet eyes, his lips the color of raspberries, his veins, his heart.

I settled on a casual look of baggy shorts and a close-fitting paisley tank top. Earlier that week, my local best friend had arrived at my door and handed me a brown paper bag with the paisley shirt. "Happy May Day," she said as we hugged and promised to see each other more.

When Alex opened his apartment door, he remarked, "You look lovely." He'd never commented on my appearance.

Embarrassed, I thanked him. A big closet lily adorned an end table, and the living room smelled like lemon polish.

Grinning, he put his hand on my elbow and steered me to the bathroom.

"What's going on?" I said.

He stepped on the scale and pointed at the number. "I gained six pounds in the last three months."

"Bravo!" I clapped.

Though unlikely, maybe in Alex's lifetime solid treatments would render HIV less of a death sentence, as had happened with diabetes. Maybe, as with polio, someone would develop a vaccine.

And what had become of Olga's buyers' club? Had it really helped? "Do you have any leftover medicine from Olga?"

He rummaged in a drawer and found a pinch of greenish powder. "It melted."

Before he could stop me, I used my pinky to scoop a grain of powder and licked it. "Kind of sweet."

"I could have been the taster, Beth."

"I know. Safety first. It's just weird that the movement is so incommunicado."

"I know."

Alex gave me a plate with enough food for a bodybuilder.

When the last bite of omelet was on Alex's fork, he gave me a fond look.

I pushed myself away from the table. "Let's go somewhere." I was afraid to stay inside because we might move closer to each other.

He took me to the wilderness preserve, where we seemed to be the only ones. Climbing, we reached a peak overlooking downtown, a clever maze of shapes and geometric patterns, like an Escher drawing. A trail wound away from the vistas down into the woods, navigating around knee-high prickly pear with their lemon and cherry-colored flowers. A tea-colored stream murmured nearby as we clambered to a high rock shelf, a king-size stone bed.

"Talk about firm mattresses," I said.

"I'll take off my shirt and we can use it for a pillow." He shed it and held it out to me.

"No, you use it. I have more fat for a cushion."

"I'll use the shirt, and you use me." He patted his chest.

I lay down gently on his warm skin, and he wrapped his arm around my shoulder. "You smell good," I said.

He put his nose into my hair. "You do too."

I let myself doze. When I awoke, the sun was setting. Though the air was cooler by the stream, it was still oppressive. The side of my head that had been on Alex's chest was damp with sweat.

Discreetly, I wiped it off. "I guess we should go."

Back at Alex's apartment, it would have been natural for me to give him a kiss or a hug goodbye. I waited too long, gave it too much import.

Alex stood with his arms by his side, as stiff and reserved as he'd appeared the moment we first met. He'd risked enough already.

Detective Ferguson held up a photograph of a woman standing in a yard—long brown hair, dark eyes, hollow cheeks. "Do you know this person? Helena Callas?"

"No," I answered. The woman might have weighed eighty pounds. It occurred to me that it could be the neighbor I'd never seen, the Cougher. But it wasn't.

"This woman's dental records match the remains from Olga Johnson's car crash. The 'movement' dentist who probably traded out the records has entered into a plea deal."

"What are you saying?" I should have consulted a lawyer.

"We think this woman's remains were those found in the car Ms. Johnson rented for her fatal business trip. This happened around the time her medicine 'club' was on the local radar."

"Are you suggesting Olga killed her? Switched the dental records?"

"It's possible the woman passed away from her illness, but her family and I have been in communication."

I rapped Ferguson's desk with my knuckles. "What are you pinning it on Olga for? She's dead! She just wanted to help people." My legs tensed for flight.

"Your friend's pills were far from nobly saving lives. This so-called movement was preying on people's desperation. Here are the FDA's chemical analyses." Ferguson pulled out some papers and spread them before me. "Other witnesses came forward."

"You could be showing me hieroglyphics."

"The 'new' medicines they peddled were basically sugar pills at ten dollars a pop. We've frozen Ms. Johnson's bank accounts, including the foreign ones."

I tuned Ferguson out. As Olga had said once, she was giving those clients hope, and that was worth something, wasn't it?

But not enough.

Ferguson's gaze zeroed in on the sweat beaded above my upper lip. "Ms. Jacobs, are you all right? Are you ready for me to go on?"

I wanted to nod but felt paralyzed.

"We want you to help us."

I *was* freaked out about being an accomplice and wondered how the hell I'd ever stopped worrying about it.

"Ms. Johnson dealt cocaine in California. She was also involved for years in selling artwork that she falsely attributed to well-known artists."

"She's dead. What does it matter?" I stood, then sat back down. "I have to go to the restroom."

I considered fleeing the building. I pictured my mosaic of my coworker James, heard in my mind's ear the sound of my neighbor, the Cougher. On the closed toilet seat, I racked my brain for reasons why the things Ferguson claimed could be true. Was Olga an addict? Sociopathic? Filling a black hole?

And what was I? I trudged down the hall back to Ferguson's office, where she handed me a cup of water, which I gulped, and she refilled.

"Of course, having a lot of money helped Ms. Johnson get the best defense lawyers in the past. Do you have some time?"

"Do I have a choice?" My adrenaline held me upright.

Ferguson showed me a mug shot of Olga from 1985, an arrest for dealing narcotics. I'd once heard that it was easier to be rich and guilty than poor and innocent.

Ferguson played a tape recording of a testimony that must have been from the mother of the little girl who used to come to Olga's. Supposedly, Ferguson had hours of other testimonies from both clients and movement workers. "Should I spare you?" she asked.

"For now, at least."

Finally, she handed me a blown-up photo of the red-haired woman from Olga's memorial, clear enough for me to recognize now.

She just couldn't blend in.

"It's in your best interest, as well as the club's clients, to work with us."

I remembered the laugh that reminded me of Olga, the sound coming from Martin's hotel room in DC.

"I can't think straight," I managed to say. "Can I get back to you?"

In my car, I searched my purse for a tissue and found a scrap of paper with the number for AIDS Services. For many reasons—self-interest, good will, reparation, for James, for Alex—it was time for me to start community service and to join a support group.

As I drove home, I shouted to the Olga that might be out there, "What the hell's wrong with you?"

With James, bad luck had robbed him of growing old.

With my marriage, both my ex and I had agreed to let it die.

If what Ferguson said was true—and I was pretty sure it was—other humans served as Olga's pawns. That missing piece of her compassion rendered other people's cares as far away as the lives beyond the border of the manicured back-yard of the house she'd rented, the one she swooped into without having to give any personal references.

Half a block away, I sat on a hill where I could see the facade of Olga's house.

A Federal Express truck stopped outside Olga's gate and Martin, her damn boyfriend, wearing tiny basketball shorts, came out and signed for a box. Martin smiled, said something that made the deliverywoman laugh. As he retreated back to the house, FedEx drove away.

The street looked as placid as a still life, and I was considering ringing the bell outside the gate when the garage door began to rise, and I dashed down the slope toward the street. I was dressed as a jogger in a baggy black tee and spandex shorts, with the wire Ferguson's folks gave me taped up my midline, while they idled nearby, trying to look incognito in a ludicrous Terminix Pest Control van.

Olga's car emerged from behind the gate, and I spotted the driver's red hair. I felt the acid of a panic attack. Why the hell was she still in my town, hiding in plain sight? Money?

"Olga!" I sprinted behind the car as it moved down the street. "Olga!" I slowed down and cursed to myself, though I half wanted her to escape.

Her brake lights flashed, and she eased to an incomplete stop. What if it wasn't Olga? Despite almost nose-diving when I tripped over a rock, I reached her driver's-side window.

Her eyes gazed straight ahead at three cats sauntering across the road. Like the three bears in the fairy tale, the cats were small, medium, and large, and Olga was a sociopathic Goldilocks waiting for them to disappear.

As I knocked on the window, she gave me no flicker of recognition, and for a flash I hoped this was not my old friend. The engine whined as the car started moving again.

"Olga!" I called out.

She screeched to another stop a few yards ahead of me, and I caught up again. When she rolled down the window, a cloud of lime-scented perfume and stale cigarette smoke blew into my face.

Ferguson's van approached from behind but skirted us and turned a corner.

"Great," I muttered.

Olga flashed a toothy smile. "Beth. I was going to call you."

"You were going to call me?"

"We should talk. Is this a good time for you?"

"Well, I was supposed to have lunch with David Bowie, but I could cancel." In college, we both crushed out on Bowie. Why was I still colluding with her? I wanted to throw up and cry and laugh and punch her.

"Well, I wasn't going anywhere special. Get in." She opened the passenger door. "We can go back to my house and talk."

I held my breath as I latched my seat belt, and I side-eyed her bare legs, her very healthy-looking body.

She might kill me. Stranger things had happened. I kept my hand on the door handle. Ferguson's people told me to use the non sequitur "Radio Shack" as needed.

"I missed you," she said. "I think you'll understand why I did what I did."

"Well, right now, Olga," I hissed, "I'm furious at you."

She just smiled.

"That thought of you burning to death. I cried for you. Ray cried. I went to your fucking funeral." I pushed the cigarette lighter in, then removed it, and held it as a warning not to screw with me.

"I know."

"What do you know?'

She didn't answer.

Back in her driveway, Olga pressed a button and the garage door yawned open. "I'd think you'd be glad to see me alive."

Fumbling with the door handle, I said, "I didn't know you were so fucked up." I tossed the cigarette lighter into her lap.

She snagged it and frowned as if I were a little kid throwing a tantrum.

We passed through to the house, neat and soulless. The

painting that Martin had done was no longer in what had been my office but back in the living room.

"It's so nice out. Let's sit in the backyard."

I nodded. I pictured my knee in her chest as I held her to the ground.

She gave me a once-over. "You look good. You're kind of skinny."

"Not on purpose."

We settled into the canvas chairs.

"Penny for your thoughts."

"Are you crazy?" I stood and towered over her.

"How's Ray?" she asked.

"Fine."

"Just fine?"

"None of your business."

"I'll go get us something to drink."

She returned with a pitcher of iced tea, the limes on the cobalt plate, two thick glasses, a pack of Virginia Slims, and a silver lighter, the old-fashioned kind that my father used in his pipe-smoking days. She poured the tea. Virginia Slims, purported to be the choice of liberated women.

I wanted a beverage, but maybe she'd poisoned the tea. She poured both our glasses from the pitcher but she'd yet to take a sip from hers.

"Mind if I smoke?"

Before I could answer, I got a whiff of butane as she flicked the lighter.

"I'm not sure where to begin." She swallowed half her beverage in one long swig.

"From the beginning?"

"All right. I disappeared because I was going to get in legal trouble."

"That I gathered."

"I didn't tell anyone except a couple of movement people. Not Martin. I got back in touch with Martin a couple of weeks ago because I wanted to stay at the house. I needed some money."

Not because you missed him, I thought. And I suspected that it was more than a couple of weeks ago that she'd contacted Martin.

I held the chair arms, bracing myself. "How about the rest of your story?"

"There's not much more to tell. What do you want to know?" She drummed her fingers on her knee.

"Everything."

"I don't know everything myself."

"No kidding." How did she still look so dazzling? I upended the iced tea tray. "You stole from people who were fucking dying!"

"Is *fuck* the word of the day?"

I ground my teeth. "What the hell is wrong with you?"

She looked smug. "All I'm guilty of is giving people hope, hope they couldn't get anywhere else because no one cares. You didn't care before I brought you into the movement."

"I helped my friend James."

"You helped him die. You were always so passive."

"It's true. But I'm acting now."

"Don't be mad at me." She grabbed my hand, but I shook her off.

"Why did you do it?" If she were innocent, I would be vindicated too.

"I've told you."

The Olga I'd adored was dead, and I could admit I'd used her too. But our crimes were unequal.

"Are you deciding what to think of me? Do you like my new hair?"

"You've hidden so much," I said.

"Who told you that?" She lit another cigarette and held out the pack to me, which I ignored.

"I'd rather not say."

She downed more tea, as if she'd just driven through the desert in a car with no air conditioner. Once, long ago, I'd driven through Death Valley in August. In that heat, you'd kill your best friend, so to speak, just to get a drink of water.

"Who are you protecting?" Olga asked.

"Maybe your so-called clients. What a joke."

"Did Ferguson plant this nonsense? They're just trying to make an example here. It's in their interest to crush the hope we're building." As if her cigarette were a hope, she stamped it out, then lit another one. "I can't force you to believe me, but we've always been such fast friends."

"Not recently, of course."

The telephone rang behind the glass sliding door, which vibrated like the tuning fork my son liked to play with. She ignored the interruption. "We can pick up again! Let's clear the air. What else is bothering you?"

I paced, being careful to keep to the manicured part of the lawn. "Who's Helena Callas?"

Olga straightened up. "What about her?"

"You tell me."

"All right." She made a chapel with her fingers. "She had CV and was very, very, very sick. She lost her vision, and I think she had dementia. Very sick. We tried to help her." Olga's eyes filled, on cue. "We couldn't save her."

"How come you never mentioned her when we were working together?"

"It was too depressing. She died at just about the time I got a subpoena. Nobody wanted her body, so we borrowed it for the cause. She was dead, anyway." Olga leaned forward and rested her elbows on her knees, covered her face with her hands for a few seconds. Then she sat up straight, pulled by invisible strings. "And that's that. God, I wish life wasn't such a mess." She lit cigarette number four.

"So, you're in hiding for the rest of your life?" I hated how much I wanted to hurt her.

"No. But I'm doing a pretty good job of it."

"The movement's still operating?"

"We're still trying to do our stuff and help out. At this point, we couldn't be in further shit anyway."

"What about selling coke?" Already off-script and a hypocrite. I wanted to pummel her with questions.

"Did Ferguson tell you that? How embarrassing." She blushed, which made even more light pour from her skin and eyes. It hadn't been her hair that was so captivating, it was her face. "Drugs should be legal. I've always thought that. We weren't pushing or selling to anyone who didn't know better. We didn't force pills down the throats of little babies."

"There was that little girl."

"What little girl?"

"Pink cowboy boots!"

"I can't possibly remember everyone." Uncrossing her legs, Olga stood. "Now, here's what I wanted to ask you." She moved toward me.

I blinked, started to back away, then stood my ground.

"Why don't you come work with us again?" She extended her hand, and I ignored it. "We can give you a bigger part, more money. I hate to think of you working all those temp jobs. You must be exhausted." She came closer. "You deserve better, something more meaningful." The flecks of yellow in her green eyes were crystals, prisms. "You're still my best friend."

I couldn't move.

"What do you want me to do? Just say it! We've always been friends. Don't you remember how everyone used to say our names together like they were one name? *Beth-and-Olga.*"

It had been *Olga-and-Beth.*

As I walked away, she called out, "How's Alex?"

I turned around. "He's starting to get some treatment from AIDS Services. You know the place that opened? The legit one?"

"I guess I'm not up on the news," she said, blowing a smoke ring.

She trailed behind me to the gate that kept out the riff-raff. I heard it rattle shut behind me.

As I drove away, my throat stung, the way my fingertips had smarted when, early in my Austin days, I insisted on touching tiny, fine cactus needles to see how they felt. They pierced my skin and hid where no tweezers could reach them, till at last, days later, they miraculously disappeared or disintegrated, proving that, in some cases, if I ignored a hurt long enough, it might fade by itself.

When I got home, I phoned Alex to tell him the story.

"Would you like me to come over?"

"You might gather that trust is an issue for me."

"I can understand that," he said. "Me too."

"I'll be in the back. Bring some old dishes you want to break."

"Is this an anger-management technique?"

We both laughed. "I'm getting into mosaics," I told him.

After I hung up, I hid in a corner of the closet till I could breathe in, breathe out.

In the backyard waiting for Alex, I relished the wonder of the dog galloping to fetch the old ball, and I welcomed the sound of the Cougher.

I approached the fence that shielded me from her and called out, "Are you okay?"

"Good enough," she answered in a serene voice that surprised me. "Thanks for asking."

Throw the ball, and the dog brings it back. Throw it again.

Maybe Alex and I could grow closer without hurting each other any more than two people get hurt by letting themselves care. I felt strangely peaceful about how much I couldn't know.

A TIME AND PLACE

BY JACOB GROVEY

Braker

I t was an unusually rainy day in Austin. The lightning was appearing as steadily as camera flashes during a Hollywood red carpet event, while the bass of the thunder shook the ground like subwoofers in someone's trunk. The clouds had bullied the sun into hiding, and I was totally unprepared for all of it. I made sure to watch the local news before I left my house that morning and the meteorologist specifically said we could leave our umbrellas at home, but Austin has always been a rebellious city that does what it wants. It was weird in that regard, but weirdness is part of the charm all of us Austinites fight to maintain.

In the midst of the rain pouring down, my car decided it was time for an energy boost. So, in spite of me wanting to get home as soon as I could, I stopped at one of the many gas stations on Braker Lane to get a fill-up. Although the rain continued to pour down, I begrudgingly went inside the convenience store to pay because I never trusted the card readers at the pump.

I planned to pay for the gas and leave, but for some reason, a one-dollar can of tea was calling my name. I wanted to avoid consuming a bunch of empty calories, but working twelve-hour shifts at a stressful job will sometimes have you doing things you don't necessarily want to do. Perhaps my body was craving something it knew it shouldn't have to serve as a substitute for the bottles of alcohol I had recently stopped giving it.

I know it's almost cliché for a cop to be an alcoholic, but in my defense, my bout with alcoholism was something that just happened. I only started to know alcohol because of the sadness that seemed to be with me my entire life. When I think about it, my sadness had to be partially because I never felt worthy of anything positive. I don't know why, but I had always convinced myself I was a fraud, and it was only a matter of time before everyone else realized it.

The other major cause of my issues had to be the blatant racism I dealt with from the people in my precinct.

Ninety percent of the time, I found myself the only Black person in a room, and my colleagues never made the slightest effort to make me feel like I was a part of the so-called brotherhood. In fact, most of them made sure they gave their best efforts to find a way to make me feel like less than a person every time they saw me. They would laugh as they asked each other if the room suddenly got darker when I entered it.

I thought about quitting every day, but then I remembered why I joined the force in the first place. I joined for many reasons, but it was primarily so the little Black and brown kids in my community would feel a bit safer when they saw a cop, instead of always fearing for their lives. For that reason alone, I couldn't make myself leave. As much as I hated it, I had to suffer through their bullying, at least until I was able to figure out a way to move past it all.

"Hello, sir. Is this gonna be it for you today?" the kid at the register asked.

I was so caught up in thinking about work, I had zoned out and forgotten I was even in the store. The guy was probably in his late teens or early twenties, which meant he technically wasn't a kid, but when you get to be a certain age, almost everyone seems like a kid.

"Let me also get forty dollars on three," I told him.

While I was grabbing my debit card and drink, more people walked into the store. The small place already had quite a few people in it, and having more enter wasn't unusual, but for some reason something immediately felt different.

It was still raining outside, so the new customers were drenched, but they were also practicing the Covid protocol of the store, so their masks were covering the majority of their faces. I could only see their eyes, yet there was a strange sense of familiarity with one of them. I didn't want to be the weirdo who stared at someone in a convenience store, so I started to move toward the door. With each step, it was almost as though I could feel my brain cycling through all of the people I had ever met just to see if anyone matched. Then it hit me.

"Tyler! Tyler Castillo, is that you?" I asked as I moved away from the door and back inside.

One of the guys became a deer in headlights while the person he walked into the store with kept on moving around to get whatever he came in there for. The guy who I thought I recognized stared at me without saying a word. Either he was stunned I was able to recognize him even though he was wearing a mask and I hadn't seen him for years, or he was a complete stranger who was annoyed at me for wasting his time.

"Who are you?" he asked.

"I know this is gonna sound crazy, but I think we went to high school together. Yeah, you had to go to Connally! It's me, Seth Tennon. Remember how we both hated going to the new school our senior years, but we ended up loving it? C'mon, man! We were lab partners in Mrs. Troy's AP chemistry class and we almost failed the first semester because neither one of us knew what we were doing. I haven't seen you in forever! What have you been up to?"

I had the excitement level of a five-year-old who had just been told they could have all the ice cream they wanted, but the person I was talking to wasn't reciprocating my joy. Out of nowhere, he suddenly pushed me to the ground.

Immediately, the tough guy buried deep inside of me wanted to show my authority. But before I was able to do anything, the guy he walked into the store with, who was now situated at the back of the store, made sure we all recognized his presence.

"Everybody get on the floor, now! You already know what this is!" he announced, and raised a gun into the air.

The pandemic made a lot of people stress about money. Many of us were questioning how we were going to make it from week to week, but you have to be in an extremely dire situation to attempt to rob a local convenience store. When desperation is involved, you never know how far people are willing to go to improve their circumstances. Recognizing this, I followed the instructions that were given to us and I stayed on the ground. I prayed none of the people in the store would try to be a hero—I just wanted everyone to make it safely back home to their loved ones.

"Whatever you need from us, you got it. We just don't want anyone to get hurt," I said.

My statement was meant to keep everyone calm, but it did the exact opposite.

"What makes you think you have any control over what's going on here? If y'all get home safe, it's only 'cause we let that happen."

There was so much more I wanted to say, but I kept my

mouth closed, hoping they would just hurry up and finish what they were doing.

After a few minutes, the two robbers had their money, but for some reason they hadn't left. It was almost as though they were doing a victory lap, of sorts. Then, when they heard police sirens in the distance, they understood they should have just left when they had the chance.

"We gotta go," the person I thought was Tyler said.

As I remained on the ground, I tried my best to glance around at everyone else. I saw the look of trepidation on their faces, and whatever thoughts of leaving unscathed they had were thrown out when the sirens made it to the parking lot.

"I told you to hurry up! Now look! How are we supposed to get out?"

"Just get everything in front of the door, and I'll do the same for the back door. If we can't get out, we have to at least stop them from having an easy path of getting in. If they make it in here, it's a wrap!"

Throughout my career as a cop, I had dealt with tons of cases when things didn't work out the way I thought they would, but I hardly ever got to witness a crime firsthand. I was literally watching things fall apart right in front of my eyes. I have to admit, seeing the crumbling plan of criminals was incredibly satisfying, though it also made me even more concerned. Anguish is dangerous, especially when those who are desperate have bad intentions.

The cops who had just arrived to the scene soon started to surround the building. They hadn't yet made any attempts to get in, but everyone knew it was only a matter of time. I told myself it was time for me to make some kind of move; nothing crazy, but I needed to shift the focus of the robbers to me so they wouldn't be paying attention to the other people in the store.

I stood up slowly enough so everyone would notice. People motioned for me to get back on the floor, but I tried to let them know everything was going to be okay.

"Hey, bruh, what are you doing?" one of the robbers asked me.

"I'm Detective Tennon. I think this has gone on long enough. You're not gonna get away, and the few hundred dollars you may have gotten from the register is not worth whatever else you're thinking about trying. At this point, the smartest thing you can do is let me help you."

I had just finished my statement when I found myself being slapped with all of the strength Tyler's partner was able to gather. Being hit like that was embarrassing, yet for the sake of the others in the store, I had to act like I wasn't bothered.

"You can't do nothin' to help us!" Tyler barked.

Technically, the guy still hadn't confirmed he was my high school classmate, but at this point he didn't need to.

"Tyler, I promise I can help you two out. Without me . . . well . . . let's just say you don't want to try and handle this without me."

Tyler's partner was getting more furious by the second. "Hey, how does this dude know you? You settin' me up or something? You working with the cops now?"

"He's not setting you up, and he isn't working with me. I actually went to school with him. I just—"

"Bruh, shut up! Ain't nobody asked you for all that! Sit down before you get dealt with, for real!"

I still had a healthy level of concern, so I knew I had to make sure I was being smart about every move I made. I got back down on the ground.

"Come out with your hands up!"

The loud command from the cops on the outside made

everyone more frantic. You would think having cops around in the midst of a robbery would make people feel safer, but it didn't. Even though I knew having them near us was a good thing, I was selfishly battling a bit of personal anxiety because if they found their way into the store, there was a strong possibility I would be racially profiled. So instead of them seeing me as an innocent bystander, or recognizing me as a detective, there was a chance they would think I had something to do with the crime.

I hated that this was how I was thinking, but my experiences with my coworkers almost forced me to be pessimistic. If I all of a sudden gave them the benefit of the doubt, sadly, it could be detrimental to my own survival. Even though all of this was true, I had to quit being the focus of my own thoughts and pay more attention to the people around me.

The others in the store were starting to realize the robbers were getting antsy. I wanted to be strategic, but I also had to be realistic about the amount of time I had to make a move.

"We all know they're gonna be in here soon, so you won't be able to stop that from happening. Before they are able to move past your little barricades, you should make some sort of gesture of good will. Perhaps that will come into play when you end up in court."

I expected them to react negatively to this, but they didn't. Instead of telling me to be quiet, or hitting me again, they just listened.

"So what are we supposed to do?" Tyler asked.

"First, you have to be honest with yourselves. You won't get to keep the money you just took. And you need to get ready to do some sort of jail time because you know that's gonna happen."

I thought this was more common knowledge than breaking news, but the look of shock on their faces told me I was feeding them information they weren't necessarily ready to receive. For whatever reason, Tyler started shooting his gun in the air.

"I'm running this, not you!"

He was talking to me, but he was looking around at everyone else. Then he told his partner to grab the person who worked at the store. His actual intent was unclear, though as soon as the request was made, multiple gunshots were let out. We immediately saw that the employee had been hit several times, and unfortunately, it didn't look like things were going to turn out well for him.

Sadness was quickly making its way into my heart and tears were ready to leap from my eyes, but for the sake of everyone else in the store, I knew I had to pretend as if I wasn't impacted by seeing the young man get shot.

"Why did you shoot them?" Tyler asked.

"I had to!" the other guy replied.

Hearing the word *them* made me look around to see who else had been shot, but I didn't see anyone else who appeared to be injured. By this time, the robbers were escaping through the back door they had previously blocked off. As they did, I tried my best to catch up to them. All of this was happening while the officers outside were finally making their way inside.

My age must have finally been catching up to me because I wasn't moving anywhere as quickly as I once could.

While I watched Tyler and his unnamed partner get away in the distance, three officers finally made it to where I was.

"I thought we got here with enough time to stop something like this from happening," one of them said.

I had worked with a lot of cops during my time on the

force, but I didn't recognize any of the guys surrounding me. I may not have known them, but they all seemed genuinely disappointed in my inability to stop things from happening.

"I'm sorry, I really am. I tried to catch them, but I just couldn't. They always say father time is undefeated," I told them.

"Man, I really hate that this happened," one of them said.

"Me too! I thought I had them, but, well . . . you can see the results." I was extremely embarrassed, yet there was nothing I could do to change what had happened.

"What's your name, buddy? Who are you?"

With all that was going on, I had neglected to introduce myself, which meant they didn't even know I was one of them.

"My bad, fellas, I'm—"

"According to the ID I found in the wallet that fell out of his pocket, this is Detective Seth Tennon."

"Detective? That's interesting. Well, Detective Tennon, you are a hero, sir. We appreciate your efforts."

I thought they must have had me confused with someone else. There was absolutely no reason why they should be calling me a hero. Ultimately, all I did was let two criminals get away, and there was certainly nothing heroic about that. In that moment, I also had to deal with the unusual feeling of having other officers show me respect. It was something I definitely wasn't used to.

Solving a case isn't just a matter of finding out who did what. Generally, the most important thing we have to do is find a way to prove what we believe. This case was no exception. It was going to be difficult, even though I had a name. Proof is like having a master key: with it, all of the doors you need can be easily opened, but without it, everything you're searching for seems to be on the other side of a door you can never seem to pry open. So over the next few days, we focused on getting the proof we needed to finally make something happen.

Although we live in a time when just about everything is being recorded and almost everybody is putting their entire lives on social media, we were unable to get anything that could actually help our case. Sure, the crime was caught on the convenience store's camera, but everyone kept their masks on, so the footage was pretty much useless. The other officers who were working the case tried to get statements from the people we confirmed were in the store that day, but everyone they spoke to was seemingly too afraid to provide us with any information.

Even though I wasn't officially on the case, I took it upon myself to reach out to some people on my own. Unfortunately, none of them even had the decency to respond. I mean, telling me they didn't want to cooperate would have been better than the rudeness of not saying anything at all. It was disheartening, to say the least, though I couldn't let that stop what we were trying to do.

With each day that passed, things were looking more bleak. Tyler had seemed to vanish into thin air, which meant the probability of us finding his partner was dwindling. I already felt bad about the whole situation, then I felt worse when I found out the store employee who was shot during the robbery had passed away. Outside of seeing him several times when I went into the store, I didn't really know who he was. Yet I felt like I had some sort of connection to him.

Whatever the reason, it was there, and knowing I wasn't able to do anything to save that man's life while we were in the store together hurt me tremendously.

* * *

For the first time, my lack of a personal life actually became an asset. Without being shackled to people who loved me and cared about my well-being, I was able to recklessly throw myself into my job. Each day, I made it my goal to learn something about the case I didn't know the day before. Finding new intel was difficult, especially since everyone who was working the case had all but given up, which pretty much meant I was working alone.

The store employee's name was Jeremiah. That being such a biblical name, it felt like I had a higher calling to make sure justice would prevail. I refused to take that mission lightly.

I didn't normally go into the office, but things changed a lot for me after the robbery. Usually, I would just drive in every once and a while, but my car had broken down soon after the robbery and was in the shop. Most people would have been in a hurry to get their car back, but finding alternate methods of transportation was actually good for me.

One afternoon, I decided to take a walk around my northern Austin neighborhood. Everything seems so different when you're not in a car dodging other drivers. I had seen the same houses and people thousands of times, but there was a strange new energy around everything. I had a smile on my face as I passed by neighbors I normally couldn't stand and made my way past the newly built elementary school on Yager Lane. Hearing the kids playing outside was music to my ears.

The air that surrounded me felt fresher. I seemed to have more energy, and all the while the sun was doing its best to remind me how blessed I was to see a new day. I didn't want that feeling to leave, so after that first day, I just continued to walk.

Time passed and I found out about the funeral service for the young man whose life was taken at the store. Cops don't always go to the services of the victims of the cases we work on, but I had to attend this one. Since the services were at High Pointe Baptist Church, which is very close to where I was living, I was able to walk there.

I just stood in the back of the sanctuary. I tried my best to blend into the background, so if I wanted to leave early, I wouldn't distract the celebration of the young man's life. But from the moment everything got started, I could feel the genuine heartache that resided inside of everyone in attendance.

Although the young man's name was Jeremiah, everyone called him *Truce*. Nobody could really pinpoint when he was given the nickname, but everyone said it fit him perfectly because he was always getting other people to settle their differences.

While friends and family continued to talk about him, I replayed a bit of the the robbery in my mind. Throughout everything that happened, I couldn't recall Truce having shown any signs of angst or anger. Nobody deserved to lose their life the way he did, especially a kid who just seemed to want everyone to get along.

I ended up leaving the service early—not because I wanted to stop celebrating Truce's life, but more because I needed to get away from the reminder of my most recent failure. I should have tried to get my mind off the case when I left the funeral, but I foolishly did the opposite. I was a glutton for punishment, so I went into the station to see if any progress had been made.

"Any new info on the robbery/homicide at the convenience store?" I called out in everyone's general direction.

I waited a few seconds for a response, but I didn't get one.

On the day of the robbery, I was called a hero, but everybody had basically been acting like I didn't exist since then. I was starting to feel like I was getting what I deserved. I decided I would just carry that feeling around until it was no longer valid.

I decided to stop asking others for help on things I could ultimately do for myself. I also decided to go back to using more old-school methods of crime solving, which meant I would have to do more groundwork. So I went back to the convenience store. When I arrived, however, I realized I had no idea if there was even a purpose in me going there.

I stood very still outside of the store. I looked around and envisioned how things had been that day. Truce was there working behind the register. He smiled as he talked to the customers. He looked like he was enjoying life, even as he completed tasks that some would have thought to be tedious.

The robbery started to play out, and I felt terrible because I knew what was going to happen and I wasn't able to stop it (for a second time). Then, I rewatched Truce getting shot. Oddly, he still had the calm demeanor and smile on his face. Obviously he didn't want to die, but it almost seemed like he was okay making his transition because he knew he had tried to live his life the right way.

The past version of me got up and started to chase the criminals. Now I was able to see why I didn't catch them. I was moving much slower than I remembered. I was gasping for air and holding my chest.

"No! That didn't happen!" I yelled out loud.

Then I looked down at my chest, not really knowing what to expect. What I saw was both startling and unbelievable. Not only was I wearing the same clothing from the day of the robbery, I also had multiple bullet holes in my shirt, which was covered in blood.

I must be trippin'. Calm down, Seth. Just breathe and get your mind right.

I tried to inhale, but I couldn't seem to pull in any air. I told myself I had to be trapped in some sort of nightmare. I slowly closed my eyes and my memories paused. My body had grown accustomed to all of the alcohol and narcotics I had put into it over the years to battle my depression, so maybe the short time I had gone without them was causing me to see things that didn't actually happen.

Yeah, withdrawal is messing with me. Get it together!

I hesitated a little while longer before I continued to re-visit my memories. I continued to stare at nothing. Soon, the sounds of the world also started to leave me. It was peaceful, though the serenity of not seeing or hearing anything was not something my mind would allow me to maintain. Soon, the memory of that day resumed.

I watched my nearly lifeless body fall to the ground. As it did, my wallet leapt from my pocket. I guess it wanted to sever its ties with me as soon as it could; I don't blame it. I had always battled feelings of uselessness, even as I worked my way up to detective.

I just stood there staring at myself as the other officers came around and viewed my identification to learn who they were looking at.

". . . hero."

I wanted to laugh at myself, but I couldn't. I wanted to cry, but I couldn't do that either.

I was suddenly taken back to Truce's funeral. I had stood at the back of the room so I wouldn't get in the way, but in my new memory, I was nowhere to be found.

I was there! I remember hearing everything about him.

Then, another memory glitch took me to the precinct.

I was ignored when I was asking questions, but now I was seeing that they hadn't ignored me—because I wasn't even there.

"I am not dead!" I yelled this as if it would bring me back, but it did nothing. "What am I still doing here, then?" I don't know who I was asking. Maybe it was just another one of those questions I was asking myself, or maybe God was making me have a long-overdue conversation with Him.

Throughout the challenges of my life, I would often hear the voice of righteousness talking to me. Oftentimes I would ignore it because doing right wasn't the easiest, nor the most fun, thing to do. When things ended with my last girlfriend, I had just about lost hope, and God tried to talk to me then, yet I would always turn to the bottle or whatever pill I could get ahold of because I didn't want to feel judged.

So now, here I was, a lost soul. Not knowing which way to turn. Not knowing if there was anything left. Not knowing if the life I had lived even had a point to it.

"Why . . . am . . . I . . . still . . . here?"

Just like with the previous question, this went unanswered. Strangely enough, this time the lack of a response seemed to give me all the answers I needed.

There was no point in trying to reexamine my life because what was done couldn't be changed. There was no use wondering if I had done right by the people in my life because I knew I had a bad habit of pushing people who cared about me away. If I would have treated everyone right, there's a good chance I wouldn't have died so lonely.

"I'm sorry, Truce. I'm sorry I couldn't save you. I'm sorry I didn't do better, God. I don't know why I didn't, but I'm sorry."

I had run out of time for atonement, and yet I wanted to apologize anyway.

Growing up, I always heard older people say there was a time and place for everything. Now that my time was up, I started to wonder where my "place" would be. Maybe if I had thought about that before my life ended, things wouldn't have turned out the way they did.

I don't know what the afterlife holds, or if there even is an afterlife, but if there is, I know God has a lot to say to me. Now I will have no choice but to shut up and listen. A lot of people say they don't have any regrets because all of their choices led them to where they were supposed to be. That's not me. I regret everything, though it's too late now.

I thought I was working so hard on Truce's case because I wanted justice for him, but ultimately that wasn't it at all. My reasons were more selfish than I'd thought. That strong connection I felt to him was because we had both suffered the same fate that day.

I may not have deserved a better ending than the one I got, but I'm confident Truce did. I had to just hope that those handling the case would actually work to provide closure for his family and everyone who cared about him. I now understand that death is simply a part of life, and no matter what, when someone reaches the end, the world has no choice but to keep moving. Now, I must move on as well.

C'est la vie.

PART III

THIS LAND

I ain't leavin' here. You can't take it from me.
—Gary Clark Jr.

THE FOUNDATION

BY CHAITALI SEN

Clarksville

Cheryl

Just over forty years old, she had a very specific skill set that she owed to her theater training and unique life experience. By the time she pulled up to the cottage on Charlotte Street, she was in character, believing herself to be someone else, someone not totally unlike her true self. She pulled down the sun visor and checked her makeup in the mirror, admiring the bronzing effect of the Texas summer on her skin. After a lifetime of trying skin-lightening creams and hiding from daylight like a vampire, she could at least now embrace being as dark as her father. She ran her fingers through her curls, touched up her lipstick, grabbed her leather attaché case, and made her way up the path to the front door.

It was remarkable how different this home was from all the others around it, though it was not in terrible condition. The home's charm was obvious, even with its slightly rusted tin roof, its slanting porch, its faded yellow paint, and the siding that was buckling and coming loose at the edges. The house she had bought in the neighborhood and fixed up last spring was similar to this one. It was the same size, at least, but Cheryl painted it white and put a black shingle roof on it. On either side of the front door she trimmed each window with black shutters. She thought it a ridiculous waste of money to expand or demolish these houses. A little rewiring and replumbing and shoring up the carpentry was usually sufficient. The key was in the fixtures. That's where she had put her budget, in the fixtures, and almost overnight, the property she'd paid cash for using the profit from her Oakland house tripled in value. She had not met the family that lived in this Clarksville house before her, and did not know anything about them except for their names. Despite all her research into the area, she had not sought out any stories of the family.

She got the lead on this house from one of the realtors working the area. It was quiet behind the door after she knocked. She was a day early for the appointment, but knew that the old woman who lived here was always home and did not receive visitors until the evening. The second time she knocked, she could hear the floorboards creaking, and slow, uneven footsteps approaching the door. The woman, Mrs. Jacqueline Redding, looked frail and stooped but her eyes were bright and alert.

"It's me, Cheryl, from the foundation," she said, reminding Mrs. Redding that they'd spoken on the phone last week. The word *foundation* usually put people at ease.

"Yes, I remember," Mrs. Redding said with a wide smile. Only her back teeth were missing, and what a relief that she sounded excited. "But I thought you were coming tomorrow. I haven't started the pie!"

She would have preferred Mrs. Redding's memory to be a little less sharp.

"No ma'am, it was today. At least, that's what I put in my calendar. Shoot, maybe I'm mistaken." She pulled her phone out of her purse, pretending to examine her schedule. "Do you *have* time to meet today? My day is packed tomorrow."

Mrs. Redding looked hesitant, but pushed open the screen door to let her in. Old-timers like Mrs. Redding, even if they received their fair share of visitors, could not help but welcome more company. It was refreshing how unwilling they were to hide their loneliness.

They walked straight into a small living room. The house looked like it hadn't been refurnished since the midseventies. Everything was brown, beige, and dull orange, with only a little sunlight coming through a window that faced the neighbors' fence. The blinds of her front windows were down, and the one other window was blocked in with an air-conditioning unit, which was also much louder than its output of cold air warranted. Mrs. Redding sat in her old, worn armchair. Cheryl . . . a name she was called by almost no one . . . let her bottom sink into the cushions of the threadbare corduroy sofa. She could see into the kitchen, also orange, and the back door that probably opened to a small lot. Despite the drab decor, the house was impeccably clean and uncluttered.

On the walls were a few family photos, one of a very young and pretty Mrs. Redding almost cheek to cheek with her husband in his military uniform. His name was Oscar, she told Cheryl, and he passed away just five years earlier, peacefully, in his sleep. "I still miss him," she said with a dreamy look in her eyes. Then, it was as if she had been dropped back down to earth. "I just remembered! I asked my friend's daughter Ramona to be here. But she thinks it's tomorrow!"

"I know Ramona. We went to elementary school together, though I don't think she remembers me."

"No, she doesn't. She said she'd probably recognize you if she saw you."

"Well, would you like to call her?"

Ramona wasn't yet back from her weekend trip to Houston. Both women knew that, knew that there was no point in calling Ramona. Ramona was a local activist trying to help women like Mrs. Redding keep their homes, even though it was futile. Eventually, Mrs. Redding would have to sell. The only question was what kind of deal she would get.

"Mrs. Redding, could I show you something?" Without waiting for an answer, Cheryl took a wrinkled brown envelope out of her attaché case. There were photographs in it, all printed to different sizes and in various states of agedness, all in black-and-white. The first photograph she placed on the coffee table was of a woman in her twenties, taken sometime in the early 1900s. She stood with much poise, despite it obviously being a casual photograph. She was wearing a long, simple dress that was loose around the bodice, that did not quite look like it fit. Perhaps it was a hand-me-down. The woman stared directly into the camera.

"This is my great-grandmother, Abigail. This picture was taken not far from here, in 1915."

"Well, don't you look just like her."

Cheryl smiled. "I'll take that as a compliment, though I don't see the resemblance."

"Oh yes, around the eyes especially."

She placed two more photographs on the coffee table. One of two boys, and the other of a cottage, or a shack, with the same design as Mrs. Redding's, the front door in between two windows, the covered porch, the high-pitched tin roof. Two men's shirts were hanging on the porch, drying in the breeze. The house had been demolished sometime in the 1920s, but the houses built after that—after many of the residents were already getting displaced to East Austin—didn't stray much from this design. Even now in 2019, houses like this could be seen all over Clarksville.

"One of those boys is my grandfather, Walter," Cheryl continued. "He grew up in the house you see in this picture. Then my father, Walter Jr., tore it down and built a new one in 1976. He needed something sturdier so that he and my mother could start their family. I got to live here for the first twelve years of my life. We were happy here. You remember my family, the Bethunes?"

Mrs. Redding did not look at all sure.

"Then we lost the house. After my father died, some fast-talking real estate agents convinced my mother to make a deal. We got almost nothing for it, and the new owners tore it down and built a rental. I really admire that you've held on to your house for as long as you have."

"Where else would I go?" Mrs. Redding replied.

"But I understand you may lose the house, Mrs. Redding."

"That's what they keep telling me."

Cheryl removed a thick file from her case. Mrs. Redding had taken out a reverse mortgage eight years earlier in order to make repairs on the house and meet her living expenses, and this, along with the delinquent property taxes, meant that the house would go into a short sale for almost nothing, or get seized by the bank entirely.

"Mrs. Redding, what if I told you that you can pass this house on to your grandchildren if you would just let us borrow it for a few years. We'll pay you rent. The house will remain in your name. But you would have to let us fix it up and sublet it until we recoup the cost of the renovation. That's all you have to do."

"But I won't get to live in it."

"No, but it will be yours. No one will be able to take it from you."

"My son lives on an army base in Japan, you see. I can't live there."

"But you have a grandson here, you told me."

"He's a musician! He don't want his old grandma hanging around." This really made Mrs. Redding chuckle.

Finding a place for Mrs. Redding to live out the rest of her days might present a problem. It was a problem that had been troubling Cheryl more than usual, not only here but during her stints in Bed-Stuy and Compton as well. Management, which operated out of some start-up hub in San Francisco, increasingly pushed her to close before they'd made proper plans for the resident to find other living arrangements. That's what made her a valued employee—that she could close a deal, that she was, in fact, nicknamed "the closer." After the papers were signed, her job was done. She did not oversee the payment of the first check, and by the time the resident had to move and the speedy but extensive renovations were underway, Cheryl was off to a new city, a new neighborhood. They wanted to move her out of Clarksville soon, send her to the next hot spot in Chicago, but just that morning she'd sent management an email asking for a face-to-face meeting, where she would announce her intention to move on from the company, but not without a severance package, knowing that *severance* was not the right word for it since she wasn't going to be fired or laid off. The compelling argument she planned to present to them was probably blackmail, but there was no other way for her to get out on her own terms.

Mrs. Redding chided herself for forgetting to bring out the sweet tea. While she was in the kitchen, Cheryl walked around the living room and looked at more of the family photographs. School portraits and birthday parties, the memories the Redding family made in this house. Some of the photographs were exactly like the ones in her own parents' house in Philadelphia. The same configurations, the same colors, the same poses, the same pursed lips trying to blow out the same number of birthday candles.

Mrs. Redding came back and handed her a cold glass of iced tea and narrated the story of her family that was illustrated with these photos. "That's my grandson, the guitar player. He's a good sweet boy. Still spends every Sunday with me. We raised him here, after my daughter died. These are his three cousins in Japan. They live on a military base."

"Have you ever visited?" Cheryl asked her.

"Never got a chance. Oh, I'm too old now to make that journey. I keep asking, *Why can't they transfer you to San Antonio?* Then I could move *there*, you see, and you could do the renovations on the house."

"Yes, that would be a solution," Cheryl said, but she felt sick to her stomach. The resolve she'd always had to close the deal was vanishing. She felt weak, almost faint. "Mrs. Redding, I think you're right about our appointment time. I think I should come back tomorrow, as we planned. I'll cancel my other appointments."

"Are you all right? You look queasy. Is it the heat?"

She was sweating. Her heart was beating like it wanted out of her chest. "I've just realized that you were right, that's all. Our appointment was tomorrow. I'll come back and explain how this all works, to you and Ramona. I'd like to see her anyway." It was amazing how true this sounded and how much, for the seconds she was uttering those words, she believed it herself.

Mrs. Redding looked almost disappointed, not over the failure of the business transaction, of course, but because she was in the middle of talking about her family, her life. Cheryl would have liked to stay and hear more, but something told her she had to leave immediately.

Tracy

She was in her office on the second floor of the Austin History Center, in the middle of evaluating a set of photographs from an estate sale in Old West Austin, when they called up from the lobby to tell her a woman was here to see her. She didn't have any appointments, but when she came down to the lobby and saw the woman, she almost mistook her for Cheryl. Almost. Except this woman was obviously of South Asian descent. Her long hair was frizzy but straight, and though her accent was American and her outfit was not in any way ethnic, she did not look like she could come from anywhere other than India, or Pakistan, or one of the other countries of that region. This was confirmed when she introduced herself as Sunita Chatterjee. She apologized for not calling or emailing first, but asked if they could speak somewhere private.

Tracy led the woman down the hall to the O. Henry Room since no one was using it. They sat across from each other at the large wooden table. "How can I help you?" she asked. Now she was able to get a good look at her, and her resemblance to Cheryl was even more striking.

"I'm sorry to be so mysterious," Sunita said as she took things out of her bag—envelopes, files. A picture of Cheryl. "Do you recognize this woman?"

"That's definitely Cheryl. She came in a lot, earlier this year. Was doing research about Clarksville. She said she had a family connection to the area. Is she okay?"

"I'm not sure, to be honest. First of all, her name isn't Cheryl. This is my sister. Her name is Vanita. Last week I got a package from her with keys to a house and an address on 11th Street. She's gone. I have no idea where she is."

Tracy tried to look impassive. "I don't know what to say. She lied to me, to us." She meant the Austin History Center, because she had shown them an ID with her name on it. It was a California driver's license, if she remembered correctly. "She said she was a writer doing research for a novel based on her family history. One of those multigenerational epic novels, like a modern-day *Roots*. She must have gone through the whole archive, and she was interviewing some of the Black residents who are still around."

She did not say that Cheryl had texted her two weeks ago. It was a weird, long text message saying she was sorry for *ghosting*, that she wanted to talk and needed to tell her something. Tracy did not answer the text. She was going to write, *Lose my number*, but decided it would be more effective, more akin to how Cheryl—Vanita—had hurt her, if she simply blocked her. But she couldn't forget it. Cheryl was on her mind constantly. She was trying to figure out what had happened, what she'd done wrong. They had taken a walk around Auditorium Shores and had dinner at a little Italian restaurant on Congress. Tracy had told Cheryl everything about her large family in Houston, but when she asked Cheryl to tell her more about her own family, she said she didn't want to talk about it. She couldn't talk about any of the family she actually knew, that she'd actually grown up with—only the ancestors she said she had in Clarksville. That should have been a red flag. The following Monday, Tracy looked through census documents and couldn't find any records of a family named Bethune owning a house in Clarksville. Then Tracy constructed a whole narrative about why Cheryl was lying— that her home life had been traumatic and she was processing it by writing a mythology, an origin story, based on family lore. Tracy felt foolish then, when Cheryl didn't return any of her calls or text messages, except to say, *Sorry, need to leave town for a bit.* Tracy had replied, *Everything okay?* Nothing came back. But she felt doubly foolish now, and angry.

"There wasn't much in the house," Sunita said. "Some clothes, some files, documents for the house she bought, and a business card with your name on it."

"The house she bought?"

"Yes, on 11th Street."

"She told me she was renting," Tracy said.

"There are closing documents. With her real name."

"She lied to me about everything. I can't help you. I don't know this woman, but I hope you find her." *I hope you find her so I can strangle her,* Tracy thought.

"Please don't go yet," Sunita said. She took out a file and slid photographs across the table, reproductions of photos from their archives. The one of the woman whose first name they knew—Ella—and the unidentified boys on the street. "Could she have stolen these from here?"

Tracy shrugged. "She didn't steal them. Those are reproductions."

"Did she tell you anything about her work?"

"She said she was a writer."

"But she wasn't a writer," Sunita said. She was losing her calm demeanor. "She went to LA after drama school to try to become an actress. I tried to talk her out of it, tried to convince her to do something more behind the scenes, become a film editor or something. I told her there were no roles for Indian actresses, and I was right! She was only ever cast as an extra. She played a prostitute three times. I mean, why would you put yourself through that?"

"Clearly she wasn't a bad actress," Tracy said. But would it have taken a good actress to convince Tracy of something that she wanted to believe all along? Hadn't Tracy done most of the work for her? How could she even believe that Cheryl—Vanita—was Black?

"Then I didn't hear from her for years. We became estranged. She cut me off, cut off the family. But then one day she sent some gifts for the kids with a card saying she'd quit acting and was working for a start-up. And then she called, and we talked sometimes, not often but enough to let me know she was okay and doing well."

"Look, I have to get back to work," Tracy said. "I told you I can't help you. You should go to the police."

"I have. They won't treat it like a missing-person case because I spoke to her so infrequently. You're the only clue I have to what she was doing here. You're the only name she left me."

"We had coffee a few times after her research. That's it. I never really got to know her." Tracy grew angry with herself as she said this. Why should she become a liar now too? Her anger started seething up through her body, like a fire spreading from inside. She looked into Sunita's eyes. They were so intent, so greedy for information. "You people are so selfish," Tracy said. "Your sister lied to me. She used me. And she stole from us—she stole our stories, she stole Clarksville. I don't owe you anything."

Tears welled up in Sunita's eyes.

Here we go with the fragility, Tracy thought.

Sunita shook her head. "You're absolutely right. I'm so sorry. I'm just desperate, that's all."

Tracy didn't want to sit in this room any longer. She didn't want to get sucked in. Whatever was going on with

Vanita, whatever she was up to, it no longer had anything to do with Tracy. "I'm sure she'll turn up. If you think about it, she's done this to you before."

Sunita tried to smile. They stood up, facing each other, and Tracy extended her hand. Sunita held it for a second, and said, "Thank you for seeing me."

In the elevator, Tracy felt faint. Her breathing was labored and her heart pounded. She hurried back to her desk and grabbed her cell phone to scroll through her contacts and unblock Cheryl. *Where are you?* she texted.

She waited. No response.

Are you there?

No response.

Vanita.

I know who you are.

Are you there?

Three dots appeared. Tracy waited and waited for them to turn into words. Whoever was on the other end seemed to be typing for a while. Then a message came through, only two words: *I'm here.*

Sunita

The house, barely decorated, could have felt more like a boutique hotel than a home, yet she felt her sister's presence throughout even in its sparseness. Vanita was always a bit of a blank slate, reading the situation and the person she was with before speaking, or acting. Acting was the right word. She did not know who Vanita was. Never had. And after a while she stopped trying to figure it out. She only knew that Vanita never stopped acting; this house had become her latest stage, and this neighborhood her latest studio.

After she met Tracy, she had no more leads to follow. She

felt there were things Tracy wasn't telling her, but how could she blame her? Tracy had no reason to trust Sunita after being so coldly betrayed by Vanita.

Sunita went back to the house and FaceTimed with Neill and the girls. Seeing them made her ache with homesickness. She said she would be home soon, but she would have to talk to Neill later, after the girls went to bed, about what to do with this house. What was she meant to do with it? Everything Vanita had left out for her must have held some clues. The files from the Austin History Center. The closing documents showing that Vanita had paid cash for the house and had not hired a realtor. The seller was a private corporation that she could not reach over the phone. She was too tired now to do anything more with it. She would take it all home with her and let Neill sort through it.

She tried to take a nap in the small guest bedroom. The October weather felt like spring in Philadelphia. The bed was next to an open window. She watched the curtains billow in the breeze that came in every few minutes. Where was Vanita? Would she ever see her again? What had she done? What was she running from?

It was no use. She was tired but couldn't sleep. She decided to go for a walk and explore the neighborhood. She'd downloaded a map of the neighborhood from the Clarksville Community Development Corporation website. The history and significance of this area was not lost on her. The area had been the quarters of some of the enslaved people on Governor Elisha Pease's plantation, but was established as a place for former slaves to live and reunite with their families in 1871 by Charles Clark. In the 1920s, the city of Austin started driving residents out of the neighborhood and relocating them to East Austin, an area Sunita didn't have time to visit on this trip. She wandered without direction, check-ing the map every now and then just to make sure she didn't go beyond the perimeter of the neighborhood. She wanted to see the landmarks: Sweet Home Missionary Baptist Church and the Haskell House. The neighborhood was quiet yet ac-tive with signs of demolition. A house that looked like it had been built in the forties had a big bulldozer parked in the driveway, D.A.R. Demolition printed on its long arm, and one large destructive claw at its end. Rolls of old carpet were be-ing hauled out of another house. There were muffled sounds of hammering and drilling from a distance, though most of the houses were already finished, some obviously newly built, some expanded, some just freshly painted or repaired. A few had been left alone, and she wondered who lived in them.

When she turned the corner onto Charlotte Street, an old woman called out to her. She was standing on her porch and carrying a purse, perhaps waiting for someone to pick her up and take her somewhere. Sunita couldn't hear what she was saying and took a few steps onto her front path.

"What's that?" Sunita asked.

"You never came back."

Sunita kept walking up the path. The woman could have been senile, or mistaken her for someone else, or thought she was her sister, the one who called herself Cheryl.

When they were only a few feet away from each other, the woman said, "You changed your hair."

"Yes, I did," Sunita said.

"You never came back the next day."

"I'm sorry. Something came up."

"But I got a letter saying they paid my mortgage. And I get the check, even though I didn't sign your papers. It comes every month."

"Well, have you deposited the checks?" Sunita asked.

"Yes, but no one has come to fix up the house."

"Maybe you can hire the contractors yourself now. Maybe they just wanted to give you the money to do that."

The woman squinted at Sunita. She suddenly seemed unsure of who she was talking to. A car pulled up to the curb and a young man got out. "That's my grandson, who I was telling you about."

"Let me help you," Sunita said. She linked arms with the woman and walked with her to the car.

The woman said to her grandson, "This is Cheryl. The one I told you about."

He looked at her suspiciously, but he was polite, telling her his full name, Jerome Redding.

Sunita shook his hand. "I don't work for that company anymore," she said to the old woman, taking a guess at what she could say that might sound accurate, piecing together the little she knew about Vanita's time here. "That's why I didn't come back."

"I decided I wasn't going to sign any papers anyway. I'm too old to move."

Sunita nodded. "I think that's wise." She stepped back as Jerome helped the old woman into the car. "I'm sorry," she said before the door closed, "can you tell me your name again?"

Naturally the woman looked a little offended. "Jacqueline," she replied emphatically. "Jacqueline Redding."

"Yes, of course. I'll see you around, Mrs. Redding."

"You take care," Mrs. Redding said.

Sunita just stood there watching the car drive slowly down the short street, stop at the corner, and turn right onto 10th Street. It was a while before she kept walking.

MICHAEL'S PERFECT PENIS

BY MOLLY ODINTZ

Airport Boulevard

ngela first met Michael the second week of college, when he and his girlfriend at the time, Elise, were tripping up on the rooftop of one of the dorms, their eyes glassy, smiles big and welcoming. Michael and Elise had seemed so happy together when she first met them. Michael was a year younger and lived on campus, while Elise was a sophomore and had her own apartment off campus already. Angela was living in the honor student dorms, where she'd gotten into a second-tier honors program that promised exactly half of what the first-tier program gave to its students, but it wasn't a big deal because she'd mainly picked UT Austin for the parties, and spent her first week of school reinventing herself as a stoner.

And party she did; so much so that later that year, Angela and two of her new friends, Daniel and Martin, got kicked out of the dorms (Angela for tripping with a friend who briefly overdosed, Daniel for having a mild psychotic break while tripping, and Martin for being there with Daniel while also tripping). Martin moved in with Elise and the party got going for real. They spent all weekend, every weekend, in that dank hole of an apartment, Elise and Michael fucking in the back room while Martin crashed in the front, everyone as high and drunk as they could possibly be while still kicking ass at school. Angela would try to keep up, but mostly she'd fall asleep pretty early. She liked to joke that she was a narco-narcoleptic: every time she'd smoke too much weed and fall asleep quietly on the couch.

The crew wasn't just the apartment dwellers and dorm expats, of course. There were plenty of other folks still living in the dorms who wanted to party outside them, especially after what happened to Angela, Daniel, and Martin, and a steady stream of people came in and out of the apartment all semester long, becoming the tight-knit group that would spend the next four years hooking up and breaking each other's hearts in what felt like a more incestuous circle than the Spanish royal family.

It was toward the end of that first year of college that Angela started to see the cracks developing in Elise and Michael's on-again, off-again relationship, now more off than on. She'd never been the most observant person in the group—she slept through much of what happened and was too trapped in her own anxiety to process much of what she did observe—but some facts are just too obvious to ignore. It came to her mostly in rumors: Michael had punched a hole in a shed door, they said, when he found out that Elise had been in a threesome with two of their other friends, Sandra and Andrew, and while Sandra and Andrew never meant things to be serious, they'd underestimated the intensity of emotions underpinning Michael's happy-go-lucky interior. Really, everyone had. And if this feels like a warning, that's because it is.

Michael got together with Sandra a couple of years later, after Elise nearly drank herself to death and had to head back to small-town Texas or die trying. Her best friend and her father came and picked her up in the middle of the night and no one ever heard from her again. Sandra was the sweetest girl that Angela had ever known, and right away Michael started taking advantage. Every time Angela would go over to Sandra's studio on the rapidly gentrifying East Side, there was Michael, lazing around, smoking weed, never doing much, as Sandra cleaned around him. When Angela watched Sandra cleaning up after her boyfriend, she couldn't speak from jealousy—no one ever cleaned up after her. Angela and Sandra had lived together long enough for Sandra to figure out that Angela was too messy to share a place with, then ended the lease early, an experience shared by most of Angela's roommates.

Angela didn't personally understand Michael's appeal, but according to Elise back in happier days, Michael had a "perfect penis." She went on and on about Michael's perfect penis for an entire drunken night out on the balcony of the housing co-op room shared by Angela and Sandra one summer. The balcony was positioned directly over a tricky parallel-parking spot, and Angela and Sandra had spent the entire summer smoking on the balcony and shouting instructions to hapless drivers trying to maneuver into a spot smaller than their cars.

Angela had at one point gotten close to finding out if Michael's penis was, in fact, perfect, but after a brief make-out session, she had decided to pass, a very good decision given what was to come later.

Michael would come by the co-op sometimes back when Sandra and Angela lived together, before Sandra and Michael started dating. He'd found a plain-faced girl who calmed him down, and when Elise saw her for the first time, she wept drunkenly about being passed over for a chick that, according to Elise, wasn't even hot. Angela and Sandra, both blond, both eighteen, loved the parties at the co-op but couldn't keep up with the old co-opers. Growing up in Austin, Angela had heard legends about housing cooperatives and their parties, but it wasn't until living in one that she fell in love with the idea (or even understood what it was): residents shared management responsibilities, everyone in the house got together for meetings to democratically decide on issues, and everyone got as fucked up as they wanted in the convenience of their own home.

Michael was hot, in a pissed-off-hetero way. At least according to Angela's friend Robbie, who liked Michael the way he liked all short straight dudes who were pissed off about being short. Michael had a chip on his shoulder when it came to class (everyone was shocked to find out later that he actually came from money) and women (his mother had spent much of his childhood beating him with a telephone and it appeared to have had some effect). He especially didn't want to be with a woman who was doing better than he was financially and hassling him for rent, which was when things started getting bad between him and Sandra. She was working in a lab and finishing her master's while he delivered pizza, smoked all her weed, and didn't pay her any rent. The escalating physical threats were beside the point to Sandra—it was about money for her.

But when Angela got a call from Sandra saying that Michael had attacked her, she was glad Sandra called the cops and dumped Michael right away, even though Sandra kept saying that all she wanted was for Michael to finally pay his half of the rent.

And then, of course, he came up with the money somehow, they moved back in together, and then a year after that, Sandra was dead. Of an underlying condition, the autopsy said, that had made her collapse in her bathroom, striking her head against the side of the tub and ending, in a second, a small but promising existence. She was pregnant at the time. And Angela had always suspected that Sandra had some help from Michael in her sudden demise. She told her suspicions to the cops—they had a domestic violence charge already on file from the great rent argument of 2012—and they did what they did best: ignored her concerns and moved on to something easier. So Angela grieved, she raged, she plotted vengeance, and then she too moved on to something easier. Until one day she couldn't anymore. Because Michael was back, and still hadn't learned his lesson.

Angela had always known Michael was still in town. There weren't all that many cheap places to live in Austin, and he'd washed up in the dorm-style apartments on Riverside just long enough for Angela's friend Hailey to recognize his braying laugh from across the parking lot. Hailey had lived in a punk house with Michael and a bunch of other guys in late college, and she still remembered vividly the night he locked her out of the house and she broke in by smashing a window. He claimed to not have known she was outside, or heard her break in, but the other roommates were in the kitchen right away, ready to wrap towels around her bloody arm.

Then one day, Michael's name showed up on the minutes of a membership meeting at Angela's new housing co-op and her heart sank into her chest. She was living at Anderson Lane and North Lamar, a mile south of where someone had painted STOP GENTRIFICATION in big block letters on a wooden fence (the sign wasn't exactly working), and she was aware of how rich it was for her to be the one who now complained of invasion. Austin had plenty of student co-ops, but this one was special—it was for co-opers for life. And that's what she'd wanted to be, at the time. The co-op wasn't just cheap (only four hundred dollars a month for a room!), it was hers. She'd been a founding member. She named the fucking building, for chrissake. She'd tell the rest of the co-op members what happened to her friend, they'd reject Michael out of hand, and that would be that.

So she brought it to a meeting. She figured all she'd need was a few minutes to get him kicked off the wait list for being a potential fucking murderer, even if he was going around still playing the part of the grieving boyfriend. She told her story. Then Michael told his.

But there was a problem—the rest of the co-op decided to believe Michael. They decided to believe him when he said that his girlfriend died of natural causes. They decided to believe him when he said that the domestic violence charge on his record was a result of both parties' actions. They decided to believe him over the words of someone they'd known for years, because giving a violent man a second chance is apparently easier than listening to a woman with a bad reputation as a roommate. After all, Angela was messy AF, didn't always do her chores around the co-op, didn't smile particularly often, had already fucked anyone she was going to fuck, and wasn't planning on fucking them again. And so Michael got added to the wait list—there were always a few people waiting to get into the cheapest housing situation Austin had left to offer—and Angela figured that she had a few months at least to turn folks against having him move in.

But then Michael jumped the wait list. Two boys already living at the co-op, both of whom, Angela bitterly reflected, had lost the ability to identify as feminist forever, had decided that they could turn their two-bedroom into a three-bedroom. Michael was game to live in one of the original bedrooms, while one of the other boys moved into the living room, hastily walled off from the kitchen with plywood. By the time Michael jumped the wait list, he'd already used his tragic little tale of love lost to fuck two of the teenage punks who hung around the co-op, and he was close to fucking two more. He was invited to the weekly *D&D* games, which Angela now began to boycott. He befriended co-op residents with whom Angela immediately ceased communication. This, she often thought, was a particularly heroic stand to take, given that she was known for being incredibly talkative. She spent each evening getting drunk and high, talking shit about Michael and smoking weed with her bestie at the co-op, who was already in the process of developing the kind of crush on her that would soon make her never want to be friends with any male.

Angela still wasn't buying a single word that came out of Michael's mouth, but the other members of the co-op kept up their aggressive neutrality. She felt that neutrality to be the ultimate betrayal. They chose to believe a suspected murderer over her. That didn't mean *neutral*. That meant they were taking Michael's side and too chickenshit to admit it.

She started greeting every neighbor with glares. She went to meetings and sat silently. She turned her lack of a voice into the loudest, most oppressive nonsound imaginable. She was the French girl staring at the Nazi in *The Silence of the Sea*, except those around her didn't read her silence as a form of rebellion. They were merely pleased she had, for once, shut up. She tried to ratchet up the tension further, stalking around the commons when Michael was in there performing his shared communal tasks, warning any girl he was spotted with of his past (the barely legal punks had, alas, taken her warning as encouragement). Her friend came over once to take some spoiling food home with him from the commons fridge and was shaken by the level of silent fury she was able to make known when Michael entered the room. He'd later call it *intense*, and that was a good summary of that year, for a whole year went by with Angela watching, waiting, and hoping Michael was going to fuck up just enough to be out of her life for good.

And finally things started to change. Michael started to show his true colors. And he also developed a habit of spitting on the concrete steps of the courtyard staircase as he was headed to his upstairs apartment, and that habit turned quite a few of his new friends against him. None of the girls were fucking him anymore, and Michael had started to get increasingly withdrawn. He dropped the *D&D* game, spending all his hours on the dark web instead, or playing games, or who the fuck knows what guys do when they get depressed. The more she glared, the more he withered; the less she spoke, the more he lost the ability to communicate at all. She had finally found a path toward revenge—she would shrink herself, but it would make him shrink further.

One day an email arrived in her inbox via the co-op's email list that said Michael had talked about buying guns, had threatened his roommates and their cats, and was being evicted. Angela crowed. He left filled with shame and she laughed him off the property. She went around to everyone who'd wronged her and they told her she was right. She was ecstatic. It was a religious fervor of I-told-you-so's. She was Cassandra but now she would be heard.

Two days later, Michael killed himself. Angela's joy seeped away slowly. He had never been proven a murderer. He'd been rejected by the co-op for spitting on the staircase more than anything she'd ever said. Her neighbors, who had so gloriously told her she was right, began to avoid her again, and she couldn't blame them. She'd lost sight of her friend in all this, pretending to speak for the dead when she was really defending her own pathological need to be right.

In death, Michael had won. She would never be able to play that ultimate sympathy card of killing herself to make people say nice things about her, she thought to herself, because she had responsibilities. She had family that she refused to abandon, and Michael had rejected his own family long before. She had a cat that she loved more than her own life, while Michael had, she reflected, no love at all. Did Michael care more about his story than his existence? Or did he just have nothing other than the lies he told himself? At least now she could finally move out of the co-op. There was no one to fight there anymore. And the parties weren't very fun these days, anyway.

STITCHES

BY AMY GENTRY

West Campus

1

M uddled by the construction in West Campus, blocked first by a barricade, then by fluorescent tape, and at last by a Jurassic-looking excavator, I cut through an alley and find myself staring at the back of Apollo House.

I knew it was still standing, of course. I've driven past it once or twice this semester during my visiting professor gig at UT. Now squashed between high-rise condos, the three-story Victorian mansion with its gingerbread trim and spired turret looks like nothing so much as an abandoned dollhouse. But the past is always smaller than you think.

Seeing it from the back is a different matter. My body leaps at the memory of flying down those sagging steps from the narrow, screened-in back porch, the screen door bouncing and shivering behind me on the frame; sleeping synapses spark to life with the remembered tastes and smells of evenings spent smoking out on the porch after dinner. As I draw closer, everything from the gravel's crunch to the late-spring heat rippling through the shade trees acquires a hallucinatory vividness. Someone inside picks idly at an acoustic guitar, and I'm knocked clean out of my skin with longing. It feels like I could reach up my hand, pull aside the tie-dye curtain hanging in the window of my old room, and slip back into an older, younger self.

I lived in Apollo House for two years during college, having applied to the West Campus Co-operative Houses out of desperation after missing the freshman dorm lottery deadline. An only child from the Dallas suburbs, I had no idea what a co-op was, as ignorant of the WCCH's hippiefied reputation as I was of their principles of shared ownership and democratic governance. I quickly fell in love with the cozy house meetings, stoned conversations, and family-style meals of tofu stir fry scooped from a pan three feet in diameter at a massive wooden table to a soundtrack of Ravi Shankar or Joni Mitchell or the Screaming Gypsy Bandits. It was like discovering a new country, with its own language—*guff* for free stuff, *house love* for required labor hours, *labor holidays* for weekends spent on home repairs—a country where no one ever had to be alone again.

"Can I help you?" A short, shaven-headed person is peering at me through the flyblown screen.

Caught mid-daydream, my first instinct is to lie. "My son's thinking of living in the co-ops," I say, although I don't have children and can't imagine I ever will, at this point. Retroactively, I appoint as my imaginary son a struggling student toward whom I feel unusually maternal—I call him *the boy with his heart on his sleeve* because of his anatomical heart tattoo, though only to myself, of course.

"Would you like a tour?"

It would never have occurred to me to ask, but I don't say no.

The person adjusts owlish glasses. "Come on up. I'm the trustee—that's like an elected house manager. Suze, they/them."

I introduce myself, adding "she/her" as my students have taught me, and mount the stairs to the porch. Then I stop dead in my tracks.

The sarcophagus is still there. That's what we called the decrepit old chest freezer where Wendi always perched, chain-smoking American Spirits and holding court in hemp and patchwork like a hippie queen on her throne. In a good mood, she'd regale you with her plans to buy a VW bus off a guy she knew and sell her dresses at music festivals all the way to San Francisco. In a bad mood, she'd ash her cigarette into an upturned Frisbee and bitch about migraines and Daniel and the steakhouse where she waited tables, in an East Texas accent like a mouth full of marbles. I can see her now, rolling round eyes and flicking her butt-length hair, saying, *Five dollars on a two-hundred-dollar tab. Some people are just too mean to live.*

Wendi disappeared during the Full Moon Party, taking only the clothes on her back and the cash tips from her dresser drawer. Everyone was too busy nursing hangovers the next day to notice she was gone, and since her stuff was still in her room, it was awhile before anyone filed a report. Although the police quickly confirmed she'd never bought the van, they also turned up a juvenile record peppered with runaway attempts, hitchhiking, and vagrancy, or so the rumors said. When nobody in her family came to make a fuss, the case went cold, which is what it does when someone doesn't want to be found. Still, between that and Oracle House burning down the summer before, it felt like the end of an era. I moved out shortly afterward.

"It's not always this messy," Suze says nervously.

I realize I must be staring and mutter something forgiving. We step into the mouthlike kitchen with its red tile slashed through by industrial stainless steel, and Suze cranks up the old spiel about *communal living* and *work together play together* and *the best friends you'll ever make*, but I'm having a hard time shaking Wendi's ghost. We organized those wire storage racks together on the last labor holiday before the Full Moon Party. Wendi told me about the *Playboy* bunny outfit she was making for the party's oh-so-original "dress like a slut" theme and, in a spontaneous burst of generosity, offered to tart up the red velvet number I'd bought for five bucks at Buffalo Exchange. Remembering her expert fingers pinning the hem all the way up to kingdom come, I wonder whether they still have that party in December and hope that if they do, the boys have to dress up and freeze their asses off too.

We move on to the common areas, and I brace myself for another tidal wave of memories, but no ghosts come out to play. The wooden dining table isn't like I remember it, and most of the other furniture's been replaced. No one's around—Suze tells me everybody's off studying for finals— and the empty rooms are stuffy and littered with picked-over piles of guff left behind by those moving out. It's time for me to leave too, but there's one more room to see.

As casually as I can, I ask about the cone-shaped spire at the top of the tower.

"You can actually get into it from my room," Suze says. "Do you want to see it?"

I nod carelessly, like I'm good either way. Like the spire's not a magical place I still dream about, a wardrobe to Narnia, an inner sanctum where Daniel's friends held drum circles during parties, creating a dark, oceanic thrum that shook the whole house. I used to lie on my bed listening to that thunderous heartbeat, just across the hall, trying to work up the courage to walk over.

The trustee always lived in the spire room, and Daniel had always been the trustee, at least for as long as anyone could remember. Tall and blond, with pale-blue eyes and a ginger beard, he radiated an impenetrable, lightly stoned calm that lay over the house like a golden dust. He had a way of gazing into your eyes and nodding as if attuned to musical qualities in your voice no one had ever heard before, and under his watch Apollo House gained a reputation for being easygoing and conflict-free. We often wrapped up house meetings early and went to Barton Springs, even though Daniel himself never swam and preferred to sit on the hillside gazing up at the stars. Lying on the soft grass next to him, passing a joint in comfortable silence while our housemates splashed in the icy-cold water, felt more like home to me than anything has, before or since.

But it was Wendi, not Daniel, who finally invited me into the spire. Somehow, she wove a spell around me at the Full Moon Party that night. It wasn't just the Betty Boop–ified dress; it was Wendi herself, chattering around the pins in her mouth while she fiddled with the neckline. *I see auras. Yours is like the Joni Mitchell album—every shade of blue.* I've never made friends easily. Chalk it up to divorced parents if you want, or a distant mom, or being an only child. I only know that since I was a kid, I've felt something wrong inside, deep down, some wall I can't cross. No matter how hard I try, I can't touch other people, only watch them through one-way glass. That night, it was like the glass dissolved into mist. I danced outrageously, gulped down Jell-O shots and pot brownies, grabbed Wendi's hand and dragged her to the dance floor to gyrate against random guys until we both died laughing. One arm around my neck, she pointed at the ceiling. *Do you smell something burning? I bet Daniel's friends are dropping ash all over the spire again. Let's go kick their asses.*

I followed her up the stairs, like I'm following Suze now, into Daniel's room and then through a little door into the spire, twelve feet across at its base and shaped like a magician's hat, with red fairy lights spiraling up its walls to a disco ball at the top. Drummers sat around the perimeter, hands pounding too fast to see, while Daniel and the others lounged on floor pillows passing pipes and a bong. Wendi and I danced under the disco ball for a while, and then I got dizzy, fell down on the floor next to Daniel, and stayed there. The last time I saw Wendi, she was in a trance, dancing ecstatically in the red underwater light. Then Daniel kissed me, and I couldn't see anything.

I'm standing right where Wendi and I danced, staring at the same batiks and mirrored embroidery and fairy lights, under the same disco ball. I reach up and spin it lightly with my fingertips, and the leaping specks of light draw my attention to a piece of colorful patchwork on the wall—the one thing in the room I don't recognize. It's unfinished but beautiful, a pattern of shard-like patches spiraling out to raw edges in whorls of red and purple and gold. I lean over for a closer look and see, near the bottom, a slender patch of red stretch velvet. I touch it.

It's from my dress.

Wendi made this.

My eyes prickle. That night, for a single shining moment, I had everything I'd ever wanted. Then the clock struck midnight and the spell wore off and I lost it all. And the only evidence that any of it happened is this single insignificant scrap of fabric.

Carefully, I unpin the cloth. It's more artistic than her other work was—finer, more detailed. I hesitate for less than a second before slipping it into my bag.

"Um, I don't want to rush you?" I jump. Suze has been standing outside the door, waiting patiently. "But I have to go down and start dinner soon."

My face is red as I come out.

"Cool, huh?" Suze says. "I can't believe it's really my room. I've only lived here a couple of months, and the guy before me had it for, like, decades."

A premonition slips through me. It can't be.

"His name was Daniel," they say, and my stomach drops. "A real co-op guru. A true believer."

"He'd have to be," I murmur. We used to call them lifers—dudes, always dudes, who hung around the co-ops far too long. They were mostly harmless, elder-statesman types, but there were a few you watched out for at parties, if you were a nineteen-year-old girl. The thought of Daniel as a lifer, sitting up here guarding the spire like a gargoyle for twenty years, depresses me beyond belief. At the same time, it occurs to me that if anyone has heard from Wendi in those twenty years, it would be him.

We head downstairs. Suze tells me there's going to be a shortage of rooms next year; one of the houses is closing. "Tell your son to get his application in now."

"Thanks for the tip," I say, really meaning it. I like Suze. I feel bad about taking the tapestry, but not so bad that I don't wait for them to peel off for the kitchen so I can check the mail table on my way out. Sure enough, there's a stack of envelopes waiting to be forwarded to Daniel's new address.

I grab one from the middle and hurry out.

2

Half an hour later, I pull up to an apartment complex north of Research Boulevard, an old stucco building whose trendy black-and-white makeover can't hide its essential shabbiness. The leggy crape myrtles out front bob lazily over their beds of black pumice, as if to say, *Can you believe this shit?*

I can't. In the past hour, I've lied to get into Apollo, stolen a wall hanging from the spire, and committed mail theft, which I'm pretty sure is a felony. And now I'm hunting down Daniel, of all people, to ask if he knows anything about a swatch of fabric the size of a placemat. It just nags at me, that Wendi would put so much care into something—it's clearly hand-stitched—and then abandon it. Maybe she didn't mean to. If Daniel knows where she is, I could ask her, maybe even send it to her.

Besides, I tell myself, Daniel's an old friend—or at least he stayed friend*ly*, after what happened between us. If anything, he'd been too nice afterward, handled me too gently, gone out of his way to include me in house activities. I was the one who moved out.

But my hand shakes when I knock, and I half hope he won't answer.

"Yes?"

The voice on the other side of the door is gravelly and suspicious. What if he doesn't remember me? I start to panic. But when I say my name, the door opens and there he is— softer around the middle, golden hair graying, and most shockingly of all, with a snow-white beard, but still Daniel, his blue eyes wreathed in twenty years of smile lines.

Right now, they're lit up in surprise. "Come on in! It's great to see your face." He wraps me in the kind of hug that has fallen out of style in the age of global pandemics. *Warm*, I think, and then pull back awkwardly.

"I believe this belongs to you," I say, holding out the envelope with a flourish I instantly regret. "I'm visiting Austin, so I dropped by Apollo."

He stares at the letter, and I want to sink into the ground. But then he breaks into a beatific smile. "Thanks, friend," he says. "Can you come in and stay awhile? I could make you a cup of tea."

It washes over me—the promise of the co-ops still lingering around Daniel like a scent, a hot meal or a cup of tea or the shirt off someone's back behind every door. All you have to do is knock. Daniel waves me over to a thrift-store sofa of the kind that used to be everywhere but is getting harder to find these days, and steps into the kitchen to put on the kettle.

"Green or herbal?" he calls.

"Give me all the caffeine, please."

He sets out the tea bags. "I'm glad you looked me up. I don't see enough of the old crew."

Blushing a little at the implication that I'm part of any "crew," I take advantage of the opening to ask who he's still in touch with. He washes a pair of mugs as he talks, and I watch the rhythmic motions of his shoulders and listen for Wendi's name. It doesn't come. My heart sinks a little as he wraps up and asks about my life.

"I'm only here for the semester. I teach writing in Chicago." I was grading papers alone in my cold apartment over Thanksgiving break, thinking I couldn't face another frozen February, when the email came from one of my old professors, asking if I could take over for a visiting writer who'd just bailed. Spring semester in Austin is a no-brainer. On New Year's Day, I got in my car and started driving.

Daniel dries his hands, looking thoughtful. "I used to wonder what you were up to, hiding in your room all the time. I guess you were writing, huh?"

I may have been, when I wasn't lying on my bed listening to drums. Carefully, I say, "What have you been up to?"

He snorts. "Come off it! You know. I'm a creepy old lifer,

clinging to my youth here in the Velvet Coffin." The kettle screams, and he waves away billowing steam.

His easy self-deprecation, coupled with my favorite nickname for Austin, surprises me into laughter. "I believe the word Suze used was *guru*."

"So, you came to see the Matthew McConaughey of the co-ops? I get older, they stay the same age?" He pours the water, shimmying his hips and adding in a growly voice, "All right, all right, all right."

I laugh and protest, not entirely convincingly, as he emerges from the kitchen and sets the mugs on the coffee table.

"Seriously, though. I'm aware of how it looks." He sits down opposite me. "I just want you to know—I mean, first off, Apollo's not a party house anymore. And me, I laid off drinking years ago. I wasn't going to keep getting wasted with a bunch of kids. Or—you know." He stammers and goes red.

I flush too. He means he didn't creep on the college girls. The thing is, I believe him. That night in the spire, after we made out for a while, he told me to wait in his room. I thought we were hooking up, and, idiotically, I took off my clothes and got in his bed, where I promptly passed out. When I woke up the next morning, Daniel was sneaking into the room in yesterday's clothes, and I realized the awful truth: he'd sent me out of the spire, not to sleep with me, but to get rid of me. I faked sleep until he left and then crept back across the hall, and afterward we both pretended the whole thing never happened. Then Wendi disappeared, and the ensuing chaos saved me from ever having to ask where Daniel had gone to bed that night, or with whom.

I was lucky it was Daniel. I know that. The girls in my classes write thinly veiled stories about this sort of thing; I know how much worse it could have been. But the memory still makes me burn with shame. Every single person leaving the spire that night saw me in his bed.

"Anyway, I know I should have left years ago." He runs his hands through his hair, and his voice cracks open a little when he says, "It's just—Apollo was my *home*."

I know exactly what he means. Apollo was my home too. I left a part of me there—the red velvet me, the me who knew how to dance, to open up, to be part of something bigger than myself. I've never been that person since. Teaching is so damn lonely. The students like me well enough, but they don't really see me. It's just more one-way glass.

"Do you ever think about Wendi?" I ask.

He takes a slow sip of tea. Then he says, so gently it makes my eyes sting, "Seeing the old place got you feeling old pain?"

I stare down into my mug. "We were just getting to be friends when she left."

"Too bad. But it figures. She took awhile to warm up to people."

I laugh, remembering her holding forth on the freezer. "She always said you gave her a headache."

"Everything gave Wendi a headache."

"True." She always blamed the steakhouse for her migraines—fluorescent lights, too many angry animal ghosts, $2.13 an hour and no benefits. "No wonder she was prickly."

He grins. "Downright ornery."

"You only think that because she didn't buy your Big Lebowski act." I hold up a peace sign and mimic his blissed-out expression. "*The Dude abides.*"

"Hey now!"

We crack up in tandem, and I feel his warmth spreading

over me, like it did those nights at Barton Springs long ago.

He must feel it too, because he looks at me with a sly expression. "Want to smoke a bowl for old times' sake?"

"I thought you'd never ask."

He fishes a small glass pipe out of his pocket, crosses a lighter over the packed bowl, and hands the greens to me with a stoner's hospitality. "To Wendi."

"To Wendi."

I haven't smoked in years, and the smooth, round weight of the blown glass feels good in my palm. I hover the flame over the bowl and inhale, watching the pot spark and blacken to ash. As I hand it back, I lose control of my lungs and cough out a purplish cloud.

"Watch it, this stuff is strong."

"Now you tell me." My head is already floating away, my legs turning to lead and sinking into the sofa. It's not unpleasant.

Daniel takes a hit, holds it, and then sighs out the smoke. "You know, I knew Wendi pretty well. We moved in at the same time, and in the beginning we hung out a lot. Did you know her parents were fundies? They, like, beat her up and locked her in the closet and shit. That's why she ran away all those times. She even lived on the street for a while." He hands me the pipe and waits for me to take a hit before saying, "I'm telling you this because I think you're doing something I used to do."

"What's that?" My eyes are watering now.

"Blaming yourself. For not seeing it coming."

It hits a nerve. If I blame myself, maybe it's because I was too busy nursing my own hurt feelings at the time to question the official story. I set the pipe down. "So, why do you think she left?"

"I think she got tired of pulling doubles every day and riding the bus home with a migraine."

"But—why leave all her stuff?"

"She took her cash," he reminds me. "Nobody knows how much she had stashed away."

"But her sewing machine, and all those dresses. If she was leaving, why not at least try to sell her stuff at the Renaissance Market first?"

"It was just one of her impulses," he says. "You didn't know her like I did. After that childhood—she was one of those people who always had a foot out the door and a packed bag under the bed, ready to go. Maybe some guy at the party offered to take her to California. Or hell, maybe she just walked to I-35 and stuck out her thumb." He glances at me. "It was a wild night. A lot of people did crazy things."

I feel my face grow hot.

"I'm not blaming her," he says in his soft Southern accent. "I'm just saying that when somebody started getting too close, she got spooked, and she ran away. That's what happened with us."

He fixes his intense blue eyes on me, and I must be way too high, because suddenly it feels like he's not talking about Wendi at all. In a moment, everything turns inside out. Daniel's the one who rejected *me*. Didn't he? Or was it me who got spooked and ran away? My head swims, and I remember the slow kiss in the spire, the heat in my thighs, the awful morning after. If only I could have talked to Wendi about it. She might have flicked her cigarette and said, *Oh hon, it's just Daniel. Don't give it a second thought*, and maybe I wouldn't have. But she was gone when I woke up, and at the end of the semester I found an apartment and moved out.

If I'd stayed, would things have been different?

Our knees are nearly touching, and he's looking at me with a steady expression I recognize from that night in the spire. My skin prickles with the sudden knowledge that I could be kissing him right now.

I'm not going to lie, I consider it.

Then I reach into my bag and pull out the patchwork.

Daniel draws back when he sees it, his eyes widening so that he almost looks afraid. "Where did you get that?"

"Do you know what it is?"

"I said, where did you get it?"

"In the spire," I say, confused.

His panic turns to anger. "And you just—*took* it?"

I flush. "It was a weird thing to do, I know. I just, I was wondering—because—"

"Wendi put it in there the night she left," he says stiffly. "I always thought it was her way of saying goodbye. Why on earth would you take it out? You think she should have sold that too?"

I stammer, taken aback. "D-did you tell the police?"

"Of course I did! Jesus, what is this?" This is the most upset I've seen him. He sucks in his breath and narrows his eyes. "Have you been talking to Franklin?"

"Franklin Trueheart?" I say, confused. Franklin was a Genus House lifer and the co-op handyman, back in my day. "No. Why?"

"Because he's got a crackpot theory for everything that's ever gone down in the co-ops. And you're beginning to sound just like him. Look, what exactly are you looking for? Do you want me to tell you something awful happened to Wendi? Maybe it did. Hitchhiking is dangerous. I'm sorry you thought she was your friend, but I promise you're not going to find some grand reason why she didn't mean to leave you. She did."

Leave *you*. The extra pronoun stings.

I slowly fold the fabric into my bag and rise to my feet. "I should go."

His face falls. "Don't. I'm sorry. You just really threw me off with that thing. You have to understand, it was all I had left of Wendi for a long time."

But the temperature in here has dropped thirty degrees. "It was nice catching up," I say, walking toward the door.

He reaches it first. "Please don't be mad."

I open it and step over the threshold.

"All right," he says. "Just do me a favor, okay? Don't go asking Franklin any of this stuff. He's cracked, maybe even dangerous. Who knows what he'd come up with."

We don't hug goodbye.

3

I get in the car and drive straight to Franklin Trueheart's office.

Everyone knew Franklin back in the day. Inked up to the eyeballs and all over his bald skull, he used to travel from co-op to co-op tinkering with busted AC units, building compost bins, and fixing whatever needed fixing, always on a volunteer basis. It was unclear who, if anyone, called in these jobs; he would just show up, towing his tools behind his recumbent bike in a trailer decorated with naked Barbies. Careless with personal space and argumentative at board meetings, he had a reputation back in the day for being as addicted to causing problems as he was to solving them.

If his website is any indication, he's also addicted to hustle. According to his antiquated home page, he's an accountant, real estate agent, amateur plumber, carpenter, and investigative journalist; on the side, he refurbishes VCRs and sells them on eBay. His office is in West Campus, right behind

Genus House, and I haul ass down Lamar, hoping to get there before he leaves for the day.

It wouldn't have occurred to me to go to Franklin True-heart for either audiovisual equipment or answers, but Daniel's warning might as well be an engraved invitation. If Franklin's just a garden-variety crackpot, why is Daniel so eager to keep me away from him? He may not be lying, but there's something he's not telling me.

I arrive just before seven and wander the alleyway behind Genus, looking for an office and seeing only an eight-by-ten toolshed. Given the way this day is going, I'm not as surprised as I should be when the door of the shed opens just a bit and a hand beckons me in.

Inside the shed, a skylight illuminates mosaicked walls and a desk so large Franklin must have to leap over it to get to his chair. File cabinets, VCRs, monitors, circuit boards, and cables crowd the small space behind him. Franklin himself looks more or less just as I remember him—stocky, muscular, and tattooed—but he's grown a fringe of hair around his bald spot, covering all the tattoos except for a single eyeball on top of his head.

"Have a seat," he says. I wedge myself into the lone wooden chair as he pats a manila folder. "I've just been reviewing your file."

My jaw swings open. "My what?"

"Apollo, right? Ought one and two. Don't look so worried," he says pleasantly. "I have files on everyone. I'm writing a book about the co-ops. In fact, do you mind if I record our conversation?" He reaches for something under his desk.

"Yes, I do," I say, alarmed.

He withdraws his hand and settles into an avuncular now-then-what-can-I-do-for-you-young-lady posture.

"How did you know I was coming?"

"I monitor my site traffic." He smirks. "Never know who's watching."

Paranoid: check. Real-time web-tracking software: check. And I'm pretty sure he hit the record button just now. Better cut to the chase. "Do you have a file on Wendi Miller?"

He grins like the cat that ate the canary. "Of course."

"I suppose you knew I was going to ask that."

"Not clairvoyant, just good with dates," he says modestly. "You moved out shortly after Wendi—" He frowns and purses his lips. "Well, whatever she did."

"And what do you think she did?"

"What do *you* think?"

Fair enough. I take out the patchwork square and toss it on the desk. "Have you seen this before?"

He studies it and says, very softly, "She was an artist."

I nod. Finally, someone understands. "I found it in the spire. Apparently, Wendi left it there as some kind of farewell message. But . . ."

He raises an eyebrow. "Go on."

I hesitate. "Well . . . I guess maybe all those dresses she made would have weighed her down too much to take. But this piece—"

"It would have been easy."

"Yes! Look—it's hand-stitched. She wouldn't even have needed her machine." I rush on, afraid I'll lose my courage: "And she was still working on it less than a week before she left. See that patch? That was my dress."

"I remember." His smiles in an unsettling manner. I'm taken aback for a moment, but then he frowns and says, "So?"

"So . . ." I hesitate. All the way here, I was dying to tell someone my theory. Now, I just want to be wrong. "So, maybe she didn't want to leave that night. Maybe she was running from someone."

"And . . . ?"

"Maybe they found her."

He doesn't react, just places the fabric carefully down on the desk and smooths it contemplatively for a moment. Then he slides it over to me. "Look carefully. What do you see?"

I lean over and stare at the piece of cloth. "It's an unusual design." He nods, and I continue: "Free-form, like she was improvising as she went. The scraps are salvaged. They all have different wear levels, see? And she was still working on it. She sewed my patch right after we hung out, when we were first starting to be friends." The light from the skylight is faint; it's getting dark outside. I take a deep breath. "I have a feeling that this was a kind of diary, with scraps representing all the people she knew, the places she went. Why would she leave it behind if she was going on some big adventure?"

"Good, good." He nods, and I feel like I've passed a test. "And the bloodstains?"

"What?" I look down. "I don't see any—"

"Feel."

I close my eyes hesitantly and run my fingers over the patchwork. At first, I feel nothing. Then a few tiny spots where the nap is slightly flattened. Then more. Then the stiff seams.

I open my eyes. All day, I've been seeing Wendi so vividly, hearing her voice so clearly. More like a ghost than a memory. Only now do I realize I've been worried that she really is one.

"Is this her blood?" I whisper.

Franklin shrugs, irritated. "Do I look like a forensics lab? That's for the police to figure out."

"What do we do now?"

He leans back in his chair. "Listen. I always thought you were smart, especially for Apollo. You don't just take things on faith. You look below the surface." He steeples his fingers. "I think you can handle this."

"Handle what?"

"Wendi and I share a similar background," he says with careful emphasis. "She grew up in Aldo, Texas, a small town outside Nacogdoches."

"And you're from the same place?"

"Gary, Indiana." He smiles. "But they're both ConEx towns."

"What's that? Like the power company?"

He shakes his head and leans forward. "Concrete Expressionism. It's a cult based on the teachings of the failed modernist painter Bill 'Bibbie' Blanks." He lays a hand on his chest. "I was born and raised ConEx. I escaped as a young teen. And so, I believe, did Wendi."

I frown, remembering something Daniel said. "I thought Wendi's parents were fundamentalists."

He chuckles. "You could call them that. Concrete Expressionists believe that by eschewing abstraction and hewing as closely as possible to the concrete nature of reality, they can defeat death itself. But after Papa Bibbie himself died, cult leadership was thrown into chaos. That's when I managed to escape. It would have been easier for a boy, though. Young women were more valuable to the cult. Breeders." My aghast expression only makes Franklin talk louder and faster. "ConEx pretends to be an art school. You know those magazine ads—draw a chipmunk and get a scholarship? Come for the free art class, stay for the ConEx pitch. Only it's a lousy recruitment technique. People want to draw chipmunks, not listen to a lecture on concrete auras in the back room."

Wendi saw auras—haloes, concentric circles, exploding spirals. *Like the Joni Mitchell album—every shade of blue.* I feel lightheaded; it's getting dark outside, I haven't eaten all day, and I'm still a little stoned. I listen hard for something to grab onto in what he's saying.

"So, when Wendi ran off with her baby—"

"Wait, baby?" Finally, something I feel sure about. "Wendi didn't have a baby."

"Of course not, when *you* knew her. That's because she left him with a non-ConEx family to raise." He leans back, looking satisfied with himself. "Find the son, and you'll find out what happened to Wendi."

"I'm not looking for anyone's son."

"He'd be twenty-two. Artistically gifted, like most ConEx." Franklin gestures humbly toward the mosaic. "And he would have one of these." He swivels in his chair and lifts the back of his hair to reveal a human heart tattooed at the base of his skull. "The ConEx symbol. The true heart."

Wait a minute. I've seen that tattoo before. *The boy with the heart on his sleeve.* I look away in confusion, see the mosaic on the wall, its intricate network of fragmented tiles like circuitry, like a subway map, like Austin seen from above. It makes me feel like I'm flying, or falling. The walls start to waver, the tiles spiral and explode.

I grab the patchwork and shove it back into my bag with shaking hands. "Daniel was right: you're crazy."

"Daniel," he sneers. "That trust fund baby always did have you Apollo types eating out of his hand." He looks at me with pity bordering on contempt. "You know what all cult leaders have in common, whether they're in ConEx or the co-ops? They're here to sell you one simple solution to life's problems. But anyone who's worked a day in their life knows that nothing runs on *simple*. Things are complicated. Things are connected." He points at my bag, as if he can still see the intricate pattern on the fabric. "Wendi knew that."

"Are you calling Daniel a cult leader?" I say.

"Worse. He's *management*. Daniel got me kicked out of Genus, after all I've done for the co-ops. For Christ's sake, I built this shed! This was my *home*!" His face darkens, his eyes well with tears.

"I'm—I'm sorry."

"The board is lousy with ConEx informants," he snivels. "When my book comes out, everyone will know." Suddenly his voice goes deadly soft. "You're one of them, aren't you? Daniel sent you to spy on me."

I stand up and a head rush blackens my vision. When it clears, Franklin is staring at me with bulging eyes, his face a dull brick-red. I edge backward, reaching for the door handle.

"That's right, run. But don't forget." He lowers his head so that the eye tattoo on the top is facing me. "I'm watching you."

The door gives. I turn, stumble out of the shed, and run out of the alley and into the path of an oncoming SUV.

4

It's too late to get out of the way, but instinct kicks in, and I yell and slam my hand down on the hood as hard as I can. The SUV jerks to a halt, bumping my hip with the force of a well-thrown bowling ball. As I pull myself up and scramble over to the curb, the driver leans out the window and screams something I can't hear over the white noise in my head. The SUV slowly rolls off, the back weighted down with kegs. If it had been going faster, I'd be in trouble. It occurs to me that I might actually owe my life to some frat party.

I sit on the sidewalk for a moment, waiting for my heart to crawl back down my throat and into my chest, but the thought of Franklin in the alley behind me forces me to my feet. As I wobble down the sidewalk on rubber legs, the hammering in my ears subsides, turning into throbbing bass, the sound of West Campus waking up on a Friday night. The sun has gone down; sorority girls are pregaming on their balconies. The parties will be starting soon.

I weave my way through the never-ending construction that clogs West Campus, my hand stinging, my hip on fire. If I felt high before, now I'm practically tripping. I keep thinking of the boy I told Suze was my son, the one with the tattoo like Franklin's. Why did I pick him? Is it because he looks like Wendi, and I subconsciously recognized him? Is he artistically gifted? How the hell should I know? He kept writing stories about his dog dying, until I gently reminded him that it was a speculative fiction class, and then he wrote a story about a dog who never dies. It was beautiful. It made me cry. There are tears in my eyes right now. This new generation is so much wiser and stranger than we were. Living with so much uncertainty, they take nothing for granted. Not even gender. Not even death. They're like baby birds, walking up to bulldozers and saying, *Are you my mother?*

Without paying attention, I've arrived at Oracle House, as if following grooves my own feet wore into the pavement twenty years back during some forgotten party crawl. Oracle was always unlucky; twenty years ago, somebody threw a scarf over a lamp during a party and it went up in flames. Now it's behind a construction fence, a banner hanging on it: *Coming Soon! The Easy Answer to Better Living! THE FOUND GROUP, INC. APARTMENTS & CONDOS.*

Oracle must be the house that's closing. But not just closing—being torn down.

Heartsick, I walk toward Guadalupe and wind up at the Renaissance Market, the open-air plaza that splits the Drag in two. The murals look even more brilliant at night, illuminated by sodium lights against a black sky. A weather-beaten man and woman of indeterminate age lean against one of the murals, sharing a forty next to their sleeping bags. I imagine Wendi homeless, camping on the sidewalk, bumming American Spirits, a perpetual runaway. I wonder if they still call the homeless teens on Guadalupe "Drag rats." What an awful name. When I was in college, rumor had it they all had rich parents in Westlake, and went home to their mansions when they got tired of street life. But of course, there are simpler reasons people disappear. Maybe they moved on. Maybe they died. Maybe they grew up and turned into these guys.

A body changes its cells every seven years, but it's still the same person. What about a city where the buildings are yanked out like teeth, one by one? What if everyone moves away, like me, or disappears, like Wendi, or is pushed out, like the people who used to live here? Buildings are replaceable, but what about whole neighborhoods? Individual cells are replaceable, but what about a hand, a hip, a beating heart?

Suddenly, nausea blooms in the pit of my stomach. I've never noticed before, but in the corner of one of the murals is a mermaid painted to resemble the Virgin of Guadalupe. Tears stream down her face, and an anatomically correct heart drips blood in the center of her chest. Her aura is made of long, swirling hair, waving like sunbeams seen through water. She looks exactly like Wendi. She *is* Wendi.

266 // Austin Noir

A quote below the mural reads:

> *For the blood around the heart*
> *is, for humans, their thought.*
> —*William Blanks Jr.*

Mermaid-Wendi cries. I cry. Nothing goes together, nothing matches, everything just keeps spiraling out and out in patternless shards, and we wind up back at the same old places, learning the lessons we didn't learn before.

The mural wavers. It's not Wendi at all.

I keep tracing the invisible path until the world starts going uphill, and then I body slam the sidewalk.

Drumbeats pump against the walls, bloody lights flicker and spin. Wendi dances, a white rabbit in bunny ears. She wrinkles her nose; something's burning. She points at me and says, Every shade of blue.

The brownies hit, the drumbeats open up, and I fall right through them. I'm kissing Daniel, but it's Apollo kissing me back, the walls of the spire leaning over me like a lover as Wendi dances faster and faster, eyes staring, arms jerking like a puppet.

The drums go silent. The spire is empty. Wendi's gone.

5

I wake up with Suze bending over me. They holler, "She's awake!" and I follow their gaze to the front porch of Apollo, where several people are craning their heads anxiously toward us. "Did you hit your head?"

"I don't think so," I say.

"You were out for a few seconds. Do you want me to call an ambulance?"

After a moment of thought, I say, "I'm just really hungry."

"Hang on." Suze rummages in the pocket of their cargo pants and comes up with a smashed granola bar. I devour it and immediately feel better.

"Thanks," I say, and after a moment I start laughing. "Co-op people are so nice."

"We are!" they say brightly. "Your son's going to love it here."

That reminds me. "Oracle House. Why would the board let it go to a developer?"

Suze looks a bit surprised by my question, but then they shake their head. "It's a mess. This one co-oper who said he was a CPA was apparently doing their books for free for years. When they got audited, it turned out he screwed up royally. They sold Oracle to pay off back taxes and fines."

"Was it Franklin Trueheart?"

They look at me in surprise. "Yeah. You know him?"

"I know *of* him."

Suze shakes her head. "Franklin's all right—as long as he's not trying to do your taxes, anyway. He's been in bad shape since getting kicked out of the co-ops for fraud, that's all. Paranoid, delusional." They sigh. "I guess some people will believe anything, if it helps them make sense of the world."

And how. All day and night, I've been looking for something to make sense out of Wendi's absence. One simple solution to all life's problems. But maybe anatomical hearts just make cool tattoos; maybe Bill "Bibbie" Blanks is just another failed modernist painter. And maybe Wendi's patchwork is just a bunch of random bits of cloth, sewn together because she was bored out of her mind, and left behind for the same reason.

I find the patchwork in my bag and hold it out to Suze. "This belongs at Apollo. I took it out of the spire earlier today. I'm really sorry. It reminded me of someone I miss."

"Oh!" Suze says, mildly confused. "Thanks. But you can keep it if you want. I'm not sure whose it is. I found it under the window unit in my room, stuffed in a crack, filthy. After I ran it through the wash, I thought it was pretty, so I hung it up in the spire." They hand it back.

I go rigid. Daniel said he found the patchwork in the spire twenty years ago. Why was it under his AC two months ago?

Oh my god.

"When did the board announce they were selling Oracle?"

"Just a couple months ago. I remember, because everybody was saying stuff like, *Oracle bulldozed, Daniel leaving—it's the end of an era.*"

The end of an era, indeed.

I don't say *I gotta go* and haul off running, like they do in movies. Instead, I head inside with Suze, let them give me food and water and introduce me to their housemates while I get my strength back. I look around at the surprisingly diverse faces and remember how the co-ops used to be mostly white dudes. That, at least, has changed. I linger on, partly because I need to check some things on my phone, but mostly because I want to spend a few more minutes in a warm co-op kitchen before I destroy them all.

It's nearly one in the morning when I get to Daniel's apartment. I pound on the door and shout, "Why did you kill Wendi?" at the top of my lungs, just in case he's asleep.

Sure enough, the door opens fast, bloodshot eyes appearing behind the chain. "I didn't do it! I swear!"

"Why did you kill her?"

"Stop shouting! Please!"

"Let me in and I'll stop!" I cup my hands around my open mouth, take a deep breath.

He fumbles the chain off the hook. I kick the door open, not knowing what I want to do exactly, but wanting it to be painful. I settle on insults. "Why did you do it, you fucking trust fund baby?"

He cowers. "I never hurt her, I swear! She was my friend!"

"Some friend."

"I didn't do anything," he says, anguished. "She passed out in the spire. I found her like that."

"She had a seizure," I say coldly. I looked up the symptoms at Apollo. The headaches, the auras, the burning smell when nothing was burning. The jerking dance I saw her do in the spire that night, under the flashing lights that undoubtedly triggered the episode. "I think she was epileptic."

"I didn't know that. How was I supposed to know that?"

"You weren't." Wendi didn't even know. Waiters don't have health insurance. When they get sick, they don't stay home from work and see a doctor; they pop a pill and pray. "What you were supposed to do was call an ambulance."

"You're right. Of course you're right. I shouldn't have just left her in the spire to sleep it off. But I was pretty fucked up that night." He licks his lips and peers up at me. "So were you, as I recall."

This time I hear it. The way he probes at my sore spots, testing me to see how deep my shame goes. How much blame I'll take.

"Yeah, we were all pretty fucked up that night," I hear myself say. "But only one of us dragged Wendi's body out of the house, dumped it, and then stole all her money so people would believe she'd taken off."

His face perfectly rigid, he folds his arms. "Why would I do that?"

"The situation with the co-ops was getting worse. Oracle burned down after a party. It was a miracle no one was killed or injured. A co-oper dying at a party right afterward wouldn't have been a good look."

"So, it was PR?" His voice drips sarcasm. "Where's your proof?"

"With the police," I say. "Or it will be when they open their mail tomorrow and find that patchwork. I wonder what'll show up on it under a black light?"

His eyes bulge in terror. Then they go dead, and the blood drains from his face.

"By the way, it was clever of you to point me to Franklin, knowing he'd spin me in circles so much I wouldn't believe anything he said, and make me feel like I'm crazy for even looking for answers."

Daniel is frozen in front of me, so I go on.

"But let's say he's right about the blood. Let's say Wendi kept that patchwork with the money in her top drawer—where she kept her valuables. Whoever took the money wrapped it in the patchwork. And then, at some point in what had to be a rough night, he used it to wipe up blood." I'm watching him closely now, probing him like he probed me, looking for soft spots and watching him flinch when I hit one. It's intoxicating. "But then the person lost it in his room somewhere. And he got so paranoid that he *couldn't* leave. He had to stay up there and guard his secret." I curl my lip in disgust. "You'd probably still be up there now if they weren't digging up Oracle House. Where is she? In the foundation?"

He looks like he's about to vomit. "She was lying in the spire after everybody left, eyes wide open. She must have hit her head when she fell. I panicked. I—I didn't know what to do."

"So you shoved her in your trunk and buried her under some rebar?"

It's close enough to the truth to make him wince. My stomach heaves, and I taste bile.

"She wasn't in the trunk." He sounds miserable. "She was in the backseat covered with a tarp. I drove around for a long time with her like that. I thought—I don't know. I was super high that night. I thought I was going to take her to the hospital." He squeezes his eyes shut.

"Guess you didn't make it."

"You weren't on the board," he says. "We were this close to getting shut down. It wasn't just Oracle; there were sexual assault accusations about the parties. People were saying the co-ops were just as bad as the frats. There was an investigation, they were talking about revoking our nonprofit status." He sinks down on the sofa. "It would have ended us."

"So you ended *her*."

"Stop saying that! You *know* I didn't kill her."

My eyes burn. "You disappeared her, Daniel. You threw her in the trash. You dragged her body right past me—and then you had the fucking balls to let everyone think you were hooking up with me when you were out digging her grave." I lower my voice to keep from crying.

He whispers, "Nobody would have claimed the body. Her family wouldn't even talk to the police. They'd disowned her years before."

I close my eyes for a moment and see Wendi sitting on the freezer, ashing her cigarette. "Then *you* should have been her family. Then *I* should have been her family." I open my eyes, a fresh wave of nausea hitting me. "Daniel—were you even sure she was dead?"

"Of course she was dead!"

But his face goes gray, and I know I've found the softest spot of all. The thought that torments him in the middle of the night. I put my thumb on the spot and press as hard as I can: "Are you sure?"

"I checked! I checked!" He starts crying. "I swear to god, I checked!" He rocks back and forth on the Goodwill sofa, his shoulders shaking like they'll never stop.

"If I were you, I'd go farther than Research Boulevard. I'd get all the way out of town." I look around at his possessions, so out of place, their surfaces sun-faded in the wrong places from having been in Apollo so long. "Honestly, it's about time. They don't call Austin the Velvet Coffin for nothing."

I leave Daniel's apartment and keep driving.

Chicago is nineteen hours away. I should hit Texarkana just as the sun's coming up. I have everything I need in my car—my laptop, my suitcase. I'll turn in my grades when I get back. They're all getting A's, even the boy with his heart on his sleeve.

I haven't decided about Wendi's patchwork. I lied to Daniel; I didn't send it to the cops. The co-ops may not have been worth saving back then, but they are now. I think of Wendi and the boy with his heart on his sleeve and all the other people I've failed. I don't want to add Suze and their friends to the list. The co-ops have changed. Daniel and I are the ones who're stuck in the past.

I pat the piece of patchwork on the seat beside me, run my hands over the bumps: my dress, Daniel's shirt, slivers of castoffs and costumes and curtains, every stitch a reminder of how we made each other our home. Wendi wanted to take it and drive off into the sunset, adding to it, piece by piece. But I'll have to start small. I don't even know how to sew.

BANGFACE VS. CLEANING SOLUTIONS, LLC

BY ANDREW HILBERT

Southpark Meadows

I was sitting there, legs propped up on my desk, trying to figure out where the wobbles were, when a real ladylike knock came on my door.

"Come on now, come in. No need to knock."

"Are you Bangface? Private eye?" She glided. Shorty. Small lady, is what I'm saying.

"Well, I'm no Jimmy Dick." I smiled and pointed at the seat. "No, don't sit there. My cat, Mariposa, pissed all over there this morning. Haven't had a chance to clean it up. What's the matter? You ever pop those?" She was very confused. Didn't take a seat at all.

She covered her mouth. She had zits all over her lips. It was distracting.

"No, then they never heal."

"Better be careful too. That's in the deadly triangle. You ever hear of it? It's the space from where your unibrow is, following your nose, down to your upper lip. Low chance but still a chance that you pop a pimple in that area and it squirts back into your brain and you go vegetal at best, dead at worst. Or reverse, whichever you feel is worse."

She seemed embarrassed like I told her she was a moron or something, but I think it was more the fact that I called out her zits and her unibrow in one fell swoop. The good

274 // Austin Noir

news is she wasn't ever going to pop a zit right there, and if I was a lazy man, which I am not, I could hang up my hat and call it a day knowing I saved a life.

"That advice is free, toots."

"What happened to your face?"

"They don't call me Bangface for nothing. Got shot there. Thought I found the answer in my last adventure but that ended up flipping on me. No use in going over the past. It's always changing anyways."

"Yes," the lady said. She looked down all concerned-like. Like she was thinking about something that used to make her happy. "My husband. He . . ."

"Checking the oil at the whorehouse? Milking the cows at the wet nurse? Cheating's easy, miss. We'll call it a hundred bucks and I'll get some pictures for the divorce proceedings."

"No . . . he owns Cleaning Solutions . . ."

I jumped outta my seat.

"Cleaning Solutions . . . LLC?"

"That's the one."

LLCs are a scam. Sometimes even worse than nonprofits. Limited liability corporations. Some Young Republican starts looking for the next move in his life because wearing boat shoes is more expensive than it used to be, so he starts an LLC. Limits his liability to everything. It's a scam. You want to hold him personally liable? Too bad. Go to his LLC, which lo and behold sold all of their belongings to his person and can no longer be touched. Seen it a few times. Always gets my ears hot like a pussycat in a frying pan, if you catch my drift.

"Wow, I never thought I'd know the wife of a man who owned a cleaning company. What's the problem? Job getting dirty?"

"You could say that."

People like this. Speaking in code. Riddles. I got shot in the face and I realized soon after I woke up in the hospital that parables are for fuckups and criminals. Something was fishy about this woman the way something is fishy about all land mammals: we're cold-blooded, metaphorically, to distance ourselves from the destruction we cause.

"All right, all right. You got a business card for Cleaning Solutions, LLC?"

"I do. I do."

Fishy. Already. This lady. Carrying around her husband's business card like she's going to forget he's the guy with the bleach. Fancy card. Must've paid a dick in dimes for this thing. One side was English and the other side Russian. I couldn't read that script though. Seemed more verbose than the English side.

"Can you read this Slavic nonsense?" I stuck the Russian side in her face.

"I never even knew . . ."

Nothing fishy about that. Carrying around a double-sided business card and never thought to turn it over. Never thought to take a note. Real marbles in the skull with this one. I've lost my patience with these kinds of requests.

"I won't take the case if you won't be honest with me."

"I . . ." She paused, hovered a finger over a pimple in the deadly triangle, and then thought better of it. "I think he's doing business with Russian criminals."

Nothing on the business card would indicate that, but like I said, I can't read that shit. Never could and never even tried. Daddy used to tell me to speak more than one language, that way you knew when people were lemon-squeezing you. Never had a use for two languages. The mean things people

276 // Austin Noir

say to me are in plain English and that's about all I can take at once, thank you very much.

"You know the Insane Fruits next to the liquor store next to the Cedar Creek corner store?" she asked.

"Slaughter Lane, yeah, I know the place." Some geniuses from California saw a nutsack they could sell a pube to and thought it would be a good place to put up a bunch of empty storefronts nobody would ever buy. Sometimes the nutsack says, *No thanks, I'm good with what I got.* And that's exactly what that empty lot said. Sure, a smoke shop might do well in a back-alley-turned-front-facing-butthole but no respectable business was going to move in when Insane Fruits had the market cornered. Now that's a good fruit cup, cupcake. Spray some chamoy on that—it's free. Douse it. Just go wild. They love it. The jukebox is always playing trombone music with Spanish—now *that's* a language. One that at least shares an alphabet with mine. I can sound things out pretty good, but when an alphabet looks like English got wet, I'm out of the pool, bucko.

"He's started going to the empty storefronts right next to Insane Fruits every single night. I secretly turned on his location sharing because I knew something was up. What is he doing there?"

This was the question. Simple as the alphabet, yet it took twenty minutes to get to it. People don't get it. It's like when you're sitting down on the bus and there are plenty of empty seats all over but the guy wearing trash bags and stinking like dirty toilet paper plops right down next to you. You're sitting there trying not to be rude so you hold your breath for as long as you can before you have to suck in so much air just to stay alive that the poop scent becomes physical and you choke on it. Or when the kid at Chick-fil-A makes you quantify and name every type of sauce you need for your chicken nuggets. Most of these kids don't realize that the sauce isn't just for the nugget, it's for the fries too. And when the fries are gone, you dip your fingers in the barbecue sauce just like prom night. There was once a Chick-fil-A that changed the recipe to their barbecue sauce and I immediately noticed by the scent (I have a good nose, even after being shot, I can smell pregnancy within four weeks of the squirt date). I went up to the kid and asked what the hell was going on. The kid said he loved it. Well, I hated it. It tasted like Carl's Jr.'s barbecue sauce and Carl's Jr.'s barbecue sauce only belongs on a Western bacon cheeseburger. I couldn't complain about it to anyone because I didn't want anybody to know I still eat Chick-fil-A despite all their interest in what stiffens the interest of somebody's pee-pee. People don't get it, is what I'm saying. Get to the point. I'm busy. I'm Bangface.

"All right, dame. I tell you what. I'm a frequent customer of the gas station there. Love the place. Real melting pot of cigarette-smoking cowboys and Twinkie-eating drug addicts. I'll swing by the empty storefronts to see if I can see who's filling it up. You got location sharing, you just text me when he's there and I'll take all the pictures I need. Whether he's doing business with Russian gangsters or just paying a clown to feed mice to his garden snake, we'll find out real soon."

She looked at me and I could tell tears were welling up behind her poofy eyes. "You have kids, Bangface?"

"Where are you going with this?"

"We have kids."

I sat there dumbfounded. That didn't have anything to do with anything, but I couldn't tell her that because she thought she was being profound. Or thought it would spur me into quicker action. Every case I take is addressed with utmost care and priority. I don't get too many of them and I get less when I fuck up. Kids don't make no difference. So I said, so as not to be rude: "Okay."

She blinked like the golf ball in her head was circling the drain of her mind's toilet until she flushed again. "Okay," she said. And then she walked out. Rolled out. She was in a wheelchair.

I didn't notice it at first because I'm a gentleman. I look ladies in the eyes and I never leave the gaze until they point downward, and even then I ask permission.

"That a permanent condition?" I asked.

"Kids are, yes."

"No, your legs."

"Tripped over my kids, fell down the stairs, sprained both ankles. They're big kids. And they blend in with the floor sometimes."

"Sounds like a dangerous game, kids do."

"Yes, well. I'll let you know when my good-for-nothing sleazebag husband goes down to those storefronts."

She finished rolling away and I put my hat over my eyes, leaned back, and took a little nap.

I don't dream much anymore. Can't remember if I ever did. The incessant noise of construction and freeway and drug addicts screaming at each other and cops shooting at everything keeps me up at night, so I take a wink any chance I get. Dame or no dame, a man needs his shut-eye—that's what Daddy used to say.

I must have slept better than I gave myself credit for because it was night when my phone vibrated the coins out of my pockets. Text message. Unknown number. Must've been the broad.

HE'S ON THE WAY.

Okay, lady. Then so am I. I straightened the wrinkles out of my clothes and smacked myself in the face a few times to wake up. My office was close. It'd take no time. I left Mariposa some food and got on the road. Whenever I start my car, it screams like thousands of dying monkeys in a dungeon guarded by banshees. Loud, shrill, and ear-popping is what I mean. I could signal a racehorse in Buda if I had the money to Pavlov a racehorse into tuning into the vibrational frequency of my little put-put. Animals are smarter than they're known for tasting. You wouldn't eat a smart kid. You might think about a dumb kid if the situation was right. Most horses are slightly dumber than a pretty dumb kid, though. You'd eat a horse over the kid. If you eat Jack-in-the-Cylinder, you're already eating horse. Kid horses, at that. Smart ones, probably. They taste good if you're hungry enough to be the cause of that much pain in the world. I'm no vegan but I like horses.

I never lose focus on the task at hand, but the Cleaning Solutions, LLC, truck must have come in from a subterranean route or had some kind of cloaking mechanism because it got there without me noticing it. Backed up to one of the empty storefronts, a door down from the vape place, and a group of biker-looking nogoodniks started assembly-lining a bunch of human-sized bags moving like humans writhing in defiance and sounding like humans muffled by socks or other obstructions in their mouths.

"Doesn't look good," I said to myself, because sometimes talking to myself is the best way to untangle my mind. I've gained weight in the last few months and more things are a struggle. First, you really don't notice the pounds because it's piling on to one area of your body. Usually your stomach and never your John Dangler. But soon that stomach fills out other parts of your body and you're more round. Rolling over on purpose is harder, but rolling over on accident is easier. Funny tricks of the universe and gravity get played on you. I get out of breath tying my shoes. My hand goes into orbit around my stomach when I'm trying to guide my Nathan's All Beef to piss. It's just tough.

I shut off my car. And skulked around the darkness of the parking lot. There were no cops to worry about in this neighborhood. Whoever started development out here was actually building a prison colony. There were only two ways in or out. One was off the highway and it always got congested, and the other was off a small country road with two thin lanes going opposite directions. Woods lining both sides, and deer and homeless people would play *Frogger* in the physical plane for fun.

My stomach got to feeling goofy. A night out led to some drunken braggadocio and I let spill that I had never in my life let out a shit when I was aiming to fart. Well, the moment I tell people I ain't ever shit my pants is the moment the universe puts me on a tightrope act barefoot on razor blades trying to avoid falling into the mustard milk, like Daddy'd call it. All eyes on me just waiting for me to squeeze out some yolk with the rotten egg.

Folks, I'm not going to lie. A schedule like mine means a less-than-ideal diet. I spend a lot of time in Whataburger drive-throughs wondering if I should skip the shake in my Monterey melt meal. I'm loaded with American cheese, salt, and white bread. I shit the bed a few nights ago and that's really neither here nor there, but I just wanted to give y'all advice: whether you're allergic or not, you oughta get a hypoallergenic mattress cover. They're waterproof and they saved me from having to buy a new mattress. Had to buy a new cover, though.

Some people think talking about the ol' poo-poo is beneath a man of my age, but I disagree. I'm open about my struggles. I'm out here like anyone else, searching for meaning, pondering the great questions, and desperately trying not to shit my pants ever again. And I definitely didn't want to spit tar on this newly paved parking lot while some Ruskies did things society probably doesn't approve of.

But I have a mission in life, folks. Unlike most gumshoes, I care about the value of my clients' time. They spend their hard-earned money on the first guy that gives them a callback and I'm here to deliver. So I tightened up the old chocolate pipes and waddled to the entrance of the storefront. No overhead lights, just floodlights pointed outward at the glass. Smart crooks, these ones. Can't see shit inside. The only way in was in, folks. You can't tuck tail and run away at the first sign of hardship. When you're in my position, you're tucking tail anyways. I'm a scared man by nature, despite my tough exterior. I did get shot in the face but you already know that. Junior to no man. My name's my own. Baptized by bullets. No fun, but a good story. Like most of my stories.

I knocked a good knock, hard enough to startle whoever was in there. How do I know? They looked startled when they got close enough to see me. Guns out, big guns.

"Hey there, cowpokes. I live in the area and I can't help but—"

"Where in the area?" Square face, mean eyes, stubble like a fisherman.

"A radius."

"Never heard of it."

"Anyways, I'm here looking for this fella." I pulled out the card and pointed at the truck just in case his grasp of the English language was less than demonstrated prior.

"Yeah, he's here. What do you need him for?"

"Got a few questions. I'm running out of Windex and was looking for a subscription plan to some local brew. I'm tired of going across the highway to Target only to come out with popcorn, DVDs I'll never watch, and a handful of forgot-my-Windex."

"We're in the middle of a job."

"I can see that, Punchy. Is this going to be the new global headquarters of Cleaning Solutions, LLC?"

He shut the glass door in my face. The thing about glass doors, though, is that they break pretty easily. I rounded up my leg like I was goddamn Shohei at the mound and did one of my finest spinny kicks. Felt a little drip-drip but that was to be expected. Can't shut off the valve completely with that kind of backup. Any plumber worth his stool'll tell you. Cleaning Solutions, LLC, would confirm. I'd ask him in a minute.

I fell to the pavement. Glass unbroken. Foot feeling funky. Stinky. Uh-oh, baby. It was poo-poo.

"Help! Help!" I don't normally like screaming for help, but I didn't keep an extra pair of pants in my back pocket, and even if I did, I'm not sure it'd done any dang good. Charlie had taken over the chocolate factory and the Oompa Loompas were walking out. No smiles, no singing.

There was some commotion from inside. I could make out some of the words they were saying. Things like, "I think that guy shit himself," and another one saying, "Let me help him, it's my specialty. It's why I do what I do." The guys must have relented because out popped Michael Frances, proud owner of Cleaning Solutions, LLC. I'd recognize that mustache anywhere when in combination with that crucifix dangling out the collar of his white polo.

"Why white?" I asked. "Ain't it a problem wearing white when doing a cleanup job?"

"You're embarrassed. You're talking nonsense. This is why I got into my job. This exact thing. I was at a bowling alley."

"Save it for the DA, I'm just here to look at cleaning solutions."

"I wear white to instill confidence in my clientele that I am the cleanest cleaner in town. If I come into your job with shit all over me, you'll see it."

"What about those hands, Mustache? You're wearing black nitrile. Hands dirty?"

The neat freak paused like I'd caught him, or like he was contemplating a metaphor an outsider wouldn't understand.

"I have a latex allergy."

"Yeah, yeah. Listen up, Germy. I ran out of Windex and I'm tired of going to Target"—this weirdo was lifting up my leg and spraying stuff all over the concrete and all over my pant legs and wiping me as I talked—"and I want to support a local business. So tell me, what you got?"

"Ah, yes. Well, I used to make cleaning solutions but now I solve cleaning problems. My solutions are not for sale." He sprayed and sprayed and I could read on his bottle, very clearly printed: NOT FOR SALE. "This is my secret formula. It completely neutralizes filth. I could use your pants as a handkerchief right now and there'd be no problem." And like a good salesman, a man who really believed in this shit, he blew his nose into my pant leg. Then he leaned over into my ear and said, "I'm being held hostage in a criminal conspiracy orchestrated by the mayor and the mob."

"The Russians?"

"I don't think they're Russian. They seem pretty diverse."

"Then it ain't the mob, Fauci." I kicked myself up like

284 // Austin Noir

Bruce Lee and walked with confidence to the front door.

There had to be five men in there. The only similarities between them were that they were muscular, mean-looking, had guns and bad smoking habits. I walked into the middle of them with my hands in the air. "I'm not here to kill anyone, don't worry."

A chuckle. Some wiseguy thought I was joking.

"Guns don't scare me," I said, and pointed to my face. "Especially guns so obviously made in China." I sweep-kicked them all at their ankles, and what do you know, they all fell down. Guns put people off balance, especially the way these guys were holding them. With one hand. Look, you might think looking cool is intimidating, but it's not. A gun is intimidating all on its own. Doing a dance with it defeats the purpose. If a little sweep kick from ol' Poopy Pants can defeat you, you're shitting the bed, amigo.

They looked dazed, this ragtag group of Blue Helmets. Their guns on the floor, them looking at the tweety birds flying around their heads. I acted fast, my body faster than my brain. I started kicking the guns away from them so that when they came to they couldn't change my name to Bangbangface. Michael Frances looked scared. I could tell by the way he kept saying, "That's a mistake. I'm scared."

"Be strong. Why all the guns?"

Clean Hands Mike pointed to the center of the room. A massive hole. Big enough to dump nuclear waste into.

"What's that?" I stepped close to the edge and peered over. A writhing mass of filthy people at the bottom.

"We're cleaning up Austin," one of the meatheads said. "Got a great contract. Making money."

Money. A four-letter word so bad it got five. I scrambled up to him and got in his face, grabbed his ears, and pulled him toward my own face. Looked him square in the eyes. "It's always money, isn't it?" Wish I had some more of that stuff, honestly.

"They're not allowed to camp wherever they want anymore. We got called to clean up the bridges. But the city wanted something more permanent." Michael took off his black nitrile gloves. "I told them I didn't know how to make it more permanent. So the mayor met me at the McDonald's and told me his nephew was fresh out of college and needed some direction. I should subcontract with his company staffed by his college buddies."

College kids. No wonder they looked so mean. Kicked out of one too many bars. Now they got a bone to pick with the world and America's Taliban-like alcohol laws. "College kids with guns. Never thought our finer institutions would produce such battle-hardened criminals." I got a closer look at them. Tattoos all over. Used to be that when somebody had that many tattoos, you would cross the street just to avoid getting shaken upside down for loose change. Now you ask them who their favorite poet is.

"Who's your favorite poet?"

This group of intellectual babies started talking nonstop.

"One at a time, please."

One of these circus clowns stepped up and said a name I'd never heard before. Then second-guessed himself and asked a clarifying question: "Contemporary, or who we think contributed the most to Western verse?"

College kids make me want to puke.

"Shut up. I don't care. You'll all be writing commercials someday." I want to be honest with everyone. I actually love commercials. Some of the best writing in America is done for the screen and they are almost all commercials. You don't get commercials much anymore these days because everyone's downloading their favorite TV shows to avoid them, but whenever Hulu asks me what I want my ad experience to be, I get giddy. It's an art form. It's beautiful. It's like *Choose Your Own Adventure* for things you'll never actually buy. It's fun to watch beautiful people suck down a Bud Lite like they're on a date with God on prom night. Evolving standards of American beauty will never change a beer commercial.

"I got mixed up in this," Michael was saying to himself. "I knew this was too big a problem to solve. I should've stuck to making cleaning solutions."

"Spanky," I said to him, "you're in a hole with this hole now, and you gotta dig yourself out along with all these people."

"Too many people don't like seeing people camping underneath the bridges. It was getting to be too much. There had to be a solution."

"Look, creep, I don't like walking over people desperately pleading for pocket change to buy a case of Bud Lite either, but I don't think the Travis County taxpayer had this in mind. What's the plan?"

"This was a temporary solution until we could figure something out. We figured the hole would be a good place to hold them for a while. We drop chicken nuggets in there every now and then."

"How many pieces?"

"I don't know! Happy Meals sometimes!"

I dug into my pockets and pulled out an Andrew Jackson. Terrible president. Bad guy. Real bad guy. I don't like him one bit but I was born for a storm and a calm does not suit me, buddy. "Get these guys some Bud Lite. I saw a commercial the other day. Seemed like a good time."

"We don't drink Bud Lite," one of the poets chirped up. "Can we get a Hazy IPA?"

I pointed my finger right into this beatnik's nose. "I want beer for the hole, not for *you*. Besides, I don't have fifty dollars for a six-pack of craft beer."

Craft beer. Makes it sound like a goddamn hobby. Call it *art beer* and I'll give it a second look, but I've never seen a commercial of beautiful people making out with a bottle of microbrew. Just bald and bearded flabby men waddling around town in flip-flops like they don't respect people's need to not be assaulted by the sound of memory foam slapping sweaty feet all goddamn day.

"You've seen too much, Bangface." A woman's voice. Very familiar. It was Wheels. But she wasn't on her rolly chair anymore. She was practically doing somersaults into the building. I gotta say, even a brain as high-functioning as mine could figure out why she would send me here to spy on her husband. A guy with a mustache as well-groomed as his could never elicit the arousal of even the perpetually horny. Behind her, the mayor was doing jumping jacks and flouting the very rules of social distancing he tried to get us all to do. He was nibbling on her ears. *She* was the cheater. Classic case of misdirection.

"I had my husband take this job. Solving cleaning problems was too small-game. I wanted to live in a gated community. I wanted to drink Hazy IPAs out of tulip glasses. He wanted to continue cleaning crime scenes and the pants of men who shit standing up."

"Darla?" The pain in Michael's voice almost broke me. For a minute I sympathized with the cross-wearing weirdo. But then I remembered that any fella who spends that much time grooming his upper lip has a bad case of I'm-in-love-

with-a-look-nobody-but-a-masturbator-could-find-sexy.
Freaks and weirdos, all the way out here in South Austin.
They're infiltrating everything, folks. These are the people
wanting to clear out the bridges. The people who want to
pave everything into a mixed-use condominium. I'm tired
of pizza costing thirty dollars and being delivered via bike
messenger. Ain't no pig tasty enough to bathe it before turning it into pepperonis. What do they call pepperonis now?
Prosciutto. Nonsense. Bacon is pork belly. Change the name
and up the price. I like supporting local businesses tearing me
a new one, though. It's good for the economy, this organic
stuff, I guess.

"By the power vested in me by the Austin voters, I am
hereby pushing you into the hole," Mayor What's-His-Name
said right before he tickled my armpits thinking I was fool
enough to lose my balance. I'm a grown man, hardened by
disappointment and the nightmarish dystopian hellscape we
live in, and I'm only ticklish when I'm not standing fifteen
feet above a bunch of crying people.

Darla, though, she pushed me pretty good. As I fell in,
I saw Fancy Hands Mike on his knees moaning things like,
"Why, Darla! Why?"

Yeah, why, Darla? Why?

"We're cleaning up Austin. And Bangface is the dirtiest
dick in town."

Dirty all the way down, folks. If you can't trust your duly
elected government to not push you down a temporary hold-
ing-hole, who can you even trust? Made me feel stupid for
ever saying the Pledge of Allegiance as a kid. Made me wish
I'd took a few friends up on joining a rock-climbing gym.
Luckily, a pile of trash broke my fall and probably my back.

"I can't make heads or tails of this." I'd get out of this hole if it took the rest of my life. I'd get to the bottom of this by the time I got to the top of this. But nothing made a bit of sense. Maybe I'd wake up back in my office with Mariposa on my lap swelling up my eyes and making me sneeze and I'd see that I was just in the middle of another bad dream.

I was thinking too much and thought is the enemy of action.

A group of folks, the best America's got to offer probably, helped me up.

"Forget it, Bangface. It's Austin."

ABOUT THE CONTRIBUTORS

Leslie Abbott

JEFF ABBOTT is the *New York Times* best-selling author of twenty novels. He is a past winner of the Thriller Award and a three-time nominee for an Edgar Award. He lives in Austin. Visit his website at www.jeffabbott.com.

Joe Worthem

ACE ATKINS is the award-winning, *New York Times* best-selling author of nearly thirty novels. A former SEC football player, he started his career as a crime beat reporter before becoming a full-time novelist. He's written eleven books in the Quinn Colson series and several true crime novels based on infamous crooks and killers. Atkins was also chosen by Robert B. Parker's family to continue the Spenser series in 2010, adding ten novels to that iconic franchise. He lives and works in Oxford, Mississippi.

ALEXANDRA BURT was born in the East Hesse Highlands of Europe and moved to Texas twenty-five years ago. After years of pursuing literary translations, she decided to tell her own stories. She's published short fiction, contributed to anthologies, and is the author of three novels, *Remember Mia, The Good Daughter,* and *Shadow Garden.* She lives in the Hill Country of Central Texas and keeps an eye on the world from a ridge overlooking a lake.

Matt Valentine

AMY GENTRY is the best-selling author of *Good as Gone, Last Woman Standing*, and *Bad Habits.* Her essays and criticism have appeared in the *Paris Review, Chicago Tribune, Austin Chronicle, Texas Observer, Los Angeles Review of Books, Slate,* and *CrimeReads.* She has a PhD in English and has lived in Austin, where she currently resides, for nearly two decades.

Korenn Grovey

JACOB GROVEY is a Texas-based author of twelve books, including novels, poetry collections, and several children's books. His love for writing started while he was in elementary school and his teacher challenged the class to create a poem. From that point, writing has remained near and dear to him. You can learn more by visiting JacobGrovey.com.

HOPETON HAY is a book talk show host and producer based in the Austin metro area who has been interviewing crime-fiction authors since 2009. Currently he hosts and produces the *Diverse Voices Book Review* podcast which features a monthly crime-fiction episode. He was the host and producer of *KAZI Book Review* at KAZI 88.7 FM in Austin from 2009–2021. Hay is a graduate of Xavier University in Louisiana.

ANDREW HILBERT is the author of *Inner Space, Invasion of the Weirdos, Bangface and the Gloryhole*, and *Death Thing*. You can catch up with him at hilbertheckler.com or follow him on Twitter: @ahilbert3000.

GABINO IGLESIAS is a writer, professor, and book reviewer living in Austin. He is the author of *Zero Saints, Coyote Songs*, and *The Devil Takes You Home*. His work has been nominated for the Bram Stoker Award, the Locus Award, the Anthony Award, the International Latino Book Award, and won the Wonderland Book Award for best novel. He teaches creative writing at Southern New Hampshire University. You can find him on Twitter talking books at @gabino_iglesias.

MIRIAM KUZNETS earned an MFA in fiction writing from the Iowa Writers' Workshop. Her fiction and nonfiction have appeared in *Narrative*, the *Southern Review*, the *Antioch Review*, the *North American Review*, and other magazines and anthologies. She is a psychotherapist based in Austin.

SCOTT MONTGOMERY became immersed in the crime-fiction scene while working at the Mystery Bookstore in Los Angeles. In Austin, he has continued to work as a bookseller specializing in the genre. His writing has appeared in *Shotgun Honey* and the anthologies *Murder on Wheels, Lone Star Lawless,* and *The Eyes of Texas,* for which his story "No One Owns the Blues" received an Other Distinguished Mystery Stories acknowledgment in *The Best American Mystery Stories 2020*.

AMANDA MOORE is a writer and attorney living in Austin. She holds a JD from the University of Texas School of Law. Her story "The Corner Man" won first place in the *Texas Bar Journal's* 2015 short story contest. She is a Writers' League of Texas board member and a book reviewer for *Publishers Weekly*.

MOLLY ODINTZ is the senior editor of *CrimeReads*. Her essays and criticism have appeared in the *Paper Brigade* and the *Austin Chronicle*. After five years in New York, she recently moved back to her hometown of Austin with her cat, Fritz Lang, in tow.

RICHARD Z. SANTOS's debut novel, *Trust Me*, was a finalist for a Writers' League of Texas Book Award and was named one of the best debuts of the year by *CrimeReads*. He is editing a collection of horror stories and is the executive director of Austin Bat Cave, a youth creative writing nonprofit.

CHAITALI SEN is the author of the novel *The Pathless Sky* and short stories and essays which have appeared in *Boulevard, Colorado Review, Ecotone, LitHub, Los Angeles Review of Books, New England Review*, and other publications. Her story collection *A New Race of Men from Heaven* was selected by Danielle Evans as the winner of the 2021 Mary McCarthy Prize in Short Fiction.

LEE THOMAS, winner of a Bram Stoker Award and two Lambda Literary Awards, is the author of *Stained, The Dust of Wonderland, The German, Parish Damned, Torn, Butcher's Road, Like Light for Flies*, and *Down on Your Knees*. His short fiction has been reprinted in *The Best Horror of the Year* and *Wilde Stories: The Year's Best Gay and Lesbian Speculative Fiction*. His work has been translated into multiple languages and optioned for film.

Acknowledgments

The editors of *Austin Noir* would like to thank the worldwide crime-fiction community, without whom this book would not exist. Additional thanks go to: Austin community radio station KAZI 88.7 FM, whose support of the *KAZI Book Review* talk show gave us an outlet to discuss crime fiction, and to KAZI program director Marion Nickerson for supporting the show; mystery bookstores, for bringing us together; and the wonderful folks at Akashic Books and Holly Watson PR for making our dream come true!

Lastly, we'd like to thank our families for encouraging and supporting us: Leslie Hay and Maya, Camille, and Justina; Fran and Alan Montgomery; and Mark Odintz, Jenny Odintz, and Fritz Lang, the Best Cat.